I0780257

SEVEN DAYS OF MERCY FOR THE APOSTATIC PRIEST

THE DIVINE HERETIC
BOOK ONE

Z. BENNETT LORIMER

HIGH TRESTLE
PRESS

This is a work of fiction. All of the characters, events, and organizations portrayed in this novel are either products of the author's imagination or are used fictitiously.

SEVEN DAYS OF MERCY FOR THE APOSTATIC PRIEST

Copyright (c) 2025 assigned to High Trestle Press LLC

All rights reserved.

Cover design by Aicel Escalada

A High Trestle Press Book
Address
Ames, IA 50010

The scanning, uploading, and distribution of this book via the Internet or via any other means without the permission of the publisher is illegal and punishable by law. Please purchase only authorized electronic editions, and do not participate in or encourage the electronic piracy of copyrighted materials. Your support of the author's rights is appreciated.

ISBN 978-1-968122-02-7 (Ebook) | ISBN 978-1-968122-03-4 (Trade Paperback)
First Printing, January 2026
Printed in the U.S.A.

For Liz

CONTENTS

PROLOGUE

You are more.

More than your skin and bones. More than your name. More than the words you speak and the thoughts in your head. You are more than the actions you take. More than your choices. More than memories. More than pleasure and pain. From the ecstatic shudder of your conception until your last stubborn bone rots back into the earth, you are *more*.

You don't see it, and well you shouldn't. Sight is a privilege, and we lost ours long ago. But you wonder, don't you? And sometimes you grasp.

It wasn't always this way.

Your forebears stared into the firmament and saw the truth of their divinity, a darkling hint of the vast eternity contained within every thriving soul. No such certainty exists anymore. Not in the night sky or anywhere else. Believe me. I've looked. The stars are only lanterns now, and the gulf between them, an abyss in truth. When we exorcised our G-d, we were nothing if not thorough.

We are artifacts, you and I. Fossils of a murdered deity rendered down to mud and stone. Irreducible reflections of a divine spark, beautiful and terrible. Fallen and pure. It is a lonely condition—containment. To be both blessed and forsaken, haunted and ignored. Our fallen G-d still reaches for us across that infinite gulf, and we are cursed to reach infinitely back. Nature abhors a vacuum, and we are nature and this abhorrence both. This is why the Selki still speak the old hymns, and the Huskan Clerics their feral mantras, reduced by time and memory to an insensate blur. It's why the Lucente poison themselves with lichen, lying wasted in oneiric fog. It's why the Elan Friars spend their lives painting votive murals only to see them burned. After all this time, The Karochan kantors still sing in trope, and the Celukids hang new ribs from their Abattoir with every passing moon. Prayers by a thousand names, cast in as many tongues into the same deaf void.

My job is to keep it that way.

CHAPTER 1

THE ETERNAL VALLEY

We planned for the worst but succumbed to a failure of imagination.

The ten-day journey out of Nurindra stretched over a month. Weeks of narrow mountain passes and barren steppe ground us down by inches. Not nine days in, a stranded wraithling cowl caught our scent on an unfavorable wind. Unable to stay ahead of their hunt, we retreated back to the mountains and selected a bottleneck to stage our defense. I killed two and frightened off the rest but broke my arm in the process. Gerritt's art spared me a sling and a period of convalescence we could little afford, as he found reason to remind me at least once per day. By the time we reached the fertile Ohtahp Valley, I would have traded his self-satisfied crowing for the sling.

Pockets of civilization welcomed us with open gates and empty promises. Gerritt convinced me to decamp inside walled Rovan against my better judgment. Before I could change my mind, he vanished into the Red City's warren of brothels, gambling houses and hash tents. It took him less than half a day to get caught swindling a shell game, provoking the local Varag. I cut down six Varagin warpigs to save him from a summary gelding and barely carved our way clear of the undercity before the lockheeds got word to drop the bronze portcullis.

Gerritt jangled his purse, now leaden with Rovan's copper coinage. He seemed too pleased with himself by half. "Awfully sensitive here."

"I need to keep you on a shorter leash," I said.

"Prettier girls have tried," Gerritt quipped. "Nicer ones, certainly."

I elbowed him hard in the gut.

"I'm starting to regret mending that arm," he grumbled.

At least that was the last I had to hear about his healing.

A safe distance from Rovan, we found the snaking line of the Tigrante River and followed it until we reached the first nexus of the Shevat Zubaydin. Silty river valleys and chaparral forests transected leagues of thirsty desert, where the great cities of Ohtahp endured a slow period of languorous decline. The migratory tribes of the deep desert swelled reciprocally as the cities emptied, and so it was mostly these nomads we encountered along the Shevat. Surrounded by so much civic decay, the pristine condition of these pathways unsettled me. By some lost art, the Shevuot withstood the ravages of time far better than the cities or the people. The Mysin Theocrats of antiquity tattooed the land with a skein of stone roads, demarcating paths of pilgrimage that outlived their divinity, connecting razed cities to temple ruins. Only the Shevat Zubaydin still saw any use, for its timeless path ended at Mahakalpe's stone gate. Priapic waystones marked the Shevat at every league. We read their skritglyphs by the light of zimcrab shells collected at their bases. No one knew who maintained them.

Time sped up along the Shevat. We soon closed on an aromatic cloud of pilgrims from Samarja or Arrek or some equally desolate Ohtahpi Creche. Gerritt and I were only two. We moved faster than the caravan and would soon overtake them. My instinct was to slow our pace and allow the pilgrims to gain, but we were already running late, and the syzygy wouldn't wait to accommodate our caution. A pair of young women wrapped head-to-toe in stoney shalwaz robes eventually broke from their caravan to hail us. Heedless of my reluctance, Gerritt accepted the invitation to join their camp, and once again I lacked the reserves to argue. We'd been on the road for over a month. We were both tired, and I was ornery.

The Shevat Zubaydin drew us up along a sheer sandstone cliff abutting the dead waters of the Karioch Sea. From the promontory where the tribe made camp, I could see the faded outline of Mahakalpe's flat walls twisting on the western horizon like some tantalizing mirage. How many generations of pilgrims had taken in this same vista on the final night of their journey? How few looked upon it with irreverent eyes? The nights had gone quiet since we left the banks of the Tigrante, but the noisome chatter of insects now reemerged to fill the evening with song. Surf lapped against the cliff walls below. The crash of boulders calving into the hungry sea punctuated the din as time and motion worked their jaws, devouring this land by inches and feet.

I watched the pilgrim camp erupt like boils. Beiyit tents sprang up by virtue of a clever drawstring contraption that allowed the tribesmen to pitch and collapse the low canvas shelters in the blink of an eye. Gerritt broke away to regale a small group of huntsmen armed with simple wooden spears around one the camp's seven fires. I overheard bits and pieces of our escape from Rovan, the familiar beats of the story seasoned with Gerritt's personal brand of embellishment.

Four young men with broad shoulders and strong backs were the last to enter the camp. They carried a palanquin supporting a tall wooden ark painted red and gold. The men set their burden down near the center of the camp with its seven skritglyph grammatons facing west toward distant Mahakalpe. The ark must have held the tribe's only clone of the Tractate, the Karochan faith's most sacred text. They wouldn't have left their creche without it.

I filled my canteen from one of several hanging bladders carried by the tribe's small cohort of bactrians and walked out beyond the outer ring of beiyit tents, keeping company with the white churn of surf. One of the pilgrims found me before long to present a generous offering of flatbread and a green knob of bactrian cheese.

"I didn't see you eat," he said, which I took to mean he'd been watching.

I wasn't really in a position to turn down the meal. We were planning to resupply in Rovan, but our hasty departure didn't allow for it, so we'd been rationing ever since. "I didn't want to impose," I said as I accepted the food.

The man's wrinkled grin revealed three missing teeth. "No imposition. All men are brothers on the Shevat Zubaydin, and we invited you to join our camp." He gathered the ends of his shalwaz robe and sat on a stone with an aged groan. Not wanting to loom, I followed suit. I didn't think this man so many years my senior, though his weathered face showed the cast of age. The Ohtahpi desert had a way of using up young bodies so that the years sat heavier than they otherwise would. I knew little of the desert tribe's honorific traditions, and each creche practiced its own idiosyncratic rites, but this man's wrapped headdress had once been red, even though his time on the Shevat had caused the dye to fade to brown. The red wrap carried the same meaning from the walls of Mahakalpe to the blasted foothills of the Camelback Range. Here was a cleric, one who had completed a pilgrimage to the ruins of Ish Dabar.

"You shouldn't be so trusting, Teacher."

"Oh?" His mouth wrinkled as he tasted my warning. "Planning to rob us within sight of the Holy City?"

I stared at him for an uncomfortably long time before answering. "You lucked out this time, but the roads are crowded with creatures of ill intent."

The cleric chuckled and shook his head. "Not this road."

"Then it would be a lonely exception, and I've walked my fair share."

"I don't doubt that," he said. "What's your name, traveler?"

"Ruxindra," I answered honestly.

He nodded, tucking a loose black ringlet of hair back inside his headwrap. "The *Hesserat* cities have opened their gates to many outlanders, but I do not think you came from Rovan nor Uruz..." He let the implied question dangle.

"Your intuition serves you well."

He pressed his foot against the leather greaves lining my pants and eyed the unmended gash in my vambrace, a memento of the wraithling's attack. I wasn't carrying Caledin Vane. I'd left the sword in a bundle beside my pack back at the camp, but I hadn't taken any pains to make its cache discreet. "Dressed for violence," he mused. "Fearful of the open road. We didn't expect news of the Eidolon's emergence to remain bottled inside our G-dling Cradle, but one does wonder just how far the song has carried."

"We came from Nurindra," I said, again honestly.

He shook his head. "I do not know it." I shrugged. "Do they read the

Word in Nurindra?" I knew he meant the Tractate, just as Ohtahp became the "G-odling Cradle" in his desert vernacular.

"Some do," I said. "Others?" I shrugged again and began eating my bread as another long silence settled around us. The Cleric remained at my side, though he let me work my way through my meal without further interruption.

"Arrekot?" I finally asked when I could no longer bear his patient regard.

He nodded. "You know something of our land, then? Half the *Hesserat* in Rovan couldn't parse an Arrekot from a Uruzot." He laughed then, but I didn't get the joke. "Our creche is a hundred leagues across the desert, beyond the last fertile valleys of the River Narir. We passed many empty creches along the Shevat Zubaydin. I suspect my tribe will be among the last to reach Mahakalpe."

"Let's hope the Mahak hasn't run out of space," I said.

His lips turned down, and I feared my response had been too glib. The Arrekot had shown us nothing but kindness, and my war was not with them, but their G-d. Some might see it as one and the same, but I did not. In the distance, another rock lost its grip on the cliff and tumbled fatally into the sea.

The cleric turned his head toward the sound. "Even the land bows before the Eidolon," he said.

"I think it's the sea that demands obeisance." I couldn't help myself.

The cleric raised his finger to me in good-natured reprimand. "Ah, but is not the sea his instrument, and the waves his dauntless will? The waters erode the land and grind it into sand to deposit on some heathen beach, a reminder that change is the only eternity, even for stubborn stone. The cliff's edge creeps ever closer. Someday even the great Shevat Zubaydin will crumble."

"That will make it harder for the tribes to reach Mahakalpe," I said, eager to drag the conversation out of the cleric's numinous cant.

Then he said something that surprised me. "When that day comes, the Holy City will be a ruin to match all the other extinct vortices of our faith."

I paused from chewing the last sliver of bactrian cheese. "You expect Mahakalpe will fall?"

He took a moment to consider his answer. "Mahakalpe will outlive its usefulness for a time, but yes, it will eventually fall."

"Why do you say that?"

His eyes pinched together in a befuddled expression that rang discordant with his sagely performance. "I thought you would have heard?"

"Heard what?" I pressed.

"This Eidolon will be the last," the cleric said. "So he has told us with the thousand mouths of the desert, and the sages have judged it true."

The cleric already had my ear, but now he had my attention. "How can that be?"

"How can it be? Or how can it be *known?*" His eyebrows drifted upward. Karochan clerics all shared a habit of answering questions with questions. Perhaps that's why the faithful call them *teachers* instead of *priests*. "Change," he repeated.

I should have let the discussion fade at that point. He offered me the opening, but I didn't take it. "The Eidolon has yet to reach the altar of Mahakalpe. He is not yet invested and may still fail." As many before him have, I didn't add.

I expected another rhetorical question, but the cleric instead glanced down at his hemp sandals, at his blackened toes encrusted with sand. "We've kept faith with a dead G-d for this long..." He shrugged.

The cleric left me to my silent consideration after that. In time, I drifted back toward the camp, roused by the sound of drumming. I returned to find a group of youngling Arrekot dancing and whooping in a tight circle, banging out a mantric rhythm on tambourines and goblet drums of every size and make. The dancers had discarded their androgyn shalwaz in favor of immodest hide breach cloths and narrow cream slips. Men and women alike exposed their chests, possessed by the spirit of the night and the freedom of the open road. The Arrekot elders watched the performance approvingly, a few tapping their feet to the rhythm of the drums. I saw my cleric sitting cross-legged among three yellow-scarfed women who might have been his wives. He bobbed his head to the drumming, beaming up at the dancers.

I found Gerritt standing amid a band of Arrekot near the Ark of the

Tractate. He drank eagerly from a jar of cloudy arak that they passed between them. Gerritt was always quick to make friends. That's never been my strength. I suppose it's one of the reasons I kept him around, despite all the trouble he made for me.

"Rux!" He summoned me over and offered the jar, but I declined. I'd had my share of Ohtahpi arak, and every dram tasted like fermented piss. He claimed my sip for himself. "You'll want to watch this," he said, waving the arak in the direction of the dancers.

I squared up beside him and watched the circle converge and retreat, the tempo of their drumming increasing with each repetition of the cycle. After one final convergence, the younglings expanded their circle to the edge of the fires abutting the dance, and another young Arrekot appeared in the center of the ring as if conjured from drumming and dirt. She wore a dress purer than it had any right to be after enduring the dusty Shevat Zubaydin, white as mother's milk but for a single red dot impressed over her navel. Firelight transmuted her wicker crown and the dun bronze pendant that hung from her shoulders into platinum and gold. The dancers circled her, and she spun with them, arms extended in cruciform, not quite dancing but revolving like a clockwork gear at the center of some holy machine. Oiled hair crashed in waves of perfect dark against her shoulders and gown. Her smile never faltered, pinned without blemish at the corners of her face.

Comeliness takes many forms in many cultures, but true beauty is an immutable spark, as constant as it is ineffable. This girl possessed it —the Arrekot embodiment of the good, the beautiful, and the true.

"Such a shame," Gerritt lamented. Shaking his head, he took another sip of arak.

"Not to your taste?" I asked.

He waved the bottle at the dancers again, this time indicating the girl. "The girl is *lehakva*." I didn't recognize the word, but Gerritt knew I wouldn't, so I didn't ask. "There's no easy translation. A virgin. A gift. A G-dswife. The tribe will give her to the Mahak, and the Mahak will present her to the Eidolon. Apparently, it's quite the trend. All the pilgrims are doing it."

I tried to picture a revenant G-dhead leaving Mahakalpe with an entourage of Ohtahpi wives and couldn't make any sense of it. "What does the Eidolon need with a throng of wives? Sounds like a burden."

"Perhaps, but only a temporary one," Gerritt said. "They'll all be sacrificed around the Altar of the Demiurge. Burned alive, as I understand it." Gerritt finished the jar of arak and wiped his lower lip with the back of his hand, marking the dancers with heat.

I turned back to the circle, watching the performance with fresh disdain—the dancing, the drumming, the foot-tapping tribesmen and their bobble-headed cleric. My eyes came to rest on the girl—this *lehakva*—decorated and beaming brighter than the gibbous moon.

How happy she looked.

CHAPTER 2

THE HOLY CITY

We arrived at the Shevat Gate of Mahakalpe seven days before the Syzygy of Avum brought the twelve celestial wanderers into alignment across the firmament.

Mahakalpe occupied a narrow isthmus squeezed between Mount Yotan and the Karioch Sea. Her boundaries once marked the western terminus of the old imperial demesne, and as such, the Mysin Theocrats fortified her stone walls to provide a bulwark against Celukid sea raiders and the tempestuous Varag. Those battlements endured as surely as the Shevuot. They kept the Mahaks in power, while the other Ohtahpi dynasties succumbed to their cities' decay. In anticipation of the pilgrimage, the Mahak had thrown the city gates wide and withdrawn his Jassanid guardsmen to the grounds of his Sahir. The Holy City welcomed all supplicants without scrutiny, for the Eidolon belonged equally to all. And so it was that we entered Mahakalpe unmolested, watched only by expressionless clay totems impressed into the walls, our passage flanked by bronze-banded gates of heavy stone.

Ohtahp was a land of pathways. The rivers. The Shevuot. The vortex of Ish Dabar. A kingdom of veins pumping people and prayer with Mahakalpe at its beating heart. The land so reviled stillness that no other sedentary destination could survive it. Perhaps that's why the nomads thrived while the cities failed. In this truth, I heard echoes of the Arrekot cleric's declaration that only change was eternal and transition the true face of the Divine.

The Arrekot caravan dissolved into the crush of pilgrims descending on the Holy City, and we soon lost sight of them in our efforts to squeeze our way through. I was happy to be rid of them, and not because their generosity complicated my resolve. My priesthood trusted me with a task, and I would not abandon it for a mouthful of flatbread and a night's rest beneath a beiyit tarp. It was the *lehakva* that unsettled me. Not for its cruelty—though, surely it was cruel—but because I could not fathom its purpose. The sacrifice of man—the spilling of innocent blood in worship or in prayer; the oldest plates of the Tractate forbade it. Those prohibitions stretched back to the time of Old Mysin when the Karochan faith was still young. Virgin gifts and votive pyres—it all stank of eldritch rites, and I was not eager to see the two sorceries mix. Even so, the *lehakva*'s fate did furnish me with the first rough outlines of a plan.

The bones of Mahakalpe moved us along with hundreds of shalwaz robes, down a corridor described by towering aqueducts and up a switchback staircase that climbed the Middle City's retaining wall. Our crowd shed pilgrims in clumps like a Subakkan pelt, each tuft of headwraps and shalwaz drifting off through the branching pathways of the bagra slum. By the time we reached the Middle City's open plaza, our band had rarefied enough to merge with the native bustle.

Old cobblestones, worn flat, lined the plaza in concentric rings, expanding out from the lip of the retaining wall to form the shape of a rising sun. Rays of hardpack road left the plaza, extending into the urban abyss. Merchant carts crowded the periphery, identifiable only by the chanting proprietors offering food and wine and wicker ornaments to the disordered shoppers clamoring to spend their coin. Many Ohtahpi faces, certainly, crowded by coarse beards, headwraps and tasseled tahliz scarves, but men of foreign cast, as well, and several creatures more exotic. Two muscular Varag in hide breach cloths, their green chests strapped with bandoliers of knives, crossed the plaza carrying a butchered boar across a litter. Beside the monger's cart, a small pack of dog-faced Subakka pawed at each other over a plate of kebabs. Amid the shopping masses, a lone Sylphid wandered aimlessly, looking lost with her pointed ears irate, glass wings fluttering nervously. Mahakalpe sat at a crossroads, and Ohtahp was no longer as homogenous as it once had been. I still wondered how many of these outlanders came through the Holy City by habit, and how many had arrived to witness the G-dhead reborn. In antiquity, the living Demiurge touched every creature on the face of Hebdomar, but Old Mysin had been an Empire of Man.

At the plaza's apex, a long-eared gargoyle spouted water from its nostrils and mouth, feeding a gray stone basin of newer vintage. Another crowd of mostly Ohtahpi women surrounded the fountain, waiting impatiently to fill clay urns while their children scrawled skritg-lyphs on the base with yellow chalk. One of the Mahak's urban magistrates stood by, identified by a white headwrap and bronze stole. He brandished a flexible rattan to warn the women off filling more than one jug. I watched him swat a small boy with braided hair who drew too near the lip of the basin with his chalk.

Beyond the plaza and an uneven expanse of domed residential roofs, another retaining wall loomed, this one crowned by hanging ferns and fruiting palms—a lush swathe of thirsty green. The Theocrats had built this city in layers, and upon the highest sat the Mahak's palace—his Sahir.

There are old Mysin histories that speak of seven Sahirs scattered throughout the empire, but the antique histories are not reliable, riddled with ingratiating embellishments and outright fabrications. Many buildings claim descent from these symbols of lost empire. At the center of Rovan, there is a strange whorehouse with cyclopean stone columns and bathing pools that never cool. The coliseum of Uruz stands atop an older structure rebuilt to service those few champions who live long enough to retire from the sport. Either building might have been a Sahir, though I saw little value in conjecture. For all righteous purposes, only one of the fabled seven still stood, and I gazed upon its verdant foreyard from the center of a mercantile plaza shaped like a birthing sun.

I realized I'd lost track of Gerritt some ways back and left my scouting to find him. One of the Subakka snapped its jaws at me irritably as I passed. I turned in challenge, flipping back my cloak to expose the red pommel of Caledin Vane, and the Subakka lumbered back to its pack, brown fur bristling. I found Gerritt standing atop the retaining wall, gazing wistfully toward the bagra's eastern bloc. He'd perched himself directly over one of the clay pipes through which the Middle City dumped its waste into the open-air sewers threading the bagras below. The vile smell made it an odd choice for a contemplative moment, but Gerritt was nothing if not odd.

"We're just in time," he said, sensing my arrival without turning.

"We have seven days to get our affairs in order," I said, still shielding my nose from the stink. "After that, it gets more complicated."

He extended his arm toward a single point on the eastern horizon, a caravan of shadows marching down from the mountain pass. "Our G-dling aspirant has concluded his prayerful vigil. He comes. Tonight. Now."

Right on schedule.

I sometimes wonder if our ancestors—our liberators—truly understood the fate they'd sealed for their progeny. I do not question their righteousness nor their valor; the Demiurge of Old Mysin needed to be destroyed. But deliverance charged a heavy toll, and G-ds are ever restless, even in death. The G-dhead's fall began a new cycle of investment and rebirth. These Eidolons who emerge from the deep desert in every age carry inside them a divine seed. The annals name dozens of pretenders over the years, imposters judged false by the Ohtahpi sages who commune with the desert's thousand tongues. Those Eidolons judged true follow the Path of the Prophet along the Shevat Zubaydin. They cloister themselves inside Mount Yotan's Broken Temple until the time is ripe to descend the mountain and impregnate the Holy City.

At the center of Mahakalpe lies an altar forged in prayer and cast in stone. The Eidolons are called to present themselves upon that stone at the Syzygy of Avum so that the seed within them may germinate among the faithful and sprout.

Seven days. Until then, the Eidolon was just a man. A promise. Potential.

It's far easier to slay a man.

Gerritt hopped down from the retaining wall and brushed off his trousers. "You're sure about this?"

I wasn't. Offered brute force or trickery, I'd choose force every time, but this land was foreign to me and I needed to get close. "If you've got a better idea, I'm listening."

He batted the suggestion away with a scoff. "You never like my ideas."

"That's because they're usually dumb."

He shrugged with no argument, then visored his hands and scanned the plaza we'd just left behind. "There's a thaumaturgical in the bagra that should meet our needs—assuming the clerics haven't flushed him out. We can call on him in the morning. I don't imagine anyone in the city's keeping their shop open tonight."

"*Uch.*" I disliked thaumaturges and their low art.

Gerritt cocked one thin eyebrow at me. "You're picky now?"

I threw up my hands in surrender. "Chthonic?" I asked.

He shook his head. "Agnostic, I believe."

"Fine." No one should ever say Ruxindra l'Maer was not a pragmatist.

"Grand." Gerritt clapped his hands together then drew back his chin-length hair and tied it quickly in a chestnut bun. "Then I'm going to find us somewhere to sleep before all these nomads snatch up the choice accommodations."

"Now?" I stopped him before he could saunter off. "You don't want to watch the procession?" I glanced back beyond the walls. The Eidolon's caravan continued its course down the pathway from the mount. They'd breach the city gates within the hour.

Gerritt flicked one gloved hand in dismissal. "You've seen one, you've seen 'em all."

I glowered at him. There hadn't been an Eidolon in Mahakalpe in almost 300 years. I should know. I carried the sword that killed him. "How old are you, Gerritt?"

He flashed the same wry smile that always answered the question, and then he was gone. I let him go. Mahakalpe contained at least as many paths to trouble as Rovan, but they were more circuitous by far, so

I clung to hope that Gerritt would not have the patience to navigate them.

CHAPTER 3

A PROCESSION OF THE MEEK

I tracked the edge of the Middle City's retaining wall along a narrow promenade dressed with lacquered signage and shuttered shops. The cobblestone walkway dead-ended between a dark residential alley and another switchback bagra descent. I nodded to a bronze-laden magistrate who let me pass without harassment. Cities were not so dissimilar in their stratification, and it was always easier going down than up.

I landed on a hardpack road flanked by more aqueducts and rivers of sewage. So overwhelming was the stench that I quickly went blind to it. The road branched into a half-dozen snaking passages too narrow for carts—barely wide enough for two men to walk abreast. With no signage to direct me and no crowd to follow, I picked one that I hoped might draw toward the Mountain Gate. No such luck. The road's course twisted and instead of reaching the outer walls, I found myself mired in the dim bowels of Mahakalpe's sprawling slum.

I found the bagramate. The city's fecund underclass lived in piles of shemechas—Ohtahpi mudbrick hovels with square roofs and shared walls. The shemechas sprouted in risers, their alleys linked by wooden ladders and crumbling brownstone steps. Some shemechas rose two stories above their entrances but no higher, a defense against fire, that persistent threat of urban life. I couldn't say how many Ohtahpi lived in each hovel, though I did see a woman ushering six younglings no taller than her knee inside a single shemecha. Each bagra block might have accounted for over a thousand souls, and there were dozens of these blocks on the city's eastern flank alone.

I saw fewer shalwaz than I had among the nomadic tribes and in the Middle City's mercantile plaza, and no tasseled tahliz. The married women weren't veiled, though some wore their uniformly dark hair bound back with roughspun cloth. Those who could not afford religious garb wore their piety in blackstem tattoos, skritglyphs impressed on their knuckles, forearms, and calves. With no water to waste, robes and underclothes hung in rows from shallow balconies to absorb the cleansing sun. The pleasant music of distant chatter and competing drums seasoned the air.

Again, the road I'd taken forked. At the dead end, I stopped in front of a narrow building with a domed roof. The local still, I assumed, from the collection of young men in hemp sandals and canvas rags, all waiting to fill urns of creamy arak from a forty-gallon jug. I passed a few more of the Mahak's bronze-laden magistrates, but too few to police such a vast and complicated bloc.

After so much aimless wandering, I reached a wider street that smelled of salt and cooking meat, home to chanting street mongers minding hand-crank spits and open vats of millet grain. One solicited my attention, brandishing a carving knife with flare. He shaved a crispy wedge of pork and offered a sample. The meat tasted well-seasoned if a little dry. I declined a full serving but tossed a copper in his urn for good will.

A long, single-story building dominated the next block beyond the street mongers. Someone had knocked down the shared walls between an old row of shemechas. No signage marked the longhouse, but I judged it a brothel by the florid perfume wafting from its entryways and the gaggle of light-skinned bastards throwing sticks out front.

I suspected that I'd turned down the wrong path when I left the last mound of shemechas to wander a narrow corridor penned by old walls of mortar and stone. Deep fissures stuffed with rolls of weathered parchment webbed the cracking mortar, as if the bagramate hoped to maintain the walls by script and prayer alone. The corridor offered no outlet. I should have turned back, but curiosity drew me along its spiraling path until I reached an open yard planted with short olive trees and aromatic jasmine. The well-kept garden surrounded an odd structure, a black cube cut in perfect dimensions, each face crowded with fading skritglyphs etched into the smooth, ebony stone. Some kind of Karochan shrine, perhaps. A tile floor surrounded the cube, fanning out from its square base for several feet before dissolving into the hard-pack dirt of the bagra road.

I circled the shrine once, looking for an entrance, but instead found a man bent over one of the tiles at the base of the cube, taking a rubbing of the floor's design with charcoal and vellum. The pilgrim didn't appear to be Ohtahpi at a glance. His skin was darker than the sun-kissed nomads of the desert, and he wore a tight purple toga and matching kufi hat with a silver pin clipped at its side. I watched him methodically running his charcoal wedge across the rubbing until my creeping shadow invaded his workspace, drawing his squinting attention my way.

"Can I help you?" he asked, not impatiently.

Taking a page from the Karochan clerics' book, I answered his question with one of my own. "What are you copying?"

His expression brightened. He set his charcoal to the side and stood up, presenting his vellum. The rubbing showed a snaking pattern of interlocking coils. I could tell the symbol once boasted greater detail, but time had worn those markings down to a nondescript blur.

"You don't recognize it?" he asked.

I turned up my hands. "Should I?"

He raised a finger, then bent to rifle through his satchel until he unearthed a small leatherbound notebook. He quickly found the page he was looking for and thrust the notebook in my face. I drew my head back and squinted at a black sketch that resembled the design on the bagra tile, but with all the faded accents restored. In the drawing, the twisting coils became a triad of serpents bound in knots, their heads set with triangular fangs, bodies inscribed with writing that didn't look like Karochan. The looping characters linked by diacritical markings better resembled older tongues—Ibreic, maybe, or Sylphid Aleel. I still didn't recognize it, so I shook my head.

The man withdrew his notebook and launched into an explanation with a scholar's zeal. "It's the *naga'tlat*—I'm certain of it. Eldritch arcanum." He turned to glance up at the black cube looming over us. "These seals are the oldest structures in the city. Older than the Sahir and all the Mysin walls. The only artifacts the Theocrats didn't raze or otherwise defile."

"These?" I asked.

He nodded enthusiastically. "Mahakalpe contains three of them. Another in the Middle City's orthodox ziggurat and a third inside the Mahak's Sahir. I've not been granted leave to visit the last, but hope springs eternal."

I looked at the shrine—the seal, he'd called it—too dark and smooth to be as ancient as this strange man claimed. "I take it you aren't here to witness the Eidolon's investment."

The man had already returned to his rubbing. He grumbled dismissively.

"Where'd you come from?" I asked.

"Originally, Nysei," he said. "My research brought me to Ohtahp, and here I've remained going on twenty years. I study gnostic artifacts —like these."

That made more sense. Nysei was an island city off the coast of distant Gozalam, home to a hermetic academy that trained thaumaturges and sophists. This man seemed more like the latter. "Do you find many gnostic sites in Ohtahp? Seems an unlikely place for them."

"Hmm? Yes, perhaps," he muttered, only half listening. "There." He completed his rubbing and set his tools aside again, looking up at me with renewed vigor. "The Theocrats were not as thorough as they would have liked the world to believe. I've found dozens of sites like these scattered throughout the river valleys in the east, but this is the only place I've found an authentic *naga'tlat* outside the Tomb of the Strigoi."

"What does it mean?" I asked.

"It's a *ward*," he said, eyes gleaming with a religious fervor I would have rather expected to find on the faces of the Ohtahpi adulators. He traced the lines of the symbol with a finger. "The winged serpents represent daemonic forces, and the knot their obfuscation. The words on this one are too weathered to translate, but if their ken is a match for the sample I recovered from the tombs—and I'll bet the last shekel in my pocket it is so—it was once a gnostic bloodbind."

"Binding what?" I asked.

"What, indeed!" His purple kufi shifted with the pumping of his brows. "Time is a thoughtless steward of truth. All we have are theories."

"And you have one, I'm guessing?"

He scratched the black stubble on his chin. "Perhaps the preservation of the seals was no oversight. Perhaps the Mysin Theocrats had a reason to leave them be."

A ram's horn bellowed in the distance, its long report followed by a stream of honking blasts. I looked up at the low walls surrounding the yard, tracking the sound. The Nyseian scholar didn't seem to notice, or else didn't care.

"Sounds like the Eidolon's caravan has claimed the bagra gate," I said.

"Hmm?" He was still staring at his rubbing, careless of the divine arrival.

The ram's horn sounded again.

"What's your name?" I asked the sophist.

"Senex Amari Desta," he answered, almost absently.

I left the Senex to his studies, tracking the bleating horn until I joined a tide of unwashed bagramate adulators surging toward the Mountain Gate. The sound of the ram's horn emptied the piles of shemechas, and now the narrow streets overflowed with bodies, a clutter of limbs and stench that threatened to suffocate me until the flow at last spilled out into wider thoroughfare. An entire maniple of the Mahak's Jassanid guardsmen kept the entrance clear, driving the eager mob of onlookers onto a dusty embankment that drew up against the Middle City's mudbrick retaining wall.

I caught a glimpse of Mahakalpe's open gate at the end of the road and the line of bactrians padding in from the Shevat beyond before one of the Jassanids caught me with the butt of his spear, ushering me up the embankment with the rest of the adulators. I was one among thousands—perhaps tens of thousands. Bagramate beggars in their dusty rags; merchants from the Middle City wearing pristine shalwaz bound with braided belts; nomads in their tribal clusters, dressed the same as the merchants but showing the sweat and soil of the open road; small packs of the orthodox with their sober expressions and tasseled tahliz.

The adulators continued to flow from the inner city, their phalanx parting like cornsilk around the advancing line of Jassanid guards. Nearer to the gate, the porcine heads of a Varagin cohort bobbed above the crowd, and across the plaza a few clusters of slender Sylphids shone like wan blue lanterns amid the wash of muted Ohtahpi.

The ram's horn sounded again, and I tracked its origin to a line of clerics along the adjacent rooftops. They bent their red-wrapped heads in unison to press pursed lips against their massive carved horns.

I settled in next to a nomadic tribe, so like the Arrekot but for a small tweak to the knot of their shalwaz robes. A stout woman I took to be their matriarch wore an ora bark circlet and a gauzy yellow veil that trended down to her pronounced bust. She stood out to me not for this identifying raiment, but for the intensity of her gaze, turned not toward the advancing caravan, but toward a lower section of the crowd. Deep lines tightened around her hazel eyes.

I fought my way free from a pile of headwraps obscuring my view until I saw what caught the woman's attention. Several paces ahead of us, three Inaghke Shades polluted the crowd of adulators, their shoulders hidden beneath the pointed epaulettes crowning their matte capes. I didn't need to see their fanged expressions nor the glowing coals of their eyes. The backs of their heads were confirmation enough: three clusters of gray tentacles, eyeless tangles gnawing the air around them with lipless mouths.

When Mysin collapsed, the hard borders of empire crumbled with it, and in the ages since, other cultures seeped through the cracks to dilute the native Ohtahpi stock. The people of Mahakalpe had grown accustomed to benign intercourse with the Subakka and the Sylphids— even the Varagin warpigs, that neutered ancestral threat. Old Mysin touched each of these peoples, vesting them with interest in the G-dling's rebirth. I could not say the same for the Inaghke.

Hebdomar is a world of a thousand sorceries and as many spirits presiding over their practice. These spirits do draw worship, and many fell peoples treat them as G-ds, but there is only one creator to whom that title rightly belongs. The Demiurge is that from which all else emanates and back to which all eventually returns. Mysin embodied the G-dhead and so allowed him to be destroyed, but there are older people who preceded this embodiment. Not older than the Demiurge himself, but older than his mortal empire by far. These peoples endure in enclaves scattered throughout Hebdomar, and they bow at altars far crueler than creation.

The Inaghke unsettled the nomad matriarch, as well they should.

"He comes." A thin voice reached my ear from the tribe of nomads to which I'd unwittingly attached myself.

My eyes left the Inaghke to find the edge of the caravan working its deliberate path down the open plaza between the flanking crowd of adulators. The Jassanids formed battalion lines on either side of the plaza, struggling mightily to keep the surging adulators back as the Eidolon's caravan entered the city—one thin row of bactrians surrounded by apostles marching on foot.

I have witnessed many honorific processions: Nurindran circuses led by mastodons with painted clowns on nine-foot stilts; Belleteyne parades awash in colored confetti and nude bodies furiously copulating as their orgy barges rolled down the street; Maltane legions marching in Triumph, their Consul armored in gilt, draped with leys of precious gems and a crown of living flame. The Eidolon's caravan seemed crafted almost in counterpoint to all these vaunted displays. Among his apostles, I saw orphans and beggars; sunken faces and protruding ribs; branded thieves and collared whores; amputees hobbling on crutches, proudly displaying the stumps of severed limbs; a pair of lepers so disfigured they must have been blind. It was a celebration of humility—a parade of the decrepit and the meek. It fascinated me. Apart from their caravan, each member of the Eidolon's entourage would have been repellant—even by the standards of the bagra slum—but in the aggregate they became something holy, something *more*.

And there he was.

Most of the bactrians carried supplies or those apostles too lame to endure the march, but atop the last beast bringing up the caravan's rear sat the Eidolon, a revenant G-dhead, thin and unadorned. He turned his shaved head from side to side, smiling to the roaring adulators, raising thin fingers in salute. I thought him small at a distance, but soon realized he was just a boy, no older than twelve or thirteen, with a beardless chin and glowing cheeks.

An armed sentinel led his bactrian by the reins, and he alone looked formidable in his hoplite armor. Straight black hair fell to his shoulders beneath the brim of an agen helm. This guardian was too fair for an Ohtahpi, and I disliked the methodical way he scanned the crowd. His gloved hand never left the sword hilt at his hip.

As the Eidolon continued down the thoroughfare, vaxillium banners unfurled from the rooftops, their grammaton skritglyphs declaring his forbidden name. I watched him as he passed and felt a pang of sadness at the guileless smile that met my stone-faced stare. I thought he'd be older. For no other reason than I hoped it would be so.

With the caravan pushing deeper into the city, I heard that thin voice again behind me. "He's so beautiful."

I glanced over my shoulder to see a young Ohtahpi nomad dressed in virginal white. A wicker crown matched the auburn highlights of her hair, and her green eyes sparkled when she smiled at me. I turned quickly away, cursing under my breath, for I knew what she must be.

With the caravan out of sight, the Jassanid guards began to permit the crowd down from the penned embankment. I searched the commotion for the Inaghke, but they were gone.

CHAPTER 4
THE UNSEEN WORLD

Just as Gerritt feared, the proper inns of the Middle City were oversold, so we had to settle for a bagra flop house wedged between two piles of shemechas. The dormer included neither kitchen nor commons, but at least we procured a private room. The bagramate celebrated the Eidolon's arrival well into the night, while I slept fitfully on a straw palette, plagued by drumming and maudlin Karochan trope.

Six days to revelation.

We awoke at the first slap of the morning sun. Gerritt led me through the bagra's western bloc, beyond the last riser of shemechas and through a dry culvert that ran beneath the hardpack street. Beyond the mouth of the culvert, we entered a hidden cul-de-sac tucked between an abandoned gatehouse of the outer wall and an empty basin. I scanned the foreboding storefronts: a sawbones, a Runic calligrapher, a relic monger, and Gerritt's thaumaturgical, outed by the iron talismans nailed into the frame of the front door.

The charmed door swung open with the jingle of bells, and we entered a small vestibule draped with hanging fetishes and lined with scattered urns. My ears popped as we passed beneath the craftsman's wards, through a beaded curtain and into a dim, windowless chamber at the back of the shop.

Gerritt's thaumaturge waved us inside his laboratory without looking up from his canted crafting desk. He looked to be hard at work mending one of his fetishes with wax and flame. While we waited to be tended, Gerritt quietly drew my attention to a line of shrunken Sanduvali heads hanging from the rafters by the stiff bristles of their bleached hair. The heads watched us in turn, and one of them cracked a sly smile with sewn lips.

It was no wonder I felt the pressure upon entering. Clashing arcanum littered the laboratory, and I began to wonder if the phalanx of fetishes was intended to keep questing sorcerers out or restless powers in. I saw a shelf of Runic talismans above a disorganized pile of Shoni votives. Beneath a Mithrite totem of the Iron Ram, a Kemetic scrying dial lay abandoned in a bin of white sand. Through the glass door of the tincture cabinet, I marked potion labels in at least a dozen tongues. Agnostic indeed.

The hunched thaumaturge took a moment to finish his work before removing a pair of magnifying specs and rising to bar the door behind us. When he passed back into the laboratory, the beaded curtain became a solid pane of blue glass. Gerritt slumped down in a wooden armchair without invitation and casually crossed his legs, leaving me to stand before this thaumaturge for appraisal. His bald head bobbed up and down as he dry-washed his hands, beady eyes flitting between Gerritt and me.

"Right on time—just as I promised," Gerritt said. He raised his hand to the thaumaturge. "This is Master Glavion, a thaumaturge of the Third Order—or is it Fourth?"

"Th-third," Master Glavion stammered. "Third Order."

"Excellent!" Gerritt said. "And this is Ruxindra bin Vargas."

I've already admitted that I'm uncomfortable with thaumaturgy, and this craftsman's squirrely antics did little to set me at ease.

Master Glavion looked me up and down before his eyes jumped back to Gerritt. "Th-this is...your sister?"

"I'm afraid so," Gerritt said, feigning sobriety. "You can understand our predicament."

Master Glavion's head bobbed up and down again. "Where did you say you were from?"

"Azytanthum," Gerritt said, launching seamlessly into every unnecessary detail of the story he'd concocted. "We're minor nobility—money lenders with a starving ledger. The jealous Graces cursed my parents with six daughters, each homelier than the next. I haven't the wealth to care for a litter of old maids into their dotage, so It's been my life's great labor to find suitable husbands for the lot. I'm pleased to say, I've been largely successful in my negotiations. Azytanthum is rich with desperate landlords and gullible amirs. Only poor Ruxindra remains. With her fertility waning, I hoped to find her an Ohtahpi magistrate given to exotic tastes."

"I suppose she is a bit long in the tooth," Glavion said, squinting into my rictus grin. "But she doesn't look so homely to me."

"You're kind to say so," Gerritt cut in. "Fair enough on the outside, I suppose, but I'm afraid our dear Ruxy's attempts at courtship have all been frustrated by a foul temper and loose morals."

"My brother talks too much," I seethed.

Gerritt shared a knowing glance with Master Glavion. "You see what I mean?"

The thaumaturge nodded ebulliently, then turned to his cabinet to retrieve several opaque vials of tinted glass. "You have a suitor picked out?" he asked.

"I believe I do," Gerritt said, too pleased with himself by half. The bastard was enjoying this. "But I fear my dear sister's impurity may present an obstacle. These Ohtahpi do trend toward the traditional."

Master Glavion snorted. "That's putting it delicately." He carried the tinctures between his fingers to a small iron cauldron and began pouring them out in precise proportions. "She'll have to disrobe."

"Not a chance!" I snapped.

"Now now, Ruxy." Out of the corner of my eye, I saw Gerritt wagging his finger. "Do as Master Glavion says."

Grumbling, I began removing my outer layers, stripping down to my underclothes.

"That's a good girl," Gerritt chided. "If you'd been this guarded with your maidenhead, we wouldn't have to be here in the first place."

The cauldron began to steam with the admixture, and Master Glavion approached with a long tape measure extended between his hands. He stopped short, eyes painting the array of scars on my naked body.

"Something wrong?" I prompted.

Instead of answering directly, he glanced over my shoulder at Gerritt. "She's a bit...well-traveled."

"She can speak for herself," I hissed. It was no great struggle to play the shrew as Gerritt had cast me.

"Her suitor is aware of the damage," Gerritt said, ever quick with an improvisation. "I believe he finds some carnal appeal in the scarring. To each their own, I suppose. Far be it for me to judge another man's fetish, especially when it serves me."

The thaumaturge's eyes narrowed. He withdrew half a step to study us both anew. "I hear the Mahak is planning a blood rite to accompany the Eidolon's investment... A virgin sacrifice by fire."

"Oh? Sounds colorful, if a bit wasteful." Gerritt's voice inflected the perfect blend of surprise and indifference, but Master Glavion's suspicions had already been aroused.

He took another step back from me and resumed dry-washing his hands. "You must understand...my work endures at the sufferance of His Holy Majesty. He turns a blind eye toward our little heathen enclave, and we take great pains to avoid provoking him."

"A sound business practice if I've ever heard one," Gerritt said. "But what does it have to do with my dear sister's pending nuptials?"

Master Glavion's throat bobbed as he swallowed. "Which magistrate did you say it was to whom she is troth?"

Gerritt exhaled. He slowly dragged himself out of his chair and crossed the laboratory to stand between me and the reluctant thaumaturge. He produced a heavy purse from his satchel and pressed its jangling contents into Master Glavion's pudgy hand.

"No more questions," Gerritt said.

The thaumaturge peered up at his intense expression, weighing the purse in his hand. With a sigh, he vanished the small fortune into one of the myriad pockets of his coat and returned to his tape measure.

Gerritt restored his pleasant grin and retreated to his armchair while Master Glavion silently took my measurements. I gritted my teeth as he methodically poked and prodded me with clammy hands, recording my bust and inseam, as well as the breadth of my hips and the short distance from my navel to my waist. With a nervous cough, he directed me to spread my legs and checked the circumference of each thigh. With those numbers in hand, he returned to his cauldron and began shaving the edges of a yellow fungus into the concoction with the blade of a silver knife.

"This will take a moment," he muttered.

With the craftsman tending his cauldron, I began pacing the laboratory in my underclothes, peering inside vases and scanning the shelves of inarticulate arcanum. I reached for the only vial in Master Glavion's cabinet with a label I could read: *Tears of Yorona.*

"Please don't touch anything!" Master Glavion piped, as if he had eyes in the back of his head.

I replaced the milky vial and turned to shut the cabinet, when a wooden stand supporting three black tablets caught my eye. A small pile of stone filings surrounded the stand, as well as a set of metal etching tools. I felt my heartbeat quicken as I read the symbols carved into the stones. The outer two I didn't recognize, but the third raised the hairs on the back of my neck: three serpents bound in hopeless knots, their bodies layered with gnostic text.

In my priesthood, we are not sorcerers, though many laymen assume us to be. Our rites delve the surface of many arcane wells, but we do not plumb their depths. Sorcerers and thaumaturges reach for these sources by ritual, craft and cant, but the power they seek to wield is no sessile weapon. It possesses a will of its own and often enough, it reaches back. The Unseen World speaks in coincidence and walks in allusion. I heard it speaking now, though I lacked the talent to translate its warning.

Gerritt must have read the sudden change in my bearing, because he broke character to squint at me quizzically. I turned back to the tablet, gently tracing the lines of the *naga'tlat* with a finger.

Master Glavion appeared at my side. "I thought I told you not to touch anything?"

I withdrew my hand. "What is this?"

The shrewd expression returned to wrinkle his brow, and I suspected our cover had been truly blown. I only hoped Gerritt's purse was heavy enough to purchase discretion.

"My clients expect anonymity," he said.

Even that was enough of an admission to pique my interest. No thaumaturgical curio, then. These tablets had been made to order, but for whom? I nodded, glancing back at the gnostic etching.

Master Glavion cleared his throat impatiently. "If you'll follow me back to the cauldron."

I did as I was told and endured another round of poking and prodding. When Master Glavion finished handling me, he ladled the admixture from his cauldron into a glass mister that looked like a noblewoman's perfume bottle. "Close your eyes and mouth," he instructed. "The glamor can be quite astringent."

Again, I did as I was told and felt the bright caress of the tonic's mist. The thaumaturge coated my body from head to toe. The treatment smelled vaguely floral, and across my exposed skin I suffered the prickle of a mild alchemical burn.

"That's it?" I asked. I felt no great change from the treatment, no transmutation of spirit.

Master Glavion nodded, setting his mister back down on a shelf above the cauldron. "The glamor will confound any of your prospective husband's attempts to divine your purity."

Gerritt rose from his seat a second time to judge the thaumaturge's work. He circled me once, smirking. "How long will it last?" he asked.

Master Glavion tilted his head back and forth. "A month, assuming normal wear and tear. I do recommend consummating your nuptials as quickly as possible to dissuade any future investigations."

Gerritt stroked his chin thoughtfully. I reached down for my pile of clothes, but he grabbed my arm to stop me. I nearly broke his wrist but restrained myself.

"And what if they subject her to a *manual* inspection?" he asked the thaumaturge.

Master Glavion returned holding a small fetish—a gilled mushroom cap folded back on itself and bound with a black sinew. "She should— *ahem*—insert this charm before presenting for said inspection. Once the spell is set, the charm will mimic the appearance and behavior of a pristine maidenhead straight through the consummation."

He placed a vile trinket on my palm. I stared at the fetish, then up at the thaumaturge. "You expect me to put this inside my vagina?"

Master Glavion winced with Gerritt chortling along like a buffoon.

"Surely not the strangest thing you've had inside yourself." Gerritt laughed again. "Don't look so morose! Your future husband awaits. If you require assistance applying the charm, I'd be happy to lend a hand—"

I closed my fist around the fetish and punched him right between his ribs. Gerritt's laughter ended with a pained *horf*, and Master Glavion ushered us out of his laboratory. No craftsman has ever been so happy to see the back of us.

CHAPTER 5

LINES IN THE SAND

Then came the waiting.

We passed the rest of the day in the western bagra, guarding our intentions, hiding in plain sight. Gerritt attached us to a blended congregation of urban Ohtahpi and their nomadic cousins from the Yusakot Creche. The merry band had procured a butchered goat, which they cooked over a spitfire in the middle of the street. We watched their drumming and dancing, much like the Arrekot's performance on the Shevat Zubaydin. They graciously shared their feast, shaving thin cuts of meat into a set of communal bowls that they seasoned with coriander and kurkumin root. We mimicked the Ohtahpi, who took turns scooping morsels from the bowls with pockets of manakeesh, a spongy flatbread that tasted like wild yeast.

As the feasting wore on, a Yusakot cleric sang a short sermon with the aid of her young husbands. The notes of Karochan trope always sounded melancholy to my ear, but the Ohtahpi faces surrounding me all warmed to hear the verses performed in their dead religious tongue. Gerritt had wormed his way among the young men of the creche as he was wont to do, and I soon found myself stranded among the unmarried women in their veilless shalwaz. A short girl with emerald eyes and a wicker circlet approached me as the sermon wound down and the drumming resumed. She looked no older than fourteen, with short, dark hair, recently washed, and supple olive skin, unblemished but for a small beauty mark upon her cheek.

"You are Ruxindra?" she asked brightly.

I confirmed it with a curt nod, for I already suspected what she must be, and I began to lament the way her ilk kept finding me.

"Your brother tells me we are to be sister-wives," the girl said.

"My brother talks too much."

The girl giggled like the child she was. "That's all brothers, I think. Those are mine over there." She pointed down the street where five young men with the same coarse hair and matching beards were grappling over a goblet drum. "Be grateful G-d only saddled you with the one."

I said nothing, for I hoped that she would leave, but of course she did not.

"I'm Liyah," she said. When I did not continue to engage, she began rocking on the balls of her feet and glancing around the gathering. "Can I show you something?" she finally asked. "Sister-wife to sister-wife."

I sighed. Seeing no way to extricate myself without giving offense, I acquiesced and followed Liyah up a maze of brownstone staircases threading the adjacent block of shemechas. Our path climbed through the alleys, crossing row after row of mudbrick hovels until we reached a flat wall set with a lattice of protruding stones.

"I'll go first," Liyah said, boldly hoisting herself up the stone ladder. "Try to follow my steps. The stones are not all stable."

We climbed the stones until we reached a summit of uneven rooftops. From this vantage, I had a full view of the familial gathering below and several similar gaggles coalescing around bagra crossroads throughout the western bloc. How small they looked from so high—and so at ease. Beiyit tarps cluttered the edges of the wider streets, their canvas walls pitched too close to the open-air sewers. I expected the Ohtahpi to greet their G-dhead's rebirth with some degree of solemnity. Instead, the Holy City thrummed with celebration. Perhaps the arousal would diminish to a more prayerful timbre as the syzygy approached, but looking down on the raucous carnival of adulators, I wasn't so sure.

I crossed the rooftop to stand at Liyah's side. We faced the retaining wall upon which sat the Middle City, with a clear view of an open plaza guarded by Jassanid spears. Some sort of shelter had been raised at the center of the plaza, a vast canvas tent dyed vibrant shades of red, purple, and blue. Offerings—or else mere decorations—had been placed around the base of the tent: cabbages and piles of fresh fruit, bundles of palm fronds and willow branches bound with myrtle and jasmine sprigs.

Liyah's gaze possessed an intensity unbecoming of her youth. A warm breeze rippled across her short hair, and she brushed a single tear from her perfect cheek.

"What is that?" I asked, nodding at the distant shelter.

"The *Cikkot*," she said. "That is where we will meet him, and where we will be given to the flame."

No tent, then. A pyre. The festive shelter took on an ominous cast. "Were you given a choice?" I asked foolishly. "Do you want to be *lehakva*?"

"Were *you*?" Liyah asked with surprising irreverence. She closed her eyes and inhaled the warm breeze. "It is an honor to be married to G-d."

"It is not an honor to burn," I said, perhaps too bitterly.

"My father says that we should think of it as a release," Liyah said. "The flames will break our mortal chains and deliver our souls unto him."

"And what do you think?" I asked.

She peered at me quizzically as if no one had thought to ask her that question, and I was sure they had not. "I think...I would have liked to endure these chains a while longer. They do not chafe so badly." She craned her neck to look up at me. We stood so close. If she expected comforting words, I had none. I did not deal in platitudes. I offered something greater, for success in my mission would mean that Liyah and every other *lehakva* in Mahakalpe might be spared.

"It does not seem holy," I said, hoping I might appeal to her sense of piety. The Ohtahpi nomads kept every extant clone of the Tractate, and even their younglings would know its prohibitions well. Her eyes pinched inward, curious. "We are forbidden blood sacrifice," I clarified.

Liyah shrugged her small shoulders. "We live in scripture," she said, turning back to the distant *Cikkot.* "Our G-d is reborn and our faith with him."

Not yet. Not ever, by the vigilance of my line. "An Arrekot cleric told me something similar," I said. "But change seems a weak foundation for any faith."

She shook her head. "I would not question your teacher, but perhaps you misunderstood. Our language may be dead, but our stories live. Karochan grows in layers like an elder ziggurat." She stacked her hands in demonstration, one over the other. "Each stone level placed atop the last. The older faces become obscured, but they are never gone."

All the ruined ziggurats of the Ohtahpi desert said otherwise, but I didn't feel the need to spoil her metaphor. "You believe this Eidolon will lay a new stone?" I asked instead.

She laughed then, not bitterly. "We are ever building—each of us. The Word provides the foundation, a Tractate pressed in stubborn bronze. In the time of the Second Temple, the desert sages reread the Twelve Plates and wrote the *Midras* with ink and scroll. Twenty generations hence, the Uvvas of the Scattering revisited the *Midras* and wrote the *Tachne* with fingers and sand."

"*Sand?*" I didn't mean to sound so incredulous.

Liyah's gaze wandered back to the *Cikkot.* "I forget how little you *Hesserat* know. Not literal sand. The *Tachne* are oral traditions. Rereadings of the rereadings. The details yield with each telling."

I cocked an eyebrow, at least a little intrigued. "Isn't that a bit flimsy for divine wisdom?"

Liyah shrugged her knobby shoulders again. "Some clerics consider the *Tachne* our holiest scripture, for its words absorb the wisdom of every age."

I'd read the *Midras* in Nurindra. Parchment traveled better than plates of bronze. They were the only Karochan texts that passed beyond the mountains of Ohtahp and so formed the foundation of every foreign congregation—the "*Hesserat,*" though only the Ohtahpi used that pejorative term. I'd never heard of these *Tachne* before, and I doubted anyone in my priesthood knew of their existence.

"How old are you?" Liyah asked after a long pause.

"I'll be thirty by the Ides of Tamzu," I said, translating my birthdate into the Ohtahpi count.

"So old," she said, and from this child's perspective, perhaps it was true. "I have that advantage, at least."

"Oh?"

She smiled sadly. "I know little of what I'll miss."

I had no response to that, and so I kept silent, waiting for an opportunity to escape, but Liyah's green eyes held me fast.

"I do not think you will see the Ides of Tamzu, sister," she said.

The Ohtahpi seemed determined to pursue their revelry deep into the night, but I eventually managed to peel Gerritt away from his arak and coax him back to our dormer. He learned from the Yusakot that all pilgrims were called to present their *lehakva* at the Sahir the next morning. My sister-wives and I were to be renditioned to the Mahak's benevolent custody for two nights of preparation and pampering. On the third day, we'd meet our G-dling spouse.

I watched Gerritt trying on the costume he'd acquired for the next day's performance. The blue embroidered tunic looked stiflingly hot as did the cream cravat, but he certainly looked the part of an Azyti moneylender from a house of fading renown.

"Where did you even find that in Mahakalpe?" I asked.

"The Holy City is a cosmopolitan thoroughfare!" he said, tying a fanciful knot in his ruffled cravat. "You can find all manner of odds and ends if you know where to look." He glanced down at his leather boots and frowned. "The shoes do clash, but it's a long walk from Azytanthum. I suppose they can be overlooked." He turned to face me with arms open wide. "How do I look?"

"Like a usurious peacock," I said.

"Perfect." He pumped his eyebrows, smiling with all his burnished teeth. "Wait until you see what I found for you."

Gerritt frustrated me to the brink of lunacy, but he had his uses. Each time one of his unsavory vices complicated our errands, I had to remind myself that he was a sorcerer of no small talent with a nose for uncovering the matériel of our trade. He'd seen more of Hebdomar than any man I'd ever known, and he had a keen memory for its every uncanny nook. More often than not, the value of Gerritt's company outweighed its considerable cost, but I found myself frequently checking those scales to ensure that favorable balance remained.

And so I checked them once again as he produced my costume from a crate atop his sleeping palette. He held the garment up by the sleeves, his lascivious grin peeking over the swooping neckline. I'd been expecting a simple gown with modest accessories—something akin to the white dresses worn by the Ohtahpi offerings. Instead, he'd conjured up a lurid yellow dress sewn from thick silk brocade. The lace silhouette would have been scandalous on any woman, but I stand nearly six feet tall, and I knew at a glance the gauzy fabric would barely brush the tops of my knees. Elliptical cutouts framed the slim bodice, which was also backless but for three thin straps.

I glowered at the garment with such heat that I was surprised it didn't burst into flame. "What is the matter with you?" I snapped.

"You don't like it? You wouldn't believe how many crates I had to dig through in the Middle City's garment den just to find it!"

"I told you to get something *virginal.*"

"And so I did." Gerritt gawked at the dress then back at me, apparently shocked by my dismay.

"I can't present myself to the Mahak in this!"

"Why ever not?"

"Because I'll look like an Arrami circus whore!"

Gerritt chuckled dismissively. "Don't be ridiculous, Rux. You're playing the part of an Azyti bride. I can't truss you up in white like some Ohtahpi crecheling. The noblewomen of Azytanthum are not so reserved. Have you ever seen an Azyti betrothal? Profligate affairs—and the young nubiles all dress in canary, not gutless white."

"Half the dress is *missing,*" I hissed.

"Windows to the unspoiled flesh that awaits!" Gerritt traced the thin bodice with his hand. "It's the cutouts that complete the disguise."

I closed my eyes, massaging my temples, and spoke very slowly. "I'm offering myself in symbolic union to the Demiurge reborn, not spreading my thighs for some *gouty water baron.*"

"The Eidolon is a man like any other until he's invested. At least in this—" he dangled the dress from two fingers, "—you'll stand out."

"I don't want to stand out," I said, close to seething. "I want to get close enough to kill him."

"And so you shall!" he said. "You'll certainly catch his eye. How else do you intend to compete with a menagerie of olive-skinned beauties half your age?"

"I'm not planning to seduce him, Gerritt. I saw his caravan enter the city in the eastern bloc. He's just a boy."

He lowered the dress, all the mischief and good humor vanished from his cast. "A *boy*?"

I nodded and sat back on my pallet with a deep sigh. "No older than twelve or thirteen by the look of him."

Gerritt set the dress aside and took a step closer. "Does this...complicate your task?"

"Of course not," I answered too quickly. "We didn't come here to slay what is, but what will be."

Gerritt nodded slowly. He knew me too well.

I peered up from my boots. "Canary?" I asked to break the tension.

"The color of yolk," he said. "Of hatchlings and spring."

"Fine," I said, laying back on my pallet. "I'll wear the dress."

Night wrapped our bagra chamber in perfect dark, and I lay awake listening to the sound of Gerritt's steady breathing. I knew he hadn't found sleep either, for the man snored like a broad-toothed saw. I'd grown used to it over time, and the quiet breathing proved more disruptive by far.

"What?" I said, still staring at the inky ceiling over my pallet.

"I didn't say anything." His disembodied voice wafted in from the darkness, perfectly alert.

"It's your silence that's keeping me awake," I lied.

I heard him grumbling, then the shifting of his roughspun blanket as he sat up on his pallet. "I dislike leaving you to fend for yourself in the Sahir," he said.

"You don't think I can handle the Mahak and his slave soldiers?"

A long pause answered my boast. When Gerritt's voice returned, it seemed to cross a distance that didn't exist within the cramped confines of our dormer. "Something isn't settled... This city's older than it has any right to be. I'm...*interfered* with."

Gerritt wasn't often given to a sorcerer's numinous ambiguity, which served us well as companions, for I rarely had the patience for it. I rolled over on the pallet, turning my back to him. "We need to sleep."

I never heard him slip back beneath his sheets.

CHAPTER 6

LEHAKVA

Five days to revelation.

We dressed in our costumes an hour after dawn. Gerritt helped me with the straps of my dress, while I tugged fruitlessly at the ridiculous skirt, hoping the fabric might bend to my will and stretch to at least breach the knobs of my knees.

"I have something for you," Gerritt said, producing a small black taffeta from his tunic. He unraveled the cloth to present a fine gold chain tied to a crystal pendant. He passed his finger over the frosted crystal, and it glowed softly in response to his touch. "I found the stone at the Runic shop in the heathen bloc." He held the necklace up by the chain. "May I?"

In answer, I turned my open back to him and gathered my hair over one shoulder. The stone felt nearly weightless against my breastbone as he latched the chain around my neck. The soft pads of his fingers lingered on my skin, withdrawing only once I turned around to face him. "Another Azyti tradition?" I asked.

He shook his head once. "I invested the crystal with a charm."

I took a step back from him and covered the pendant with a palm. "You know I don't like to be ensorcelled."

He rolled his eyes. "You're not *ensorcelled*. You're wearing a talisman."

Semantics, as far as I was concerned. "What if the Mahak detects its geas? Or the Eidolon?"

He raised his hands, placating. "It's quite artfully done. Not even a Magnamaegi could sense it without inspecting the stone."

I chewed my lower lip, still skeptical. I trusted Gerritt's judgment where arcana were concerned, but only just. "What sort of charm?" I asked.

"A translocation. After the deed is done—or if you find yourself backed into a corner—break the crystal and you will be transported back to this room. If you find yourself staked to a pyre, the heat should break it for you, though I expect you'll endure some discomfort in the interim." His eyes drifted up to the ceiling, and I sensed him probing some power far beyond the boundaries of our dormer. "The old Mysin walls of Mahakalpe confound the spell. I would have preferred to have you whisked away to some safer redoubt, but I couldn't manage it. We'll have to escape the city on foot. If you're successful—"

"*When* I am successful."

He allowed it. "*When* you are successful, this city's going to erupt. We'll be hunted by every adulator in Ohtahp."

I closed my palm around the pendant, testing the feel of its jagged lines. Gerritt's intimation bothered me, however well-intentioned. "You think I need a safety net?"

"Wouldn't you rather be prepared for any outcome?

I wasn't being obstinate. I'd already caked myself in thaumaturgical glamor, and no spell came without its attendant costs. The Eidolon's convergence had inundated Mahakalpe with esoteric art, and sorceries did not blend well. Even a charm so small as Gerritt's translocation could have an unpredictable effect.

"Just humor me, Rux." He was pleading now. "If I can't stand by your side, at least let me help in my way."

Again, I acquiesced.

We left the bagra, returning to the switchback stairs that climbed the retaining wall to the Middle City where so many of Mahakalpe's pilgrims converged. With the Syzygy of Avum approaching, the pilgrims tightened their hold on the city. Bodies choked the road up to the Sahir —lean Ohtahpi in their tribal clusters, but also barrel-chested Varag, irritable Subakka, and foreign men betrayed by native garb. Many of these interlopers crowded around the low stone wall that ringed the foreyard at the foot of the Sahir, voyeurs straining to witness the offerings of sundry *lehakva* delivered to their fate.

Emboldened by my submission to his charm, Gerritt entered character, affecting a haughty indifference for the swarming masses, deflecting every unwashed body with the arrogant sneer pinned to his cheeks. It was well enough that he was such an eager performer, for performance was never my strength. Neither was subtlety nor petty deceit.

I already felt naked in the dress, but it was worse without my sword. I knew that I would be denied any proper weaponry in the presence of the Mahak, and I didn't relish trying to explain why an Azyti noblewoman required a fine Nurindran blade. But I still had a job to do, so I pinned up my hair with a whalebone clip, its long central finger capped with tempered steel. Disarmed, but not entirely defanged.

Caledin Vane is a blessed sword—as much a relic of my priesthood as a weapon of war. If the Eidolon completed his investment, I would require its deicidal report, but I didn't intend to let the ritual get that far. Until then, this G-dling boy would still bleed, and I was deadly with any edge.

We approached the gatehouse in the curtain wall footing the cliffs of the Sahir, and a Jassanid guard raised his gauntlet to halt us beneath the teeth of a raised portcullis.

Gerritt tilted his head to the guard in a not-quite-bow. "Lord Vargas of Azytanthum, presenting my sister Ruxindra bin Vargas in troth to the Eidolon on the occasion of his investment."

The armored Jassanid's docile expression paired eerily with his heavy bronze plate and muscular build. His head moved in my direction, eyes shielded by the brim of his helmet. Without speaking, he shifted the gleaming head of his spear from one shoulder to the next and turned to lead us through the gatehouse and into a small foreyard at the base of Mahakalpe's highest retaining wall.

Rows of olive trees and flowering jasmine recalled the bagra plaza where I encountered Senex Amari Desta and his gnostic shrine, but with added splashes of hibiscus and orange bell poppies crying for attention beyond the lines of cut bluestone edging their beds. The Jassanid deposited us with a lockheed in a bold red robe displaying Mahakalpe's Yucca Palm. I heard the word *lehakva* pass between them before the Jassanid departed, returning to his post. The lockheed wore some kind of ceremonial mask, a bronze cage capturing his bald head.

I cleared my throat, eyes flitting to Gerritt, who shrugged in return. My question was too obvious to give it voice. The Mahak's retaining wall offered no obvious ascent—no switchback stairs or armored doors. From edge to edge, I saw only stone.

The lockheed's eyes shifted behind the thin bars of his mask. "His Holy Majesty is not expecting tribute from Azytanthum," he said.

Gerritt stepped in front of me. "Why would that be?" he asked, inflecting a stroke of defiance.

The lockheed cocked his caged head, peering at me over Gerritt's shoulder. "It's very far," he said flatly, returning to Gerritt.

"A credit to us for making the journey on our fair city's behalf," he retorted. "I believe the occasion justifies the hardship. We were told that all who follow the Word are welcome inside the walls of Mahakalpe, and that all men are brothers along the Shevat Zubaydin."

"And you bring *lehakva*?" the lockheed asked. I wished I could see more of his expression, but the caged mask prevented it.

"As all pilgrims are called to do," Gerritt confirmed.

"*Lehakva* must go to the Eidolon pure."

Gerritt nodded. "And so she is."

I felt the lockheed's hidden eyes probing me again. "She is old," he said.

"You dare question my sister's chastity?" Gerritt sounded convincingly aghast. "What manner of discourteous lout does His Holy Majesty employ? I demand to speak with the Mahak."

"She is old," the lockheed repeated.

"More's the blessing of her forbearance," Gerritt shot back. "Now if you're quite finished insulting my sister—"

The lockheed raised a thin hand leaden with chains and gold rings to forestall the outrage. "The palace kantors will have the truth of it."

He produced a heavy stone key from beneath his robe and mounted three small steps to a tiny platform that footed the retaining wall. Huffing with feigned impatience, Gerritt returned to my side, and we watched together as the lockheed pressed the key against unbroken stone.

The stone *yielded*. The key sank into the retaining wall, and as the lockheed turned it, a seam appeared. The stone peeled back like the edge of a scroll, revealing a steep, cyclopean staircase that rose hundreds of feet to the city's final plateau.

I preceded Gerritt onto the platform and gazed up the dizzying ascent.

"The Mahak awaits," the lockheed said.

"I'll be sure to mention your insults levied against our G-dling bride." Gerritt spat his retort in passing as he mounted the first of many stairs.

No one who has seen as much of Hebdomar as I have would dispute that it is a fallen world. The great cultures of antiquity are ash, their advancements lost or maligned. Our modern sorceries grasp the Unseen World by its thinnest threads, and our G-d is dead. So rare are the occasions to look upon a pristine capsule from our golden youth that it's easy to forget their splendor. Perhaps it is a gift that memory sands the sharpest edges from the sublime. Dun recollections soften to better blend with the banality of our time. The Sahir of Mahakalpe was one such relic, as much a fortress and a palace as a vortex of the Divine. Fluted columns in holy proportions. Marble stairs and floors of polished glass. Artisan statues of Mysin Theocrats and ancient heroes I could not name. A great gold rotunda, as lustrous as the day it was raised.

Such wonders our ancestors created. Nevermore. Every dilapidated artifact claiming descent from these pinnacles invited a regrettable comparison.

We faced the Mahak's full court in the Sahir's hypostyle. Ohtahpi magistrates and palace functionaries filled the risers to either side of the marble receiving floor, a great host presiding over delivery of the *lehakva*. Fountains poured from the mouths of hanging statues to join a thin moat of running water transecting the hypostyle. The stream flowed between two arched tunnels, its waters vanishing into the palace walls to be refreshed in some deeper cistern or well. If not for his gilded seat, I would not have picked out the Mahak from the crowd. His Holy Majesty, last of the great regents of Ohtahp, latest in an unbroken line stretching back to the time of Old Mysin, made no great impression. He was thin and bearded, dressed in a brown headwrap and cream shalwaz that might have belonged to any Middle City merchant. He sat among his highest courtiers upon a raised, white dais beyond the moat. I counted nine before Gerritt nudged me to follow him into an obsequious bow. We both knelt before the court, pressing our foreheads to the polished floor.

"Rise," a young vizier commanded. The hypostyle echoed with the rapping of his scepter against the floor.

We stood as demanded, and Gerritt quickly claimed the floor. "Holy Majesty. The faithful of Azytanthum attend the resurrection of our G-d, and we bring a gift as all pilgrims are called to offer." His eyes drifted up to the frescoed dome of the rotunda. "It is the honor of a lifetime to stand within these hallowed halls."

I scanned the dais again. In addition to the red-robed vizier, three other magistrates wore the same caged mask I'd seen on the lockheed beneath the Sahir. I saw a cleric in red and shalwaz beside three young girls in palace dress. The Mahak sat between his wife, the Mahakva, an aging Ohtahpi beauty with full gray hair, and a younger man suited in golden linen, his hide belt clasped with a buckle shaped like the Yucca Palm. Some princeling, perhaps, dressed to outshine his father. The Ohtahpi practiced plural marriage, though either man or woman might become the nucleus of a familial pod. Only the Mahak bound himself monogamously, a hedge against the discord of surplus heirs.

My gaze lingered on a Sylphid Slayn, the only foreign dignitary present, her station identified by her emerald tiara. She caught me staring, and her blue lips turned down, glass wings vibrating at her shoulders.

"Holy Majesty," Gerritt continued. "I offer my sister, Ruxindra bin Vargas, in troth to the Eidolon, and as *lehakva* anointing our G-dhead's return."

I felt the weight of a thousand judgmental eyes as the Mahak edged forward in his throne. For a moment, I lost myself in the regent's soft, brown eyes—almost kindly. I heard Gerritt clear his throat, and realized he had extended his arm, summoning me forward. The Mahakva folded her arms across her chest as I approached.

Once again, the vizier's sonorous voice filled the chamber. "Mahakalpe welcomes all pilgrims, but perhaps our *Hesserat* cousins mistake their charge. *Lehakva* are not despoiled. They must go to their G-dling husband pure. This offering—"

The Mahak raised his hand, silencing his vizier mid-sentence. He covered his mouth with a fist and gently coughed. "I doubt our cousins misunderstood the requirements." His voice was much softer than his vizier's—as kind as his curious eyes. The entire court leaned in to capture every word. "It is not our place to question *lehakva*'s purity. The kantors will confirm it." He lowered his hand, and two of his masked attendants came forward, crossing the moat by way of unseen stones concealed by flowing water. I glanced back at Gerritt standing stoic as they led me to the dais to present me before the throne.

The Mahak spread his arms and proffered a grandfatherly smile. "Ruxindra is a beautiful name," he said. "Nursili to my ear, though I am long absent from the world beyond our G-dling Cradle. Times change, as do names, I suppose."

"Yes, Your Holy Majesty."

"Tell me, Ruxindra—why do you wish to be wed to our Eidolon?"

I wasn't expecting an interrogation, but I didn't think it wise to lie. I was beginning to suspect these caged masks identified Karochan kantors, and too many sorcerers had an uncanny ear for falsehood. "I—I don't know that I do wish it," I said.

"Oh?" Lines formed across the Mahak's aged brow.

"I come before you to perform a duty, Majesty. We all must serve."

He nodded thoughtfully and raised one finger, a signal for the masked attendants to escort me beyond the hypostyle, through a narrow corridor concealed behind a curtain of falling water. We walked the winding hallway until we reached a canted marble slab at the center of a small, round room where the kantors instructed me to disrobe. As an added precaution, I tucked Gerritt's necklace inside my folded dress.

The androgynous magi both had shaved heads like the lockheed, but I could glean through their masks that they were women. They instructed me to disrobe and lie naked across the cold stone slab. The revelation of my scars passed unremarked, as one bent to light a silver thurible of incense, while the other unboxed a phallic wooden instrument carved at the handle with Karochan skritglyphs.

The first kantor dangled the thurible over my body, perfumed smoke billowing from its silver pores, burning my eyes to tearing and prickling my sex. She dressed the ritual inspection with muttered notes of Karochan trope. When the kantor's puissant chant concluded, a small stone ingot crowning the thurible turned from jet to maiden's red. She nodded to her partner, who then knelt at the base of the slab and thrust her masked face between my legs. I braced for violation as she peeled back my petals and stuck her wooden wand inside me. I felt a painless crack within my pelvis, and the kantor withdrew her instrument. I lifted my head to see the false blood of the thaumaturge's charm webbing the kantor's wand.

"She is unbroken," the second kantor said, rising steadily to her feet.

They helped me dress and marched me back through the winding corridor to the hypolyte. Upon returning to the dais, I saw that Gerritt still held his position across the moat. I tried to catch his eye while the Mahak received his magi's report with a broadening grin. He clapped his palms together. "*Masra elohaim*! That makes thirty wives to be delivered to our revenant Lord."

The Mahakva didn't look half as pleased as her husband, and the princeling audibly yawned. I bowed my head in deference, evading any further need to dissemble.

The Mahak rose from his throne and surprised me again, grasping me by the arms and pulling me into a warm embrace. He kissed the center of my forehead. "You may take a moment to say farewell to your brother before joining your sisters inside the keep."

"Thank you, Holy Majesty."

He directed me to the hidden stones within the moat and left me to cross to Gerritt alone. As soon as I reached him, Gerritt pulled me into an embrace much tighter than the Mahak's. "I hope that wasn't too uncomfortable," he whispered in my ear.

"Your thaumaturge did well," I said.

"You're on your own from here."

"Just me and twenty-nine sprigs of virgin kindling."

He kissed my cheek to make it look authentic. "I won't be far. Don't forget the charm."

CHAPTER 7

GARDEN OF PLENTY

J assanid guards materialized from their hidden posts, and I was once again led from the hypolyte, through the winding marble halls of the Mahakalpe Sahir. The soldiers directed me through an arched doorway and into a vast, enclosed atrium open only to the sky. The Mahak's water garden was lush and verdant in a manner that bordered on the obscene. Soft foreign grasses cut by narrow stone pathways. Fluted columns draped with hanging vines. Fruit trees and flowering shrubs in abundance around shallow ponds crowded by lotus blossoms and lily pads. Not even the fertile river valleys of eastern Ohtahp could compare.

A harpist in palace red sat beside a tall stone fountain, plucking pleasant notes to accompany the chirping of frogs. I saw no Jassanid spears in the garden, though I suspected they must be close. The whole Sahir had been built with subtle alcoves masked by falling water and expert masonry. I saw only young women, a nubile menagerie dressed almost entirely in white. My sister-wives to be, at least for some short time. *Lehakva.*

Four Ohtahpi girls who might have been sisters in truth sat beside the nearest pond, weaving chains from flower stems and crowning each other in turn. Elsewhere, a tall woman in green with fairer skin than the

Ohtahpi helped a shorter girl reach a ripe pomegranate from a hanging branch. Most of the other girls engaged in idle chatter over silver platters piled high with figs and cheese. I recognized the sun-haired nomad I'd brushed up against at the Eidolon's reception. She sat among a handful of her sister-wives watching the harpist play, barefoot and bunching soft grass between her toes. I searched for Liyah, but didn't find her. Perhaps she'd yet to be delivered, though I hoped she'd escaped, that she was free.

It is both strength and weakness that I am not easily saddened—not prone to melancholia nor bouts of general malaise. As I watched these offerings taking their leisure in the Mahak's garden, I felt nothing but rage. This sacrifice by fire reeked of eldritch sorcery, but it was a familiar stench, for every culture on the face of Hebdomar still carried foul hints of its sordid bouquet. All manner of blood has been spilled in pursuit of divine favor, but an inordinate share belongs to women—to the young and the pure. Men great and small tremble before the mystique of female sexuality. They seek to squeeze it and bridle it—to see it throttled and, yes, destroyed. I do not deny that some mean spark may be released in its destruction, but to see such a power nourished? To cultivate it? To guide it through its fullest bloom? There lies a power to debase every haughty sorcerer and necromage—to bend every monarch and send crass thaumaturges screaming for their middens.

I kicked off my shoes and sat on the ledge of the fountain beside an unclaimed platter of goat cheese and bread. A small blue frog leapt from its lily pad with a chirp to escape my company. A few feet away, one of the Ohtahpi *lehakva* smiled wistfully as she tossed crumbs of manakeesh into the water, feeding red anguills that surged to the surface to gobble them up. I didn't recognize her at first, but she recognized me. She abandoned her crust of manakeesh and slid across the fountain ledge to join me.

"It's you," she said.

I did recognize her, then. The Arrekot *lehakva* I'd seen dancing on the Shevat Zubaydin. Those slender curves and flowing tresses of dark hair left an impression. She still wore her wicker crown, though its color had faded to light brown without the gift of moonlight.

"I didn't realize you were to be wed to the Eidolon," she said. "I would have introduced myself."

I tore a piece of manakeesh from the platter and slathered it with goat cheese. "You have me now," I said before taking a bite.

"I'm Dahlia." She helped herself to a sliver of fig and slipped it onto her tongue.

"Ruxindra," I said. "Rux, if you prefer."

I watched her slender neck tense as she swallowed. "Why would I prefer to mutilate such a pretty name?"

"Breath is precious." I stretched out my legs and took another bite.

She mimicked me, sidling closer across the ledge. "You *Hesserat* have everything backwards." She giggled. "It's words that are precious. Names should only grow over time. I will not help you diminish your own."

Dahlia's white gown fell nearly to her ankles, and I found myself reaching for the yellow lace of my skirt trending scandalously up my thighs. "I never gave it much thought," I said.

Dahlia slipped another sliver of fig between her lips. I could tell she had a dozen questions burning on her tongue; soon enough, one found its way to her ripe lips. "Is it true you've never looked upon the Twelve Plates? That you've never read the original Word?"

"We had the *Midras* at my temple," I said evasively. I knew shrinkingly little of how the *Hesserat* practiced their faith, and I did not think my cover would survive an inquisition.

Fortunately, with her question answered, Dahlia did not pursue. She dipped her hand into the fountain and jumped when one of the lurking anguills rose to nibble her fingers. She glanced over at me, blushing.

I laughed despite myself. "Don't worry," I said. "They're toothless eels—pleasant ornamentals. They only eat the dead skin." Dahlia's complexion paled. "Watch," I told her.

I rotated my body to face the fountain and dipped my bare feet into the water, barely breaching the surface. Three slender anguills slithered over, fish lips puckering to meet my calloused soles. The fountain bubbled with their ferocious nibbling, tickling on the cusp of pain. "The women in Nursin—" I caught myself, "—in *Azytanthum*—they use them as cosmetics. Given enough time, they'll polish even the most haggard feet."

Dahlia peered down at the splashing frenzy with reticent intrigue.

"Try it," I said. "Those pretty feet can't have emerged from the Shevat Zubaydin unblemished."

She hesitated but eventually joined me, pressing one high-arched foot against the water and then the other. More of the anguills swarmed, and one even abandoned me to explore the fresher snack. Dahlia's whole body tensed as the anguills began their feast, but she quickly acclimated to the sensation and began to relax. She giggled once again in that same girlish trill.

"Finally another northerner!"

I retracted my feet from the fountain and turned to find the fair-skinned woman in the green dress standing over us. She thrust one open hand in my face displaying a gaudy diamond ring. "I'm Maddux DiLenus of Oksa," she said.

Maddux expected me to reciprocate, so I clasped her hand and shook. "Ruxindra," I said. "Of Azytanthum."

"An Azyti!" Her thin face lit up with recognition. "My mother trades with the Spicer's Guild in Azytanthum. Spectacular city! Gateway to the Lapis Road. Do you know Tajjar Sabahn bin Khalik?"

"Azytanthum is a big city," I said.

"It certainly is," she agreed, moving on. "You can call me Mads, by the way."

I shared a knowing glance with Dahlia before returning to Maddux to introduce my new acquaintance. "This is Dahlia from the Arrekot Creche."

Maddux's expression soured as her eyes fell on Dahlia, and I knew the look of a woman threatened by the beauty of another. Maddux was still my junior by several years, but she was among the oldest of the *lehakva*. She turned quickly back to me, restoring her solicitous grin. "Another spare daughter to a pious merchant, then?"

"Something like that," I said.

Without seeking leave, Maddux threaded her arm through mine and scooped me off the fountain to carry me away from Dahlia and my plate of cheese. "Aren't you a strong one," she said, probing the lean muscles of my arms. "I do like the dress. You Azyti are always so unencumbered…"

Maddux had an officious way about her that I found refreshing amid all these demure Ohtahpi. I let myself be dragged to the far end of the garden where a golden pitcher of honey mead sat untouched atop a glass pedestal. She poured two cups, again without asking, and thrust one into my hand. Maddux lifted hers immediately to her mouth and drained it.

"Go on," she coaxed. "Just because these boring Ohtahpi don't imbibe, doesn't mean we have to pass our time like ascetics."

I ventured a small sip—dry with just a hint of crisp fruit. A far cry from the bagramate's dishwater arak.

"By what route did you make the pilgrimage?" she asked.

I searched my mental map of the region for a plausible path and decided it was better to keep things vague. "We took a trader's route through the Camelbacks until we reached an outer creche. From there, we followed the Shevat Zubaydin all the way to Mahakalpe's gates."

"Those are troubled passages through the mountains." Maddux clucked her tongue, gently swirling the dregs of her cup.

"My brother accompanied me."

"He must be formidable," she said. "My mother's caravans don't test those trails without a company of armed serai."

"He'd like to think so," I said. Maddux snorted and poured herself another cup. "What about you?" I asked, deftly guiding the conversation away from myself. "It's a long walk from Oksa."

"We took the old Mysin Road out of Arram. I traveled with half my congregation," she said. "In the company of the Slayn."

I perked up at the Sylphid's mention. Sylphid rangers traveled far and wide, but rarely in groups. I'd already seen several in Mahakalpe, and the presence of their Slayn suggested they'd brought forth an entire Swarm. "I saw her in the Mahak's hypolyte," I said, fishing for details. "Any inkling why they've come? I did not think the Swarms followed the Word."

"The Sylphids don't follow anything," Maddux said. "They *study* Karochan—like some base discipline. As if the *Midras* were some reliquary of ancient truth."

"...Isn't that exactly what they are?"

Maddux smiled cruelly. "I don't think the Slayn brought her Swarm to Mahakalpe to witness the Eidolon—at least not principally."

That was interesting. "Seems an unlikely coincidence," I said.

She shook her head. "They're a cryptic bunch. Kept mostly to themselves, but I did overhear a few of them speaking Mysinic. They seemed less concerned with the Eidolon's investment and more curious about whatever comes *next*." Maddux crossed her arms and scanned the panoply of virgin brides taking their leisure about the garden. Her nostrils flared. "Look at them all. Grazing like guileless pigs awaiting slaughter."

I took another sip from my cup to conceal my scowl. I would not have described any of the girls I'd spoken with as guileless, and they were none of them pigs. "That sentiment doesn't sound very holy, sister." I sipped again, this time to hide the grin.

Maddux drank deeply from her cup and when she surfaced, her haughty bearing seemed to deflate. "Not much that's holy about any of this," she muttered.

I lowered my cup and cocked my head to her. I had not expected to find another reluctant bride. "You do not wish to wed the G-dhead?"

She actually scoffed. "Did you see his entrance?" I nodded. "He's a child. I'd be surprised if the Divine Spirit didn't split him down the middle. Not that any of us will live to see it. His guardian, though..." she let the thought dangle unfinished as she chewed her lower lip between two teeth.

The guardian stood out to me, as well—dark-haired and vigilant. If it came to blows between us, I wasn't sure my hairclip would suffice.

A bell chimed from somewhere within the garden, and some of the girls began stirring to answer its call.

"Onto the next facade," Maddux said. She finished her mead and set the empty cup down on the pedestal. "Come on."

The girls all funneled out of the garden through another arched doorway, this one crowned by a marble carving of the Yucca Palm. Maddux remained at my side as we flowed with the other *lehakva* down a broad corridor that led to a steaming bath. That bath was built into the floor of the Sahir, wide enough to comfortably fit twice as many women as we had in our cohort. Vents in the floor tiles refreshed the heat from some buried furnace.

Standing mirrors ringed the bathing chamber, so I seized the opportunity to examine my reflection. It was the first time I'd really seen myself in over a month. I do not carry a pocket mirror among my traveling supplies, and Ohtahp is not rich with placid waters. I can't say I much cared for the image looking back. My skin was dry and blotchy, unevenly bronzed by so many days beneath the cloudless Ohtahpi sky. Dark circles bracketed my eyes, and my hair, typically a wine-dark red, hung listless against my shoulders, sun-bleached and frayed with split ends. I angrily prodded these blemishes with the pads of my fingers, keenly aware of every perfect body undressing behind me. I never thought of myself as vain, but I did take pride in my appearance. A certain hard-bodied appeal had served me well in my priesthood, and in my many tasks as a peripatetic sword. I found no reason in that mirror to be prideful. I looked rundown and, as I'd been frequently reminded, old.

I cut myself off from the mirror and disrobed to join my sister-wives in the bath. Better nude than another moment in those harem silks. Gerritt's talisman, I kept around my neck.

The water's warm report quickly banished any lingering distemper. With an earnest moan, I slid down the blue tile, submerging my body to the chin. I allowed myself to close my eyes, and for one shining moment, the gravity of my environs and my task vanished from sight. Alas, both were waiting when I opened them again.

The bath had filled with soaking *lehakva*. Some of the younger girls played at modesty, sinking their breasts beneath the water and clinging to the corners like frightened moths. I caught my first glimpse of Liyah stretched out lazily along a wet step, her short hair sopping. Not free, then. Far from it. It was ever a pointless dream.

Two female servants in palace garb and chain belts emptied libation urns of scented oil, enriching the bathhouse odor with potpourri and lime. Eager to mark me as her pair, Maddux swam over from the other side of the bath and sat her skinny rump beside me.

"This is nicer than the baths in Oksa," she said. "And fewer flatulent merchant wives seasoning the broth."

I laughed. I was beginning to enjoy her irreverent sense of humor. "The Mahak certainly knows how to treat his *lehakva*."

Maddux cringed. "Don't use that disgusting Karochan slur."

"It's what we are, isn't it?"

"*Ugh*." Maddux moaned and submerged her head beneath the bathwater. When she popped back up, she let her small breasts breach, pink nipples prickling the surface like angler's floats. "We're *brides*," she said. "Betrothed to the Eidolon."

I did not feel the need to point out that we were sacrifices, as well. Maddux surely knew it as well as every other young girl acclimating to the heat of the bath. It is no easy thing to go willingly to one's demise, and if denial helped Maddux live out her term at the Sahir, it was no kindness to take it from her.

"Do you think he'll consummate the marriage with all of us?" she asked.

Until that moment, I hadn't even considered it, and just as quickly, I dismissed the possibility. The blood rite called for maidens, and ritual fire was ever a jealous mate. This conceit of marriage to the Eidolon seemed more the feint. It was the pyres to which we were truly consigned, but that wasn't what Maddux wanted to hear. "I don't think he'll have the time or the stamina," I said.

Maddux frowned. "He'll have us for three days. Surely, the boy will be eager. Look around." She drew an arc through the bath water. "Who could resist such a bounty?"

Her hand shot out with surprising speed, and she tweaked my nipple. Hard.

Maddux's sly grin suggested she had no notion of the danger she was in. I'd killed men for less. The sheer audacity of it—and my inability to respond—drove me to laughter. My first honest laugh in forever.

Maddux's grin broadened. She leaned back against the tile, extending her legs until her feet breached the surface. Between the bracket of her toes, I saw three bodies approaching the bath.

All the girls swimming and soaking around us scrambled to attention as the Mahakva walked up to the rim of the bath flanked by two Jassanid guards. She looked down upon the collection of nude *lehakva* with an upturned nose. Her plump face appeared pinched, gray hair pulled up in a tight gold circlet. Silence gripped the chamber but for the splashing of sheepish girls drifting toward the back of the bath.

The Mahakva huffed, fists propped on wide hips. "You all seem to be enjoying yourselves." Her voice carried the timbre of accusation. "*Masra aruir!* No palace should bear the burden of so much untamed flesh." The Mahakva snapped her fingers, and a line of female attendants entered the chamber bearing towers of absorbent robes. A second set collected the scattered garments pooled along the tiles of the bathhouse. "My holy husband has ordered that you be pampered, and so you shall be, but I will not stand for any profligacy." The attendants holding the robes formed a silent ring around the edge of the bath. "Dry and cover yourselves. Your bridal gowns will be cleaned and returned. The servants will see you to your chambers, where you will remain until called upon for evening prayers. You're to keep to your wing of the Sahir while you await your *fate*."

The Mahakva inflected this last word with such venom. Not a soul in the bath missed her meaning.

A small sound piped out of the bathwater, and I realized a thin girl soaking next to Liyah had begun to cry. Liyah wrapped a comforting arm around her sister and permitted her to weep into her shoulder, pointedly avoiding the Mahakva's judgmental gaze. More tears soon followed from many other girls. Their whimpering echoed off the bathhouse tile, became a feral dirge, another maudlin verse of Karochan trope. The Mahakva's cruelty had breached the thin veneer painting this dire congregation, unleashing a deep well of mourning and despair.

Maddux didn't cry, but she sat in silence beside me, staring daggers at this careless regent.

The Mahakva looked over the baleful display with open disgust. She scoffed loudly and turned on her heels to exit the bathhouse, her Jassanid guards in tow.

CHAPTER 8
SHADES

We walked the halls of the Sahir in silence, a gallows march of virgin girls in plush, tan robes. I expected to be delivered to some pillow-laden harem or else a communal dormer of feather beds stacked in rows, but the Sahir's keep was even bigger than I imagined. The Mahak's servants found private chambers for each of us.

I regrouped with the other *lehakva* for a brief evening service presided over by a bearded cleric in a red headwrap. The kodesha temple in our wing of the Sahir was narrow and spare, but I suspected a more opulent hall of worship existed elsewhere on the grounds. Our cleric performed the entire service in Karochan. I understood none of it, but I followed my sisters through their motions: chanting atonally along with call-and-response prayers; tracing my fingers through a tray of olive oil to paint slick lines across my brow and cheeks; kneeling before the bima to accept a sacrament of bread and salt. The service at least seemed to calm my sisters' nerves, and for that I was grateful.

I returned to my chamber after dark to find a plate of pork and whipped yams awaiting me beside a splashing bowl of pure water and a corked bottle of golden mead. It had the feel of a gaolhouse meal, if a rich one. I'd been expecting some communal feast to celebrate our arrival, but perhaps the Mahakva intervened. We wouldn't want to seem *profligate.*

Waiting bothered me—more than anything else. I am a woman of action, ever unsettled alone with my thoughts. I ate everything and searched for other ways to pass the time. My dress hung from a clothes hook over the chamber armoire, cleaned and steamed as promised. I knew I'd have to don the garish silk once again to meet my G-dling spouse, but for now the Mahak's red linen slip would suffice. How I longed for a pair of trousers and a boiled leather cuirass! I retied the knot in my hair and secured the violent clip. Gerritt's arcane bangle still hung against my breast.

I remembered that we'd been granted freedom of the *wing*, and so we had, for I found my chamber door unguarded and unsealed. Eager to return to motion, I struck out for the keep's hall, dimly lit by tall brass braziers simmering between smooth columns. The firelight revealed only the edges of the colorful frescoes painted onto the arched ceiling. From what little I saw of each scene, the artwork did not appear to be Karochan; too many chiseled nudes unburdened by headwraps or shal-waz. Even the blue strip of sky seemed something foreign to this land, thick with white clouds, too rich with moisture to have formed over Ohtahp. Like so much of the Sahir, the fresco seemed older—belonging to some lost tradition more ancient than Mysin and more joyful by far.

I passed many doors kin to my own and heard the voices of my sister-wives congregating within. Their girlish chatter diminished as I turned down a short set of marble steps into an empty chamber shaped like a diamond. At the center stood a tall black statue of a faceless woman draped in billowing shrouds. Whether the image had been shaped that way by its creator or worn expressionless by the passage of time, I could not say, but I felt its empty gaze haunting me as I circled the room.

I did not know how deep into the Sahir our purview extended, but no red-robed servants nor Jassanid guards emerged from their hidden alcoves to turn me back. So I continued on, down a second corridor askance from the diamond statuary, nearly blackened with its braziers unlit. The hallway swept in banking curves, up a gradual incline that carried me to a dead end—or what seemed like one at a novice glance. A small pool at the end of the hall collected falling water from a hanging gargoyle's mouth. Five-eyed and many-horned, the hideous stone emptied itself between two curved fangs that looked sharp enough to gore a man. The falling water produced a white churn that echoed down the empty hall, but through its obfuscating din I heard the unmistakable sound of heated voices. I half expected to be accosted by a decade of Jassanids and dragged back to my chamber, but no slave-soldiers materialized. The voices seemed to be coming from inside the stone of the Sahir—beyond the waterfall.

The Sahir is a marvel, fortified by elevation, sorcery and stone. Each of its halls was yet another constituent fortress, guarded by illusion and brilliant design. I stood in the throes of one such illusion, but the realization was enough to dispel its mundane glamor. I slipped behind the waterfall, and a new passageway unfurled: a stone descent lined by torch-bearing sconces.

The voices came clearer from this vantage, rebounding up the spiral staircase. I followed the sounds until I entered a domed chamber at the foot of the stairs, and there I found the Mahak engaged in a spirited discussion with the Sylphid Slayn. The two monarchs stood before a great stone cube, smooth as glass and darker than jet. A gnostic shrine. Another seal. The perfect twin to its bagra pair. The Senex Amari Desta had been waiting for his chance to behold this relic for two decades, and here I'd found it in little less than four days.

"...it will be," the Mahak said, a note of urgency inflecting his steady voice.

"How can you be certain? It's a wonder the seal has endured for this long." The Slayn's windchime voice sounded smooth but brittle, a pane of glass on the verge of shattering.

"It is the sacred charge of my line to see that it holds," the Mahak said. "Some duties are older than G-d."

"I dislike it," the Slayn chirped. "This Eidolon's investment weakens chains that were forged in the blood of my people."

The Mahak glanced up at the cold black stone, stroking its smooth face with reverence. "Chains can be reforged."

He turned from the seal and saw me lurking in the entryway. A cock-eyed expression greeted my intrusion—quizzical, though I didn't sense any ire. Only the Sylphid Slayn seemed ruffled by the interruption. Her pointed ears fanned out from her head, and she beat her wings in agitation.

The Mahak removed his hand from the seal and squinted at me until recognition widened his eyes. "Ruxindra? Are you lost, dear?"

"No, Holy Majesty," I said, hanging my head. "I heard voices."

Conscious of the silent Jassanids keeping vigil at the edge of the room, I stepped slowly into the chamber, cautious not to rouse any violent response. The floor of the shrine was unlike the marble tiles lining the upper layers of the Sahir. These looked more like the tiles of the bagra plaza where I'd encountered the first seal, clay panes carved with the same inscrutable gnostic script.

The Mahak looked at me with gentle scrutiny. "You would have had to wander quite far to overhear us in this pit."

"She shouldn't be here, Sharif." The Slayn's wings fluttered as she spoke. "Send her back. Under guard."

Apparently, the Mahak thought differently. "Peace, Illusitar." He stepped toward me, and I sensed the subtle shift in the ring of Jassanids aroused by my proximity. "It's not uncommon for *lehakva* to discover untapped wells of gumption as their bridal rite approaches. She has as much right to be here as we do. More, perhaps."

"Hardly," the Slayn—Illusitar—said.

Ignoring her protests, the Mahak extended his arms to me. "Come. You've discovered our buried temple. You might as well explore it. We have nothing to hide."

I stepped past him, scanning the cube and the gnostic symbols surrounding it. Given enough time, I did not doubt I would find the *naga'tlat* among them. "What is this place?" I asked.

"An agiary," the Mahak answered.

There was a term I recognized. Agiary. *Uhtashgah. Dar-es-Freyj.* Many words for the same thing: a gnostic fire shrine, though I saw no sacred flame.

"Have you seen its like in Azytanthum?" the Mahak asked.

I shook my head, pacing the perimeter of the cube. "Not in Azytanthum...but I saw its twin in a plaza of the city below."

"Did you, now?"

I was surprised by the Mahak's willingness to indulge my curiosity. "Are they Karochan?" I asked, playing dumber than I was, but only slightly.

"No." the Mahak followed in my footsteps, again tracing the stone with his withered hand. "They are relics of a different faith, an older tradition native to our G-dling Cradle."

I looked up at him, feigning surprise. "Why would the Theocrats place heathen shrines in their Holy City?"

He smiled indulgently, and I again marveled at the plainness of this man. Many regents of Hebdomar proffer themselves as successors to Old Mysin. Petty emperors and rump state kings—pretenders, one and all. Here stood the man with the truest claim to that inheritance, clothed in hemp sandals and shalwaz rags, and perhaps that was the point. The Mahak had no need for gilt or carmine capes. Mahakalpe was his raiment, the Sahir his glowing scepter, and the Altar of the Demiurge his timeless crown. "You misunderstand," he said to me. "The agiaries were not placed in Mahakalpe; Mahakalpe was placed around the agiaries."

Illusitar shot a warning glare at the Mahak. "That's enough, Sharif."

Again, the Mahak ignored his royal guest. He took my hands in his, kind eyes flitting between my own. "I think she has a right to understand. She found this place, after all. G-d speaks in coincidence."

I swallowed. "What do I have a right to know?"

"The purpose of your sacrifice." He released my hands and shook his head. "The younger girls cannot hear it, and so I do not linger on the macabre, but you seem to have more iron in you than the others—isn't that right?"

I said nothing.

The Mahak gazed up again at the smooth, black face of the seal. "Your sacrifice is but the next phrase in a spell cast long ago. A spell we are still casting, truth be told. The Unseen World is a web of interlocking threads." He turned back to me, crossing his fingers in a skein. "Every sorcerer's spell—every note of kantor's trope—tugs on these threads, disturbing their closest neighbors. The G-dhead's rebirth will be quite a tug, indeed. Through your sacrifice and that of your sister-wives, we will ensure that the agiaries survive the reverberations. It is a noble calling, wouldn't you agree?"

Before I could answer, a piercing sound interrupted the moment—a woman's distant scream. It must have been desperate to penetrate this deep into the bowels of the Sahir. More screaming followed, a chorus of shrieking in horror and pain. The Mahak's thick eyebrows turned inward as Slayn Illusitar fluttered to his side.

"Sharif!" Illusitar shouted.

The Jassanids contracted in an instant, forming a protective line of spears around the three of us. The Mahak didn't budge, staring hard-eyed at the staircase beyond his wall of Jassanid spears.

More screams tumbled down from the Sahir—louder and closer.

"The girls, Sharif!" Illusitar squawked.

The Mahak only held up his arms, guarding both of us. "Hold, Illusitar. There are 200 Jassanids defending the halls above, and twice-a-dozen kantors. We are safe right where we are."

As if in counterpoint, the screaming swelled again, joined this time by the clash of metal. I knew the sounds of combat as well as any song, and my deepest instincts pushed me to pursue. Ruxindra l'Maer drew toward violence like iron filings to a lodestone, but Ruxindra bin Vargas would not be so bold. So I hesitated, fearing to breach my cover, but the escalating cries and the clatter of arms eventually tipped the scales.

The Jassanids pointed their spears at the entrance, but they were not expecting anyone to surge from behind. I shot past the Mahak's arm and slid through a narrow gap in their phalanx, darting for the spiral staircase. I heard Slayn Illusitar squeal and the Mahak shout my name, but I was already racing up the stairs to the darkened wing of the Sahir, driving toward the sounds of disruption. I knew the Jassanids would not pursue, for they were sworn to protect the Mahak.

The screaming came to an eerie halt. I smelled blood.

In the diamond chamber, I found the bodies of four Jassanid guards, their spears scattered, entrails spilling from their ruptured bronze plates. I knelt to inspect the bodies, confirming each lifeless stare. The screaming swelled again, and I ran toward it, up the stairs and around the bend, tracking the discord to the chambers of the *lehakva*. I was grateful that my palace slip was not confining, though it would yield to metal as easily as flesh. In this sense, I was liberated, but with little room for error.

The hall of the *lehakva* reeked of slaughter. Torn limbs and broken bodies littered the floor. Every scrap of mutilated flesh belonged to a Jassanid, but for a caged head brutally separated from its kantor host. I shot through the first chamber door I found ajar, ready to remove my hairclip and reveal its deadly report.

I was too late—at least for the four girls caught unawares in this room. Their bodies lay strewn about the chamber, one folded in the corner like a discarded doll and another torn nearly in half at the waist, her severed torso collapsed beneath an overturned vanity and littered with porcelain scraps of a shattered plate. A third hung garishly from the corner of an end table, her skull stove in on its corner. The last lay across the bedspread, almost peaceful by comparison, her perfect bosom peeled open like a citrus rind. The bodies all looked like they'd been mauled, defiled by tooth and claw rather than a weapon's precise edge. I abandoned the dead to chase the resurgent sound of screaming carrying through the chamber wall.

The screams grew to a desperate crescendo and were as quickly snuffed out. I searched the next two chambers and found only the aftermath. Three more slaughtered girls—one of them Dahlia. Her throat had been torn out, dark hair unrooted in clumps, hazel eyes forever frozen in the wide cast of her dying horror. One pretty foot, polished by anguills, lay at the corner of the bed, severed at the ankle. I ran back into the hall and waited for the screams to resume so I might track the active point of contact.

I didn't have to wait long.

Frantic screams erupted from the chamber beside my own, and another sound, crass and sibilant: a daemon's feasting hiss. I burst through the door and saw Liyah backed into the corner of her room, eyes ferocious as she brandished a flimsy dinner knife in defense of a sister-wife grasping her legs in a shrieking ball. Two creatures cloaked in black closed on them, circling the bed. Pointed epaulettes crowned their fell capes, and the backs of their heads squirmed with bundles of writhing snakes.

Inaghke.

I hurled myself at the nearest Shade, toppling it before it could test Liyah's meager blade. I grasped the foul thing by the wrists, warding off its long, clawed fingers already dripping with blood and gore. The coals of its lidless eyes smoldered, black sulfur wafting from its lamprey mouth. I sensed its partner surging toward us, pivoting to address the greater threat. The creature I'd pinned began shrieking, extruding sharp fangs from the pits of its circular gums. Snakes struck from its scalp, and as I lurched beyond their range, the Inaghke slashed me across the cheek with the edge of one long claw. Enraged, I snapped both of the creature's wrists to an enfilade of tortured hissing. In one motion, I removed my hairclap and jammed its sharpened finger under the Inaghke's chin, staking shut its vile maw and breaching the case of its brain. The Shade went limp beneath me, its dun eyes smoking, fires quenched.

No sooner than I'd vanquished the Shade, its partner was upon me. It battered my hand with its boney claw, knocking the hairclip from my grasp. It seized me up from the floor by the fabric of my slip, its claws sinking painfully into the skin of my breasts. It slammed me into the wall, shrieking with outrage, brandishing its venomous fangs. I pressed one forearm across its throat, barring its teeth from finding purchase.

The coals of its eyes pulsated with surging heat as it fought against my strength. A forked tongue flashed from the ring of its maw, and a black voice slithered out behind it. *"Shibboleth..."*

I know not what it saw with those eyes. There are some who believe Inaghke Shades can read minds, but I think it more likely that they read our souls. It named my priesthood and met that revelation with renewed vigor. Hissing, it released my shoulder to grasp my barring arm with one clenched claw. I felt the ardor of its grip, and knew it had the strength to tear that arm straight from its socket. My hairclip lay useless against the opposite wall, impossibly out of reach. Fortunately, I didn't need it.

I am a daughter of the Shibboleth—an Apostatic Priest. I am charged to hunt daemons and slay G-ds, and I'd killed Inaghke before.

I hissed back in the creature's face, bearing my own white teeth. The creature's pause offered opening enough to remove my arm bar and grasp the Shade with both hands by the tentacles of its head. Serpent bodies shuddered between my fingers as I throttled them. I pulled with all my strength of arm, flexing hard-earned muscles until the tentacles stretched beyond their limit. I tore handfuls of the wriggling organs from the creature's scalp with a burst of ichor, tossed them squirming to the floor, and returned to tear again. The Shade fell to the ground, grasping its mutilated head in agony. I heard Liyah and her sister-wife screaming, as well, and to that frightened chorus I fell upon the wounded Shade, hands dripping with silver ichor, and tore at its tentacles over and over.

I didn't stop until the Shade was completely shorn and its foul body still. I stood up amid clumps of severed tentacles and pools of ichor, chest heaving with exertion inside my soiled palace slip. The spectacle left Liyah and her sister-wife breathless. The Sahir had gone silent once again.

I took a step toward them, and Liyah raised her dinner knife. "Don't come any closer!" she shouted. She looked upon me with horror I thought better spent on the Inaghke Shades.

Heavy footsteps sounded from the hallway. In an instant, a decade of Jassanid guards were crowding the room, surveying the slaughter with those empty soldier's eyes. My cheek stung where the Shade had slashed me, blurring half my vision. I stood motionless, still dripping with the evidence of my intervention, certain that any wrong move would end with ten spearheads trained on my gut. The Mahak entered the chamber behind his guards, mouth set in a graven pout. His eyes fell on the broken corpses of the Inaghke before finding their way to me.

"Inaghke Shades," I said before he could ask. "They came for the girls."

"I know what they are," he snapped. Gone was all the regent's grandfatherly indulgence.

"Sh-she killed them!" Liyah piped from the corner. "She fought them both with her bare hands!"

The way the Mahak stared at me then, I knew my cover was blown. He lifted one finger, still staring, and the Jassanids encircled me with spears raised.

"Take Ruxindra to her chamber," he said. "And this time see that she doesn't leave."

CHAPTER 9

DELIVERY

I returned to my chamber a prisoner in truth. The Jassanids barred my door, and though I could not see them, I knew they remained just beyond the barrier, insurance against my escape. With no window to the outside world, I had no way to track the passage of time, which was maddening. I paced the small bedroom, replaying the battle in my head and turning over the implications of the Inaghke's attack.

Inaghke Shades are not mindless beasts like the wraithlings I dispatched on the mountain road to Ohtahp. They are soulful creatures, as intelligent and willful as any man. My work on behalf of the Shibboleth brought me into conflict with their ilk before, but I knew little of their enigmatic designs. This band came to kill *lehakva*, though I could not fathom why. It is no small feat to impregnate the Sahir. This assault carried great risk and must have been long in the planning. I didn't like it, and not for the physical danger they posed. Mahakalpe had become an unstable alchemy, transmuted under pressure, and here was yet another volatile ingredient added to the mix.

My chamber door swung open, but only briefly. Four Jassanids pushed me against the back wall with their spearheads, while a palace servant deposited a plate of food and a fresh red slip. I heard the heavy bar fall once again upon their exit.

I changed out of my soiled robe. My chest ached with punctures, and my cheek had begun to ooze where the Inaghke slashed me.

It served me poorly to have so much time to think. As the hours of solitude dragged on, I considered breaking Gerritt's charm and returning to the bagra to concoct a new plan of attack. My cover was already blown. The Mahak was more likely to see me staked to a delta atop the Middle City's barbican than let me anywhere near the Eidolon. I fished the trinket out of my dress and cradled the small calcite pendant in the palm of my hand, staring into its crystalline depths. A cautious woman would have cracked it—unleashed its translocation before some masked kantor divined its purpose and took it away. I was lucky it hadn't been confiscated already. I closed my fingers around the talisman and began to squeeze, but only gently.

I was not a cautious woman.

I tucked the charm back between my breasts and out of sight. The Mahak kept me in suspense for this long, and cared enough for my well-being to see me fed. I would follow this path to its bitter end out of curiosity and, perhaps, a dash of petty pride. It would not do to prove Gerritt right.

Eventually, the door to my chamber opened again. Between the line of entering Jassanids, I saw the braziers burning in the hall. An entire day had passed. Four more to revelation.

I understood the drill by now and backed against the wall with my hands threaded behind my head. Four spearheads held me at bay, and behind them entered the Mahak.

He stared at me through the tunnel of spears, his plain face a mask of severity and contemplation. At last, he exhaled and raised one hand. The Jassanids parted to permit his approach.

I lowered my hands from my head, and just as quickly the spears snapped back to my throat.

"At ease," the Mahak instructed. "I do not think she means us harm —isn't that right?"

I nodded but kept silent.

The Mahak pointed at my cheek. "We'll need to see that tended."

"I would appreciate that, Holy Majesty."

His shrewd expression didn't budge. "Who are you?" he asked.

"Ruxindra," I said.

The Mahak's golden eyes narrowed. "Perhaps. But that is not all you are, I do not think. It is no small matter to slay an Inaghke Shade—let alone two of them. The Yusakot girl claims you are bedeviled. She said you fought like a harpy."

"I—I have some training in martial arts," I said.

"That much is clear." The Mahak edged closer. "The Jassanids searched the city for your brother, but he seems to have eluded us. Who sent you?"

"I came of my own volition."

I could see the Mahak's frustration in the tension of his jaw, but the modest regent was adept at maintaining poise. "I suppose we should be thanking you," he said. "You saved the lives of many *lehakva* last night."

I painted each spearhead arrayed before me with my eyes. "You have an odd way of showing it."

"A precaution," the Mahak said without a hint of apology. "You saved many, but not all. Nine girls were slaughtered—along with thirteen Jassanids and two kantors. A heavy toll."

"It would have been heavier, I assure you—had I not intervened."

The Mahak nodded his wrapped head. "My beloved wife was right about you. She sensed something amiss from the moment you set foot in the hypolyte. I've grown so accustomed to her venom, that I fear I've acquired a tolerance."

"I am no threat to you or your people, Holy Majesty. I've come to Mahakalpe to wed the Eidolon—and to serve as *lehakva* upon his investment."

The Mahak took a deep breath, twirling a single oiled ringlet of his beard around a finger. He released the coil and reached into the folds of his shalwaz, producing two black tablets chiseled with familiar designs.

"You recognize them," he said. My face must have given me away. "These tablets were found on the bodies of the Shades you slayed."

"Then you shouldn't be handling them," I said.

"My kantors have already inspected them and determined they are benign. What are they?"

"I don't know," I said honestly.

"But you've seen them before?"

I hesitated, not wishing to implicate poor Master Glavion, but I could sense my fate balanced on a razor's edge. Any dissembling risked tipping the balance. "They are thaumaturgical trinkets," I said. "That is all I know."

He hissed, holding the two dark stones away from his body like some contaminating germ. "They are a match for the arcana in the agiary," he said. He looked up at me again, eyes burning. "The agiary *you* discovered beneath the Sahir."

"G-d speaks in coincidence," I quoted, perhaps unwisely.

"Don't quote scripture to me," the Mahak snapped, his glacial patience at last wearing thin.

"I—I believe there is a third," I said. I knew there was. Neither of the two tablets in the Mahak's possession bore the *naga'tlat*.

The Mahak regained composure once again. He nodded, more to himself. "A third Shade breached our defenses. We believe it escaped after you dispatched its cohort." He returned the tablets to his shalwaz and pulled over the stool from my vanity to sit. He folded his hands across his lap and looked up at me, still pinned to the wall by Jassanid spears. "Only one question remains," he said. I thought that unlikely, for I had many of my own. "What am I to do with you?"

Every answer I came up with seemed ill-considered, so I let him arrive at his own conclusion.

"My beloved wife and my idiot son think I should have you deltafixed."

"What do you think?" I asked.

"I think I would be a fool to ignore their wisdom twice." His anger simmered again, but he breathed it back. "Unfortunately, I am not in a position to be so wasteful. Nine dead *lehakva* weakens our sacrifice to the cusp of inadequacy."

"What are you saying?"

"The kantors judged you pure, and you came to us willingly. You will be wed to the Eidolon alongside the sisters you saved, and you will be given to the flames upon the Syzygy of Avum."

I was stunned. "Th-thank you, Holy Majesty."

He scowled at me, returning to his feet. "Save your thanks, Ruxindra bin Vargas of Azytanthum. It is a high crime to deceive the Holy Court of Mahakalpe. Had I any other option, you'd already be hooded and marching for the barbican. Our circumstance only buys you time. You *will* still pay for your deception in blood, but I will see that blood is put to good use." At last, the Jassanids withdrew their spears, falling back beside the Mahak. "You will remain in this chamber under guard until morning. Only then will you rejoin your sister-wives to be delivered to your fate."

Alone again, my mind raced. I had been right about the sacrifice all along. This was no Karochan burning to anoint the G-dhead's return. The *lehakva* fueled an eldritch spell—a bloodgift intended to feed some gnostic seal disrupted by the investment. The Mahak needed my contribution more than he realized, for killing the Eidolon would surely mitigate whatever corruption he hoped to avoid.

A mender in palace red wearing the gold bracelets of her trade entered my room without the precaution of Jassanid guards. She packed the puncture wounds in my chest with a stinging black paste and cotton swabs, then cleaned and irrigated the cut on my face before stitching it with sinew. She painted over her sutures with the same medicinal paste. I tried to thank her for her ministration, but she didn't linger. My wounds already felt better. I'd grown so accustomed to Gerritt's healing that I'd forgotten how much could be accomplished with needle and thread.

Not long after my mending, the door to my chamber swung open for the final time, and a palace servant directed me into the hall where I entered a silent maniple of Jassanids marching three abreast. Day had broken once again, and the braziers were quenched. Three days to revelation.

Everywhere I looked on our winding course through the Sahir, I saw bronze breastplates and ready spears. After the thwarted attack, our Jassanid guards dispensed with all pretense of subtlety and now roamed the halls freely.

We passed by the entrance to the water garden and the wings of the hypolyte, toward the landscaped yard approaching the retaining wall where the rest of the *lehakva* awaited. The tale of my battle with the Shades had clearly spread. Each girl watched me with a different blend of fear and awe as I rejoined the cohort now surrounded by a full maniple of slave-soldiers and three masked kantors.

The girls drew away from me as I entered the procession. I caught Liyah's green eyes tracking me from the edge of the receiving yard. As soon as she realized she'd been caught staring, she looked away and scampered further up the line.

Through the row of spears and the helmeted heads that accompanied them, I saw the Mahak presiding silently over the congregation from the top of the marble cursa footing the Sahir. He stood between his son and the Mahakva, who I could only assume came to witness her palace exorcised of so much nubile flesh.

No address preceded our disposal. The Mahak simply raised one hand, and the Jassanids thumped their sandals in unison. My sister-wives and I perfected our line and began the long march to our shared fate. I drifted toward the back, not wanting to upset anyone with my proximity. Maddux emerged from the ordering to claim the undesirable position at my side. I breathed a sigh of relief to see her among the living, for I feared she might have been one of the nine dispatched by the Inaghke before I reached the hall.

She leaned over to whisper in my ear, "Such wild stories these girls tell."

"Maybe not so wild," I said, a small smile twitching on my lips. "I'm glad to see you are well."

"Slept straight through the action," Maddux said. "Had to hear about it at breakfast the next day. It's hard to believe."

"And what about this isn't?"

Maddux elbowed me in the ribs. I winced from the tug at my mended wounds, but she didn't seem to notice. "They're calling you 'the harpy,' you know? Half the girls think you're one of the daemons who attacked us, and the other half think you're some kind of savior sent by G-d to defend his wives."

"What do you think?" I asked.

Maddux stuck her tongue in her cheek. "I think...you're the most interesting woman I've met here, and I'm not really in a position to be picky."

Our gaggle lurched into motion, with the kantors heading the procession. They parted the cliffside and descended the stone steps, leading us through the foreyard and the gaping portcullis of the curtain wall. Cheering crowds of adulators greeted us in the Middle City. A second maniple of Jassanids had cleared a path through the winding city streets, just as they had for the Eidolon's entrance in the bagra below. The pilgrims' admiration buttressed the other girls. Even cynical Maddux held her head an inch higher as cheers and drumming showered our walk.

We took a circuitous route around clusters of domed houses, over commercial thoroughfares lined with shuttered shops. I suspected our path had been calculated to pack as many adulators along its flanks as possible, witnesses for the *lehakva*'s delivery to their G-dling lord. We passed a trellised ziggurat anchoring a humble enclave of the orthodox, their congregation gathered at its base in their stoic expressions and tahliz scarves. Beyond the enclave, I saw the raised mound of the Penitent Barbican ringed by crumbling fortifications. What once had been a fortress now served as a gallows, its elevated position ideal for public display. A line of stockades sparsely occupied by ruffians and thieves ringed the base of the earthen mound, while five triangular deltafixes stood atop the barbican, sunk into the ground on heavy wooden stems affixed to their isosceles points.

Our procession drew closer to the barbican, and I noticed a small group of adulators had detached themselves, interest piqued by a spectacle of a different sort. One lonely soul, freshly condemned, had been staked at the wrists to the crossbar of one of the hideous devices. Even from a distance, I saw that his legs had been broken with hammers and bound to the deltafix with thick hemp ropes. He'd been blinded, as well, empty sockets trailing bloody tears. Despite all that damage, he'd not yet stilled. His chest still heaved with ragged breaths and his head lolled side to side.

We passed beneath the ruined walls of the Penitent Barbican, and I lingered on the suffering man staked in warning, carefully mutilated to elude death's merciful release.

I knew this man.

Master Glavion, the squirrely craftsman whose low art allowed me to confuse the kantors' scrying. I watched his bleeding lips move noiselessly, whatever cursed whimper he muttered lost in the reverie of the crowd. A less seasoned priestess might have felt a pang of guilt for the fate that befell him, but I did not think he'd been incriminated for my glamor; it was the tablets carried by the Inaghke that earned poor Glavion his deltafixion, and for that sin, I shouldered no blame.

Gerritt was going to need another local thaumaturge.

At last, we turned down a wide thoroughfare that drew toward the Middle City's retaining wall. The plaza of our destination opened before us like a titan's maw. At its center stood the colorful *Cikkot*, a many-chambered tent as wide as a block of bagra shemechas.

No adulators were permitted to enter the plaza. A pair of Jassanid guards stood sentinel at each entry point, guarding against interlopers. Our own maniple fanned out to cover the rest of the plaza, and we *lehakva* at the procession's center formed a fertile line before the *Cikkot's* blue vestibule to await our G-dling reception.

All silences are not equal, and the one that fell upon that Middle City plaza then was one of the heaviest I have ever known. The roar of adulators vanished, peeling back along the path of our procession all the way to the curtain wall. Our Jassanid escort became a ring of statues, timeless as any marble art piece of the Sahir. Not even a mischievous Ohtahpi breeze dared disturb us. Skritglyph pennants hung limp from their spires as the very land around us held its breath.

I watched the mouth of the *Cikkot* with the same intensity as my sister-wives. Gerritt's pendant seemed to gain weight against my breastbone with every passing second. My red hair hung freely against my shoulders, unbound by the deadly clip I'd lost fighting the Inaghke. It hadn't been returned.

The blue canvas flap fronting the *Cikkot* stirred from motion within. A gloved hand peeled back the flap, and a head of full black hair ducked under the roof of the tent to enter the plaza. I recognized the Eidolon's guardian. Maddux might have been stuck on his strong jaw peppered with stubble or his long, raven hair tied up in a warrior's bun. I was drawn only to his hoplite armor scored with battlemarks, breastplate embossed with unfamiliar heraldry—an eagle and the aspect of the rising sun. A gold cape was pinned at his shoulders, and from his sword-belt jutted a jewel-pommeled hilt.

His sword reminded me too much of my own Caledin Vane. It even had the same red-leather grip grooved by years of steady use to fit the hand to which it belonged. Icy blue eyes surveyed the line of *lehakva*, the expression beneath them flat and unreadable.

I looked past this obstacle as the flap of the *Cikkot* ruffled once again.

Someone much smaller and less violently adorned entered the plaza behind him.

Some of the girls further down the line gasped to behold the Eidolon, though I couldn't fathom their awe. He seemed a meager thing, thin and boney, head shaved to the root, drawing attention to his over-sized ears. He wore a thin orange wrap, tied not in the complicated braid of a shalwaz but anchored around one shoulder like a Gozali toga, exposing his hairless adolescent chest.

The Eidolon walked on bare feet, passing his guardian to scan his betrothed with wide, bright eyes. Troubled eyes.

He looked every inch the child he was, overwhelmed by a lavish new toy. He opened his mouth as if to speak but shut it just as quickly. He shook his round head then turned away from us and padded back toward the *Cikkot*.

"No," he said as he passed his guardian. With eyebrows raised, the guardian watched him duck back inside the ritual tent.

The silence hanging over the plaza grew much heavier then. Some of my sister-wives began to shift awkwardly in our line. None had come here expecting rejection, but I already suspected this was something else.

The guardian turned back to us with a weak smile. He extended one arm to the *Cikkot*. "Please, come inside. The disciples have prepared your chambers."

CHAPTER 10

CIKKOT

I followed Maddux into a maze of fabric corridors, canvas walls and wood scaffolding. The *Cikkot* seemed a world unto itself, a liminal plane of beaded curtains and hanging gauze, of embroidered pillows and incense urns, all of it painted in the shifting colors of light passing through translucent dye. Offerings littered the interior corridors as without—bundles of palm fronds and willow branches; dried pomegranates and knotty gourds.

I heard voices coming from deeper within the *Cikkot*—laughter and animated chatter speckled by the clinking of earthenware cups. The voices faded as we passed through a dense curtain of wooden beads and through a thin blue corridor lined with oil lanterns spouting their unctuous flames. It seemed an awfully precarious arrangement. All these layers of overlapping canvas packed with dried offerings made the *Cikkot* a tinderbox, but perhaps that was the point. We were *lehakva*, after all. Betrothed to flame.

At the end of the corridor, we slipped through a thin sheath of yellow gauze and entered a wide chamber of plush cushions, bedrolls and floor tables, each set with humble gifts of bread and cheese beside a few horn pipes with wide, flat bowls. I saw the Eidolon's guardian at the back of the chamber, bending to light a stick of incense from a flimsy wick. Once the scented tinder caught, he blew out his starter, sending wisps of smoke up into the rafters of the tent. My sister-wives scattered in cliques to claim their bedrolls. A few swiped corners of bread or nobs of white cheese from the floor tables in passing. I picked up one of the horn pipes and sniffed its bowl—shisha mixed with sticky fruit.

Maddux hailed me from the corner of the pillow chamber, patting the empty bedroll next to hers. I abandoned the pipe and went to join her.

The Eidolon's guardian watched us all acclimating to the new environs with his arms folded across his armored chest. Once most of us were situated, he coughed into his fist, summoning our attention.

"Luka wanted you all to be comfortable." Confusion dappled the faces of the *lehakva*. "Ah—apologies. That's his name—the Eidolon. He dislikes titles."

Maddux chewed her lower lip and batted her eyes precociously. "What's *your* name?"

Some of the other *lehakva* giggled.

The guardian smiled at her indulgently, and even I had to admit, it was a comely grin. "Kenver Montaigne," he said.

"I think I'll call you Ken," Maddux said. A shame Dahlia was no longer with us to reprimand her.

"I'd prefer you didn't," Kenver said. He left Maddux's moony eyes to scan the rest of the *lehakva*. "This will be your sleeping chamber until the syzygy. You are free to explore the depths of our shelter at your leisure. The disciples who traveled with us along the Shevat Zubaydin are scattered throughout, and I'm sure they'd be interested to speak with you if you are so inclined. Luka—the *Eidolon*—has mandated there be no locked passages within the *Cikkot*, but the Mahak has requested that you remain within the plaza at all times preceding the investment." His eyes shot back to Maddux. "Don't make me come looking for you."

Maddux licked her lips flirtatiously. "Catch me if you can."

"When will our betrothed come to see us?" Liyah's voice piped up from the opposite side of the tent. It seemed no accident that she'd selected the bedroll farthest from my own.

Kenver's expression flattened. "Eh..." He scratched the dark stubble along his chin, looking slightly uncomfortable. "I am sure Luka will join you all in good time. As you can likely imagine, he is beset with the gravity of his task."

"I would like to speak with the man I'm going to marry," Liyah said. Her eyes turned down and her voice became quieter. "Even if it's only for a night."

The intimation settled over the room like a burial shroud. Even Kenver was not immune to its weight. His shoulders slumped beneath his yellow cape. "I will speak with him," he said. "And I will return. Until then, I leave you to your leisure."

I watched his yellow cape trailing as he swept swiftly from our tent.

Maddux pretended to faint with a lusty sigh. She ruffled the red fabric wall behind us. "You don't suppose they have an ice bath tucked away somewhere, do you?"

"Put your tongue back in your mouth," I chided. "This is a holy shrine."

We descended upon one of the standing tables and stuffed ourselves with bread and cheese. The other girls kept their distance, still wary of me. Maddux tasted the lip of a horn pipe and cringed, tossing it away.

"Another loaf of this damned manakeesh and I'll split the seams of my betrothal gown," Maddux said. I rolled my eyes at that. The girl was thin as a saber. She bunched up her auburn hair in two fists and let it fall against her shoulders. "I'm sick of all this *waiting* and *feasting*. The syzygy is less than three days away. When are we to wed?"

"Still dreaming of a skinny boy between your thighs?" I asked.

Maddux smiled devilishly behind her cup of wine. "It might be the boy between my thighs, but it will be Kenver of whom I am dreaming." She bit down on the rim of her cup.

"You'd better gird yourself for disappointment."

Maddux pretended she didn't hear me.

The many complications to my task were beginning to weigh on me. My hairclip had always been a sorry substitute for Caledin Vane, but now I found myself bereft of even that modest blade. I imagined myself smothering the boy with one of the *Cikkot*'s thousand embroidered pillows or else killing him with my bare hands. Both were certainly options, but neither would be quick. Then there was the obstacle of Kenver Montaigne. I did not think the Eidolon's handsome guardian would be as easily thwarted by knuckles and silk. The sooner this ritual farce ended, the better. I needed to draw the boy out and corner him. Alone.

To that end, I needed to see more of the *Cikkot*—to understand its layout and routines. I also needed a better understanding of the Eidolon's movements. Was he isolated in quiet prayer or enmeshed among his meek disciples, haunted by Kenver's watchful eyes?

I stood up from the floor table, smoothing the silk brocade of my dress.

"Where do you think you're going?" Maddux asked.

"Kenver said we're free to wander the *Cikkot*. I'm going to wander."

Maddux looked aghast. "What if the Eidolon returns? Or Kenver?"

"That's a risk I'm willing to take."

"Oh, no." Maddux hoisted herself up from the floor. "You're not getting rid of me again that easily."

She followed me out into the blue corridor, down the line of oil lamps to a multicolored crossroads of intersecting tents. The *Cikkot* unfurled like a lotus, layers upon layers of fabric and beads spiraling toward a seedy center. Muffled chatter reached our ears from some deeper redoubt. I heard dulcet string music, as well—more festive than the Karochan trope that dogged the city. We tracked the sounds around a looping passage of overlapping red and yellow canvas. The *Cikkot* swallowed us deeper, its steepled ceiling vaulting ever higher as we progressed. I sensed Maddux's footsteps drawing to a halt behind me and glanced back. She'd stopped over one of the offerings, a black-and-green mottled gourd scratched with skritglyphs and pinned with black poppies.

"*A'shana Hava-a...*" she read, turning the gourd over in her hand.

"What?"

She stared intensely at the gourd.

"Maddux?"

She replaced the gourd with a warding gesture, drawing a line around her heart with thumb tucked between first and middle finger.

"Maddux," I repeated.

"I thought you read the *Midras*?" she said. "It's the *Ashima Kov*. Funeral prayers. Depressing decoration for a wedding..."

"Come on," I said. "We're getting closer."

We still hadn't reached the center of the *Cikkot*, but we did find the revelers. We passed through a hanging flap of green canvas pinned up at one corner and entered a wide crescent-shaped chamber. Hanging wreaths of wooden beads and waxed leaves looped from the wooden rafters, the ambience dressed with pipe smoke and song. The smell of so many pipes and a steaming iron cookpot resting over a pit of glowing coals almost drowned out the ripe scent of the gathered disciples.

I stood flat on my feet beneath the entrance flap, struck by the convivial atmosphere. The congregation recalled a brothel salon or uptown hash tent more than any kodesha temple. Beggars and collared whores slurped soup from earthenware cups around the cookpot, while cripples lay recumbent upon plush cushions, passing banter back and forth with lepers and branded thieves. The string music seasoning the air belonged to a blind leper strumming a lute, his blissful expression molded from black lips and lesions. Kenver sat cross-legged beside him, nodding along to the pleasant tune, a cup of stew resting forgotten beside his knee.

The Eidolon stood out only for his youth. He sat among his disciples in no place of high regard, sharing a water pipe packed with shisha and cherry coals. I watched him cough from the pipe's harsh report, while an older woman in a purple chiton laughed at him. Luka's cheeks reddened, but he smiled through the good-natured ribbing, passing the pipe's snaking hose to the next disciple in line.

Maddux struggled to gain a view over my shoulder. I shifted my body to let her pass so she could stare open-mouthed at the gathering. For the first time since she thrust her hand in my face in the Mahak's water garden, Maddux was speechless.

I would not have described the Eidolon's tent as particularly well-guarded. His disciples were too well at ease, and none appeared armed save for Kenver. Unfortunately, the crowd was its own barrier, and I counted myself among the unarmed.

"*Masra aruir!*" Maddux swore. "What a sorry bunch..." Her eyes fell on the leprous musician, and she physically recoiled against me. "Isn't that catching?" she whispered.

I barely heard the question. I was too focused on Luka's shaved pate bobbing back and forth as he tracked the conversation around the water pipe.

One of the disciples noticed our arrival and drifted over with two cups of wine in his hands. "Salutations!" He thrust one cup at each of us. "We were wondering when we'd get the chance to engage with the blushing brides. Everyone is curious!"

Neither of us was blushing, but Maddux did look a bit queasy. This disciple was too plump to be a beggar. The old lines of a penitent brand beneath his eye marked him for a thief.

Luka had noticed our entrance, as well. His bright eyes flashed on me, stiffening his posture and wiping the casual smile from his lips.

The disciple waved his hand, guiding us deeper inside the tent with his other arm. "Come inside, come inside. We don't bite!" he insisted. "Except for Mariam, but she used to collect coin for that service. Old habits." He laughed at his own joke with a snort. "Come."

We followed him toward the cookpot. Maddux squeaked as his calloused hand closed around her arm. I watched Luka excuse himself from the water pipe to creep over to Kenver's side. The Eidolon bent over his guardian's ear to whisper something, and I saw Kenver tracking our path across the tent as he listened.

Our guide led us to a group of three older disciples sprawled out on a bed of cushions, soaking up the cookpot's ambient warmth. Gray-haired Ohtahpi, one and all, wrinkled skin and brittle bones draped in androgynous bagra rags. "At ease!" our guide demanded. "Have a seat and drink your wine. If you're hungry, Gulam's made gallons of his famous shakshak stew." He fanned one hand over the elder Ohtahpi. "This is Samel, Moshev, and Hava. They've been eager to meet you and your sister-wives."

"And who are you?" I asked, neither sitting nor sipping my wine.

His smile pulled at the white lines of his penitent scar. "I be Tajjar Shirit of Uruz." He performed a flamboyant bow. "Blessed to make your acquaintance."

Hava lowered her cup of stew, revealing a wrinkled mouth and whiskered chin. "Tajjar is it? I thought Luka wiped away all titles along with our chains and our crimes?"

"Eh-heh." Tajjar Shirit smirked at me. "Old habits—as I said. Sit, sit." He flopped himself down next to Hava.

Maddux clung to my arm for dear life.

"You better do what he says." Hava paused to sip from her stew. "Shirit doesn't take no for an answer."

"Pretty sure that's what earned him his brand," Moshev joked.

Shirit wagged a finger at him while the others laughed. "I was persecuted."

"Weren't we all!" Hava rolled her filmy eyes.

"It isn't my fault Subakka don't understand haggling," Shirit grumbled.

They all laughed at that—even Shirit.

I found myself quickly acclimating to the local musk and sundry company. I liberated my arm from Maddux's grasp and joined the circle on the floor. Abandoned, Maddux dropped to my side.

"You've had our names," Hava said. "Now who are you?"

"Ruxindra," I said. "And this is Maddux. She isn't usually this quiet."

Maddux glowered at me but offered no amendments to her introduction.

"*Hesserat*," Samel said, unfolding his aged legs with a groan. "I thought all the *lehakva* came from the creches."

"Hardly!" Maddux snorted, at last finding her voice. "Half the girls washed in from the cities. Ruxindra's from Azytanthum, and I'm from Oksa in the south of Arram."

Luka's disciples all looked at us blankly. I gathered Shirit was a merchant—or had been. He should have at least been aware of Azytanthum, but I doubted any of them had heard of little Oksa.

"They read the Word in these *Hesserat* cities, do they?" Shirit asked.

"Of course they read the Word." Hava batted him playfully. "They must be devout to send *lehakva*."

"We have a small congregation in Oksa," Maddux said. "More Karochan in Azytanthum."

"What's it matter?" Moshev said, leaning back against his cushion. "G-d is reborn in our little Luka. The faith will be rewritten. No better time to join the guild, if you ask me."

I glanced again at Luka. Kenver had risen from his seat beside the blind lutist, and they both looked enmeshed in a heated conversation I could not hear over the din.

"I would be interested to hear how you all came to be in the company of the Eidolon," I said, returning to the circle. "You seem an unlikely fellowship."

Maddux snorted, and Shirit laughed.

Hava's eyes narrowed on me as she set aside her cup of stew. She seemed the shrewdest of the bunch by far. "And what's *likely* about any of this, huh?"

I met her stare, showing just a glimpse of my mettle. "I didn't mean any offense. I would have expected the Eidolon's disciples to include more Karochan clerics. Perhaps a desert sage or two."

"Don't tell that to Luka!" Shirit said. "He can't stand the clerics—most of them, at least." He searched the room until his eyes landed on one of the lepers sitting quietly beside a row of collared whores. "Gulam used to be a tongued sage. Added his voice to the *Tachne* before he caught the scale. Curse cost him much of his faith—along with his good looks and wives."

Maddux gasped. "That leper made the stew?"

The disciples laughed at her expense, and even I could not resist a grin.

"We all took different paths to Luka's side," Shirit continued. "The four of us are from Uruz. Luka came through—what was it? Three years ago?"

"Almost four now," Samel supplied.

"That's right." Shirit nodded his head. "Just a youngling calf, too short to peer over a bima. He'd already collected a few followers by then —mostly castaways left behind by their tribe. I won't speak for anyone but myself, though you'll hear the same story from every soul in this tent or some version of it. Luka held these sabbath feasts in the bagra every week. Not exactly sure why I felt drawn to them. Hadn't set foot in a Karochan kodesha in years—not since my imprisonment. Got to talking with Luka one sabbath over goat and barley, and our conversation stretched late into the night, long after the goat had been stripped and the arak ran dry."

"Sounds more like a sermon than a conversation," I said.

Shirit shook his head vociferously. "Then I'm telling it wrong. Was me doing the talking most of the time. Spilling details about my life I thought I'd forgotten—about my family and my business. About my crime. Luka just listened, occasionally prompting me on with a question." The other three Uruzot disciples nodded along with Shirit's account. "When it came time for Luka to move on from the city, I just... went with him."

"The boy has a way about him," Hava said. "You'll see. Draws out all the heretics and the apostates."

Maddux stuck her pointed nose in the air. "I'm not a heretic or an apostate."

I couldn't say the same for myself. "What about Kenver?" I asked. "Where'd he come from?"

The Uruzot all looked at each other without answering. Hava held Shirit's gaze and eventually shrugged. Shirit turned back to me, rubbing the back of his thinning head. "Kenver was the first," he said. "Been with Luka longer than any of us."

"Some say he's the one what pulled the boy from his mam and cut his cord," Samel added.

"Nonsense," Hava said. "Luka doesn't have no worldly mam. He was born of the desert."

That sounded unlikely to me, but I didn't see any point in questioning the Eidolon's myth. "Kenver isn't Ohtahpi," I said.

"Not from the Cradle, no," Shirit said. "Camped with the man for years, and he doesn't share much. Nice enough companion, though. Ferocious in his loyalty to Luka. Hardly ever lets the boy out of his sight."

Wonderful.

"He's a monk," Samel said.

All the disciples moaned.

"Come off it, Samel," Hava chided.

"It's true!" the man insisted, sitting upright once again. "He wanders off on his own every New Moon. We was in tight quarters in Rovan. You remember. I heard him chanting over his sword. Weren't no Karochan chant, neither."

"The *Hesserat* all have their queer ways. Doesn't make him a monk," Hava said. She looked directly at me. "Isn't that right?"

I didn't answer. I was too busy watching Luka head for the exit with his dutiful guardian following close behind.

They both disappeared. When I returned my attention to the circle, Hava was still waiting for one of us to respond. "Anyone know where he's from?" I asked instead.

All four of the Uruzot smiled. "Across the sea," they said in unison.

The joint statement had the timbre of an inside joke, but I didn't see the humor in it. The Eidolon was guarded by a warrior-monk from across the sea. A man who prayed over his sword and rarely took his eyes from his charge. At that moment, I would have traded my left hand to hold Caledin Vane in my right.

The string music came to an abrupt stop as the leper bent to drink from his cup of wine. I abandoned my own and stood up from the circle of Uruzot disciples. They watched me attempt to extricate myself with near disinterest. How casual they all seemed—drinking, smoking, and idling away the time while they lived in the presence of the G-dhead reborn.

"Thank you for the company," I said.

Hava raised her cup of stew. "Come back soon. Time runs down."

Indeed.

I turned to track Luka and Kenver's path out of the tent. I wasn't sure what I hoped to find or what I might do when I found it, but leaving the tent of his disciples exposed the Eidolon by inches—even if he still had his enigmatic guardian at his side.

"Where do you think you're going?" Maddux said.

"Stay here, Maddux."

"Oh, no. You're not leaving me." Maddux leapt to my side and grabbed my arm. This time, I did not indulge her trespass. I jammed my elbow against her ribs and reversed her grip, twisting her wrist in a painful lock between my fingers and thumb.

My cover had already been blown once. The wandering stars drew ever closer to their alignment, and with each passing moment I shed strips of Ruxindra bin Vargas, exposing more of the Apostatic Priestess beneath the veneer.

To her credit, Maddux did not squeal, but I saw the way her bright eyes quivered in the torchlight, widening to look upon me with fresh regard. I could almost track all the embellished stories of my battle with the Inaghke resurfacing in her mind—stories she'd been only too eager to dismiss. A harpy, indeed.

"I said, *stay here.*" I released her hand, and she stumbled two steps back from me, looking up with wounded eyes. At least she complied.

I left Maddux and the disciples behind and entered another narrow passage within the labyrinth of the *Cikkot.* I was becoming increasingly convinced that the sprawling tent-shrine was somehow bigger on the inside than without. This passage looped in great arcs offering no obvious outlet, its canvas walls staked irregularly to the plaza ground. The ripe scent of the disciples evaporated within its winding abyss, displaced by something greasy and foul that clung to the back of my throat. I didn't place the black odor until I saw the decorations lining the corridor further along its spiraling path.

Stakes.

Heavy wooden stakes driven deep into the ground, cut from cypress or oak or some equally sturdy tree, none of which Mahakalpe grew in abundance. This lumber had been traveled with effort, carved and sunk with intention before the *Cikkot* had been pitched. The thick scent belonged to the oil soaking every nest of kindling at their bases.

The stakes stood like sentinels, silently guarding the passage, thick hemp ropes already dripping from their trunks. When Liyah first brought me up to that bagra rooftop to show me the *Cikkot* from afar, I didn't take her warning literally—that this would be the site of both our gift and our sacrifice. All the offerings of bundled sticks and dried gourds became ominous in retrospect. I didn't count the stakes I passed, but I knew that there were thirty—one for each of us, including the fallen.

The *Cikkot* was a pyre in wait. This tent was betrothed to flame as surely as we were, and by the time the wandering stars broke from their syzygy, this plaza would hold nothing but ash.

I lost all sense of direction within the tent's painted walls, but I knew this charnel hall drew toward its center. I also suspected what I'd find there.

The spiral tightened as I passed the final stake. Raised voices pushed through the canvas walls—clear as kantor's trope. It sounded like an argument—an adulator at war with his adolescent G-d.

"This is a very bad idea," Kenver said.

"I don't agree."

"You'll insult the Mahak."

"What if I don't care?"

G-dling though he might be, in that moment Luka sounded like nothing more holy than a petulant boy. Then again, there are few things more holy than a petulant boy.

"I don't like it either," Kenver said. "But this is something eldritch—tangent to your investment. We shouldn't meddle."

"I thought I made myself clear the first time."

A long pause as I approached the spiral's terminus.

"The *first* time?" Kenver asked. "You're Mysin now?"

"Aren't I?"

The spiral ended and so did the conversation. Kenver and Luka turned in unison to watch me step inside the peaked chamber at the center of the *Cikkot*. My slippered feet crunched over a canvas floor laden with kindling, just as flammable as the nests coiled at the base of each stake. A steepled ceiling drew up above the rest of the shelter, toward a gap in the canvas sheeting that opened this chamber to the sky. Dusk crept in through the skylight, painting the low stone altar beneath it with a darkling glow. Here was the narrow patch of sky where the wanderers would join for the syzygy. Their bright outlines already prickled the canvas skins along their edge as they approached their seasonal convergence.

My intuition proved out. The *Cikkot* had been assembled around the Altar of the Demiurge.

For such a sacred artifact, the altar itself wasn't much to look upon—a flat anvil anchored by seven clawed pedestals displaying seven skritglyphs: the septuagrammaton describing G-d's forbidden name. Taken together and without the dressing of interlineal vowels, they were unpronounceable—even in Karochan.

"Hello," I said.

Kenver's brow pinched as he turned his head toward me, but at least he was looking. Luka strained himself just to avoid meeting my eyes. I do not know if it was my age or the titillating cut of my dress, but he seemed almost embarrassed to look upon me.

"You're one of them," Kenver said. "Luka's betrothed."

I nodded.

"What are you doing here?" he asked.

"I thought we were granted freedom of the *Cikkot?*" I took another step deeper into the chamber. "Something about 'no locked passages.'"

Kenver glanced over at Luka, at last drawing the boy's head up from the floor. "You did say that."

Luka smiled weakly, content to watch Kenver and avoid meeting my eyes. "I'm sorry I haven't addressed the *lehakva*," he said. "I have a lot on my mind."

I snorted, hoping to disarm him. "That seems an understatement."

"Which one are you, My Lady?" Kenver asked.

I shook my head. "No Lady. Ruxindra bin Vargas of Azytanthum." I stared down at Luka. "And you are he. Our revenant G-d."

"Just Luka, if it pleases," the boy said. His eyes glanced away from me, returning to the lip of the altar. "For now, at least."

I took another step closer, keen to the swift movement of Kenver's hand over the hilt of his sword and the subtle way he repositioned his feet. Not threatening, but certainly alert. It was all very artfully done. Under any other circumstance, I might have been impressed, but the man's vigilance remained a gross impediment I hadn't yet worked out how to circumvent.

I pretended not to notice, focusing my gaze on Luka.

"Can we help you with something, Ruxindra?" Kenver asked.

"I hope that you will," I said. "It's my sister-wives. None are so bold as to impose themselves on your holy person." Luka's skinny body winced. "None except for me, at least. They wish to meet you. To look upon their husband before they are called to speak their vows. It is not an unreasonable request, I think."

"Not unreasonable, no," Kenver said, as if he'd made the very same point only moments ago.

Luka realized we both were watching him, now. He exhaled with a child's frustration. "Fine," he said. "I will come to see the girls. Tomorrow. Before the ceremony."

"I think they would appreciate that." I had nearly reached the edge of the altar. I was close enough to touch him. Not an arm's length from the man—the boy, the *G-d*—I'd come to kill. That scrawny neck looked no stronger than any sprig of kindling waiting to feed his G-dling blaze, and I knew it would snap just as easily. My right hand twitched. I was fast, but how fast was Kenver?

My window closed as quickly as it opened. Kenver moved around the altar, placing his body between me and my quarry. I glanced down at the altar, hoping to defray any burgeoning suspicion. "This is it, isn't it? The Altar of the Demiurge."

"Yes," Luka said.

I glanced up at the sky. "And that is where the wandering stars will align."

Luka nodded his shaved head.

At last, I looked into his eyes, brown and guileless. I hoped to find in those irises some hint of the divine seed within him, some spark of wisdom or roosting ghost. I saw nothing so grandiose. Those wide, wet eyes belonged to the boy he was and not the G-d he would never be. Their light would vanish as easily as all the others I'd guttered on the edge of Caledin Vane.

Luka seemed more at ease now that he'd finally met me. I had a sinking feeling that he searched my eyes in turn, and felt a pang of fear at what he might discover. "Can I ask you a question, Ruxindra?"

"I hope so," I said. "We're to be wed."

He nodded gravely. "Do you wish to die?"

"*Blade of Perris*." Kenver raised his hands to his temples, shaking his head. "What is wrong with you, Luka?"

Luka held my gaze through the reprimand, surprising me with his mettle. "I want to hear her answer."

"It's fine," I said to Kenver. "Death comes for each of us. So few get to choose its time and manner, and even fewer matter."

"And you would choose this time?" Luka asked. "In this manner?"

"I would choose to matter," I said.

To that, he had no easy response.

"You see?" Kenver said, breaking the uncomfortable silence. "The *lehakva* understand their sacrifice."

"I do see," Luka said, still watching me. "Just not what you think you are showing me. I would have liked to spend more time with you, Ruxindra. Listening."

"Then come see me again," I said. "In private, perhaps."

Kenver's eyes tightened. His hand tensed around his sword grip, and I caught a glimpse of the maker's mark impressed beneath the crosshilt. I knew it unwise, but I couldn't help but stare, for it was the same mark carved into the hilt of Caledin Vane. I gawked for foolish seconds at the familiar brand until Kenver moved to cover it with his cape.

"I would have liked that," Luka said, blissfully ignorant of the unspoken exchange between his guardian and his betrothed. "If only I had more time."

I shook myself back to the present. "Time runs down. I think I should return to our sleeping chamber."

I turned too quickly to exit, and it might have been my own nerves, but I thought I could feel Kenver's eyes boring into me from across the altar. I tried to assure myself it had been but a fleeting glance—mere seconds—and that my practiced stare offered no hint of recognition. Each self-assurance rang hollower than the last. I walked a narrow path, and this was a stumble I could little afford.

My curiosity, at least, was earnest.

The Eidolon's guardian was the last person I expected to carry a G-dkilling blade.

CHAPTER II

THE ALTAR OF THE DEMIURGE

I slept.

I'd missed my opportunity, but it was only *an* opportunity, and it was hardly golden. Even so, time ran down as Hava pointed out, and I was no closer to a vision for ending Luka's life.

My eyes flashed open. I tasted leather—a gloved hand covering my mouth. In the thin light of incense sticks and guttering pipes, I saw Kenver's black-haired head looming over me.

I knew better than to struggle. He drew one finger over his lips, urging silence.

I steadied my breathing, and he cautiously withdrew his hand. None of my sister-wives stirred from the intrusion—not even Maddux, who'd edged her bedroll a few feet further from my own. More than anyone else in the chamber, I was isolated.

"Why were you staring at my sword?" Kenver's whisper sounded taut, like the smallest string on the leper's lute tuned to the cusp of snapping.

"Kenver?" The grogginess proved an asset in my attempt to play dumb. "What are you talking about?"

"I saw you staring over the altar."

"You're mistaken," I hissed.

He pressed his finger back over his lips. "Keep your voice down." He waited, perhaps expecting me to sound some alarm, but I did not give him the satisfaction. "Tell me why."

"It looks like a fine blade," I said. There was no sense in denying it twice. He'd seen what he'd seen, and just as I feared, it had roused his suspicion.

"You have an interest in smithcraft?"

"You wake me for this?" I tried to sound sanctimonious. "This is inappropriate."

"Answer the question."

I inched up on my elbows, drawing eye-to-eye with the man. "I have an interest," I said. The best lies carried notes of truth. "My mother was a fencer. She trained me in sword forms, and I know an artisan blade when I see one."

"Your mother?" His eyebrows pinched together as if he didn't recognize the term. "An Azyti merchant's wife taught her daughter fencing?"

I raised my voice just a hair. "That's hard for you to believe?"

Kenver's eyes shot to Maddux as the girl moaned and rolled over on her sleeping pad. He waited for her to settle, then returned his focus to me. "It's unusual." He prodded the stitches in my cheek with a finger, and I winced. "This wound is fresh."

"The path to Mahakalpe is dangerous," I said.

"No, it isn't."

"Maybe not for an armed man and his G-dling entourage."

His stiff jaw shifted, nostrils flaring as he exhaled. "You will forgive my caution. There are some who wish harm upon Luka."

Indeed, I thought, *and no more likely candidate than the guardian with the G-dkilling sword.*

I showed him my empty hands with an obstinate snort. "You see any weapons here?"

Silently, he stood up. "I can't be too careful. Not when we are so close." He turned to leave.

"What's its name?" I asked. I should have let him go, but I needed to be certain.

He stopped and glanced back at me. "What?"

"Such a fine sword must have a name."

Kenver propped his fists on his hips, staring. "Caledin Bolg," he finally said, confirming my every confusing intuition.

The Caledin Swords are not common, nor are they lightly worn. Nine reside at the Shibboleth and with its ordained priests. More are unaccounted for, but not so many that I should encounter one by happenstance. These are the blades that were carried by the Fellowship of Gammoran in their brave sack of Mysinium a millennium ago, forged by the Old Smith of Heingarten and instilled with lost art. Each blade is unique, but they all bent to one purpose.

Kenver held his ground a moment longer to stare at me, and then he was gone.

Two days to revelation.

In the morning, the Eidolon came. Kenver summoned us from the *Cikkot* to meet Luka in the plaza beneath the open sky. We donned our bridal gowns and braved the sunlight—found a crew of disciples hard at work assembling a simple arbor at the top of the square. The Mahak's Jassanids still guarded every city entrance to the plaza. Their mere presence kept the adulators out, though I suspected the Mahak intended them to keep the *lehakva* in. The disciples didn't seem to mind the armed guards. They largely ignored them as they went about their task, pitching the arbor and decorating it with wreaths of vibrant poppies and angel's breath.

My sisters and I pooled in a disorganized huddle, watching the back of Luka's bald head as he presided over the preparations. After some coaxing from Kenver, he came to us looking flushed and overwhelmed. He'd swapped his orange toga for a pristine shalwaz and wore a golden groom's stole around his neck.

Luka glanced back at Kenver, seeking permission to retreat, but the guardian urged him on. He cleared his throat, the apple bobbing as he swallowed. "Thank you all...for being here." I heard some of the girls shifting awkwardly around me. "The Syzygy of Avum is less than two days away. We are to be wed. In this plaza." He walked over to the arbor and placed one hand on an upright beam. "It will be a brief ceremony," he said. "We will speak our vows to each other in turn beneath the wreaths. Teacher Gulam will preside." He indicated one of the lepers idling beside the arbor, and the disfigured man bent his head, even more ghoulish in the light of day.

Luka lingered beside the arbor—left its cover only reluctantly, determined to keep some distance between us. "After the wedding, there will be a reception in the *Cikkot*. We will only have a few hours before we are called to take our places for the syzygy, and I will have to take my leave of you all. I must approach the altar alone."

A small voice crept out of our gaggle, and I was surprised to discover it belonged to Maddux. "Might we spend some time with you before the rite, *Masra*? We have so little time."

Luka winced. "Please don't call me that." He hung his head and his shoulders like a child kicked.

Kenver drifted to his side and placed a gloved hand on his back. "We will try to spend some time in your chamber before the rite. There's much to prepare."

It proved half an empty promise. Luka never came back to see us, sending Kenver instead in his place. Our betrothed's avoidance seemed to shame the handsome soldier, but I felt a grudging respect for the effort he made to speak casually with each girl, bestowing the gift of his genial company. He drew a sizable harem, sitting cross-legged next to one of our floor tables, puffing infrequently from a cherried pipe. He listened patiently, smiling and chuckling in all the right places while each girl regaled him with stories of their brief lives. I still sensed the disappointment scorching my sister-wives, but the company of a man like Kenver proved a potent balm.

I held myself apart from the flouncing *lehakva*, cursing my inability to escape the pillow chamber unnoticed. If Kenver was here, then Luka was elsewhere, unguarded and possibly alone. I wasn't used to operating within such stifling confines, and they chafed.

I began to perseverate over my imperfect options. I could kill him between the lines of our vows. Only the leper would be close enough to stop us, and I did not think the disfigured cleric such a threat. It would be a grand performance with witnesses all around, but Gerritt's charm still hung around my neck offering at least one sorcerous path of escape.

If the moment didn't serve, I'd have to accost him over the Altar of the Demiurge. Luka would approach the altar alone. I could find him there. I knew the way. I imagined myself cracking his head over the ancient stone—the very site of his investment. Unfortunately, I suspected I'd find myself tied up at that time—lashed to a stake and wreathed in flame. Perhaps I could slip my bindings and worm my way to the center of the *Cikkot*, but that was a dangerous game to be playing. Deferring my duty to the waning minutes of the boy's mortality left little room for error.

The sun began to set over Mahakalpe, and with only hours to revelation, I was no closer to choosing a path. My sister-wives grew somber as the wedding rite approached. Shirit appeared through the tent flap covering our chamber accompanied by two more disciples, one branded and one lame. They passed beaded circlets to each of us—Ohtahpi bridal raiment. The disciples offered to help us affix them to our crowns, but most of the girls recoiled from their touch. I let Shirit help me with mine.

I felt a sharp tug as he pinned the circlet in place. "There we go," he said. "Red hair is not so easily tamed, eh?"

He was trying to keep the conversation light, but sadness prickled the surface of his gentle ribbing. We both knew where I was headed. "Our husband-to-be is keeping a pretty low profile," I mused.

Shirit's fingers threaded my hair as he finished his work. He came around to stand in front of me and sighed. "Don't be too sore on him. Luka has his moods." He glanced around at all the Ohtahpi beauties placing their finishing touches. "I think this is all a bit much for him."

"He is G-d."

Shirit nodded. "He will be. Not a doubt in my mind about that. But he's also a boy, and the seed of wisdom within him has yet to sprout."

I thanked Shirit for his ministrations and let him move on to the next *lehakva*.

Never once did I question my resolve—not even then. Luka's youth didn't move me. Neither did his bashfulness nor his sordid collection of devotees. The Shibboleth did not dispatch me from Nurindra to slay youngling Luka of the Ohtahpi Sands. The boy was an ill-placed vessel, condemned by proximity and poor, blind fate. His destruction was collateral, though no less necessary for it. A small price that any Apostatic Priestess would gratefully pay.

My priesthood's zeal is not born of mere superstition, and the G-dhead's embodied return is no idle threat. Men may be the authors of history, but we are also its most faithless stewards. Ages decay; their annals lost alongside the forgotten tongues that shaped them. Not even atrocities survive the indifferent march of time—not without extraordinary intervention.

The Shibboleth alone remembers, and we are extraordinary.

When last the G-dhead walked the face of Hebdomar, his geas changed us all. Each thread of sorcery bent to his will, and every mortal soul felt his fury. Civilizations great and small knelt in servitude. Others vanished without a trace. From the crook of Old Mysin, he expanded his reach, creeping beyond the Vale of Arram and across the violent seas. He reached for the dark places at the edge of the map, and he would have grasped them had our ancestors not intervened. No war is prosecuted without cost, even to the victors. That carries threefold for wars against G-d. We visited a great wound upon ourselves in the G-dhead's destruction, but at least we are free.

Shibboleth. A heavy word, possessed of nested meanings like some Varkutskan doll. It is a temple, a priesthood, and a maxim. Where I'm from, what I am, and to which I am avowed: *To abide no walking deity within the demesne of mortal men.* So I swore beside my true sisters of the priesthood, and so we remind each other with every Apostatic rite.

Never again.

Many were the obstacles keeping me from Luka's throat, but conscience was not among them.

Dusk painted Mahakalpe with its golden light, bringing with it the buzz of insects and the bubbling chatter of witnesses gathering outside the *Cikkot.* My sister-wives and I lined up two-by-two inside the blue vestibule.

The *Cikkot* consumed the greater share of our small plaza, and the adulators pouring in to witness the ceremony ate what little space remained beyond its sprawling footprint. I suspected thousands more gathered atop their shemecha roofs, straining to catch a glimpse of their *lehakva* as we walked to our vows and the burning death beyond.

A disembodied hand appeared, drawing back the flap of the *Cikkot,* and we entered our wedding aisle as one, a beautiful chain of the condemned. Each link pulled on the next, dragging us through rows upon rows of guarded adulators—Luka's disciples and clerics of the nomadic creches; urban orthodox in their tahliz and yellow veils; Sylphids, as well—as many as I'd ever seen assembled, their wings overlapping the caged heads of Ohtahpi kantors. The Mahak occupied the position nearest the arbor, guarded by nothing more foreboding than a line of Jassanid spears. He'd brought his wife and his vane son, but I saw no other magistrate of the Sahir. This was to be our wedding party—attendants to our marriage and our demise.

Our G-dling husband awaited us at the edge of the arbor, his slight figure throttled between his leprous cleric and the broad shoulders of Kenver Montaigne. No music greeted our procession. No cheers nor showering of grain. We walked in silence to the center of the plaza, unhooded but no less condemned. At the blast of a ram's horn, we stopped to face our husband.

Clarity, then. We'd be summoned one-by-one to take our vows.

That would be my moment.

I walked the path now, but *Shibboleth preserve me*—it was damned narrow. I am a warrior, not an assassin. I preferred to look my quarries in the eye, and so it would be with Luka. No cover stories or knives in the dark. Luka would see me plain, and in his final moments, he would know my name is death.

Kenver performed a gallant bow before attaching some ceremonial pin to Luka's shalwaz. The two companions exchanged whispered sentiments, and Kenver retreated to join the crowd, opening blessed distance between his sword and his charge. He'd granted me precious space to work, and I thanked the Shibboleth for every inch of it. I just needed that damned leper to call my name.

The boy hung his head as he was wont to do, but this time when he looked up, I saw fresh fortitude coiling within him. The leper raised his prayer book to call the ceremony to order, but Luka stopped him before he could speak.

The Eidolon stepped down from the arbor and faced us, no longer meek or ashamed.

The entire plaza froze—the disciples, the Sylphids, the nomads, the Mahak. Everyone was silent, and nobody moved.

Luka surveyed the plaza, his loamy eyes pressed to solid stone. When he returned to the procession of *lehakva,* his upper lip curled. "I am *insulted.*"

The words struck the plaza like a bolt from the heavens. Luka's lips were moving, his tongue dancing beyond their wet aperture, but his voice belonged to another man—another *time.* The sound of him consumed the silence whole, threaded every gap in the crowd and filled the plaza to its edge.

"Ohtahp. *Kariocha.* I expected better from the keepers of my Word, and yet everywhere I turn, I see only...*perversion.* How dare you?" He looked around the gathered witnesses again, scornful eyes painting the highest and the low. Jassanids and kantors. Nomads and Sylphids. The Mahak and his bitter wife. "How dare you consecrate my return in forbidden blood?"

Luka waited for an answer, but the silence that met this question was sharp enough to cut tempered steel. "Will no one speak in defense of this atrocity?"

When no one answered, he approached us—his line of betrothed— revulsion twisting his youthful features, bestowing years he'd not yet earned. "We will not wed," he told us. "Nor will you return to befoul my *Cikkot* with your sacrifice. I annul our betrothal and return you to your people. I condemn you to *life.*"

Out of the corner of my eye I saw a small patch of crowd ripple, granting passage to Kenver, who stepped into the marriage aisle, his face a bloodless mask. Luka raised one hand, and the warrior froze. "My guardian will see you all to safety beyond this plaza. Your duty has been served."

Kenver's chin dropped, his jaw unhinged. He took a moment to emerge from the shock, then began walking toward us, one hand guarding the hilt of Caledin Bolg. I looked to the Mahak—saw him white with pallor and wide-eyed with the Mahakva nattering in his ear. I heard the shifting of armored Jassanids somewhere in the distance, and Luka again raised his stentorian voice. "None will interfere! On threat of damnation, *none will bar the* lehakva's *path.*"

Kenver flashed Luka a warning look as he passed, but the Eidolon waved him onward. The guardian placed a gloved hand on Liyah's shoulder once he reached our line. He began guiding her toward the edge of the plaza, tugging the chain of *lehakva* behind her, when another body shot into his path.

Slayn Illusitar, clothed in an emerald gown embossed with precious gems. The Sylphid regent invaded the aisle flanked by two masked kantors. Glass wings fluttering, she sailed past our line and prostrated herself before the Eidolon. "Holiness, please. I beseech you. You know not what you risk. You needn't proceed with the wedding, but the *lehakva* must be burned."

Kenver jerked our chain to a halt, turning to watch this petition play out.

"I know not?" Luka's thin body began to tremble as he looked down upon the prostrated Slayn, but I sensed no fear from him. His was the tremor of a long-simmering rage—apt to boil.

"Please, Holiness!"

My body prickled with frisson. There are few sounds as unsettling as a fae creature's plea.

Luka pinched his eyes shut. "The ignorance... The hell awaiting this city has been tempered by your sin."

Illusitar looked up. From my vantage, I saw only the points of her ears and the back of her head—the half-circle of her emerald crown.

Luka raised one hand, pointing over the Slayn's bowed head at his guardian. "Kenver." Not the order of a king, but the commandment of a G-d.

"Come..." Kenver directed Liyah toward a corridor forming through the crowd. Witnesses scrambled to part before our chain, and I was jerked from the plaza. What else could I do? I glanced back, searching for the Mahak or the Mahakva—for their peacock prince—but the royal family had vanished from the square, fleeing the Eidolon's judgment.

As soon as we were clear of the plaza and the crowd, the girls surrounded Kenver. Pretty eyes glistened with tears—tears of shock and, perhaps, relief. I shared only the former.

"You heard him," Kenver said. "Off with you. Back to your tribes and your shemechas. Luka does not wish you to be present for the syzygy."

Kenver began fighting off hurried questions and grasping hands in his eagerness to return to Luka's side. I waited at the edge of the plaza outlet and seized him by the wrist, refreshing his dormant suspicion with my strength.

"Why?" I asked him simply.

I let him break my hold, and he stared at me. "Who can know the mind of G-d?"

He vanished back into the plaza, and a skein of Jassanid spears closed behind him. My heart sank into my stomach. I did not linger to see what the other girls would do. It no longer mattered.

I could not shake the feeling that Luka had somehow *known*—had looked into my eyes and seen that death awaited him. Without a single weapon drawn, he'd neutralized my threat—blazed himself an unencumbered path to the altar. The Shibboleth trusted me with a sacred task, and I was failing.

I ran down the switchback stairs of the retaining wall and through the bagra streets, darting past mobs of adulators awaiting their G-d's rebirth. Piles of shemechas streamed by, beiyit tents and cookfires blurring. I did not slow my pace until I found the crossroads where I'd feasted with the Yusakot Tribe. I climbed mudbrick stairs and cut through alleys, rising from the bagra with every step. Only hours to go until revelation, and all I could do was climb.

I found the ladder of mortared stones that Liyah had shown me and hoisted myself up to the summit. Pilgrims crowded the rooftops—Yusakot and their bagra cousins, most of them straining to gain a view of the *Cikkot* across the way.

A small group of veiled women sat in a circle chanting trope while one of them tapped a tambourine. Their cleric occupied a perch at the rooftop's northern edge, the very same place I'd stood with Liyah only days before. Some of the Yusakot recognized me. I heard them muttering as they parted, permitting me to pass through their cluster and claim the prize position at their cleric's side. The teacher watched the distant *Cikkot* and the faceless crowd around it with such intensity. I didn't think he even sensed my arrival until he spoke.

"Where is Liyah?" he asked without breaking his thousand-yard gaze.

"Not over there," I said.

He painted me with a sharp side-eye.

"I suspect she'll be back here soon," I told him.

The cleric's lips turned slowly downward. "The Eidolon rejected his *lehakva*?"

"Something like that."

The cleric took a deep, bracing breath, and we spoke no more. I remained by his side, watching the nondescript wash of adulators surrounding the *Cikkot*—the highest spires of its painted canvas walls still visible overtop the crowd. The wandering stars burned like sorcerous coldfires against the backdrop of the moonless night, their twelve twinkling eyes entering alignment in a perfect ring around the firmament.

Never had I felt so helpless, tossed from my path at the whims of celestial motion and G-dly caprice. Hours must have passed before the blanket of adulators covering the plaza of the *Cikkot* began to shift, drawing up against the edge of the city square like a rolling tide. I knew then that the Eidolon had renditioned himself within the *Cikkot*, that he'd entered alone, and that he'd face the Altar of the Demiurge to submit himself, fulfilling his birthright as a worldly vessel for an omnipotent ghost.

The distant plaza of the *Cikkot* began to glow with new light. The Yusakot around me gasped, misinterpreting the sign for some beam of G-dly investment, but I knew its shifting cast for the wild dance of flame. The blaze prickled the edges of the *Cikkot*, devouring dried offerings, inhaling the unctuous fumes of oil-soaked sticks. Flametongues licked up the canvas walls of the shelter, climbing high above the central chamber's steepled roof. A wall of heat struck us upon the distant rooftop, carrying with it the taste of charcoal and the corrupted scent of burning potpourri. Sparks streamed up to join the syzygy, as the immolation cast long shadows across the city. The *Cikkot* vanished and there was only the flame.

I closed my eyes as the gathered Yusakot began to sing their maudlin trope.

Hope is a thin tether.

Perhaps Luka would still fail. Many before him had, and if he was proven false, then the flames would accomplish my job as well as Caledin Vane. I did not think the boy a mere pretender, though. The fire might burn away his mortal shell, but the greater part of him would be unleashed.

The tambourines and the chanting suddenly stopped. I heard awed voices rising up around me and opened my eyes. The fire still burned ferociously, but every head had turned to the sky.

A comet appeared. A great ball of azure and green trailing blue streaks of stardust, cracking open the night and defacing the timeless firmament. The omen boiled to life at the center of the syzygy, and there it remained, with every wandering star arrayed in twinkling salute.

Change. The Arrekot cleric had tried to warn me.

My right hand twitched.

I was going to need my sword.

CHAPTER 12

REVELATION

I sat atop my cot with Caledin Vane across my thighs. Rhythmically, I passed the smallest of six polishing stones across her blade, an act of ritual as much as maintenance. My own green eyes stared back at me, reflected in blue steel. The Eidolon's pyre had burned away the last vestiges of Ruxindra bin Vargas. Only Ruxindra l'Maer remained, and she was damned pretty for an old maid.

Gerritt paced the length of the small dormer, back and forth, marching to the *shick shick shick* of stone on steel.

"This is not good," he muttered. "Explain to me again what happened?"

I'd already recounted my entire escapade three times over, and I didn't feel inclined to revisit it in any great detail once again. "The Eidolon sent us away. He annulled the betrothal and banished us, then he went to face the altar alone."

"Not that part," he said. "This Sylphid Slayn—Illusitar. Tell me *precisely* what she said."

I set aside my polishing stones and looked up at him irritably. "She said, 'You know not what you risk. The *lehakva* must be burned.'"

Gerritt ruffled his neat brown hair. "And you weren't burned." He stopped pacing and waved his hand over my unburnt body. "Clearly. How did the Eidolon respond?"

I paused, reliving the interrupted wedding procession. I'd been so focused on my task that I hardly weighed the cryptic conversation that passed between Luka and Illusitar. "He said, 'The hell awaiting this city has been tempered by your sin.'" I shrugged, resuming my polishing.

Gerritt gaped at me. "And that doesn't bother you?"

"Seems fairly rote—as far as divine threats go. *Woe unto the sinners. Hell and damnation. Fire and ice.*"

Gerritt stomped over and grabbed me by the shoulders. "Rux. He said 'the hell awaiting *this city*' not the 'hell awaiting the *sinners.*' Don't you find that a bit unsettling?"

"Should I?"

He threw up his hands. "Yes!"

"City's full of sinners." I tested the fresh edge on Caledin Vane against a fingernail.

"Something's off."

"So you've said."

Gerritt tugged his hair in frustration. "Something *new.*"

I snorted. "G-d is reborn. That's new."

"I don't like it, Rux. The Jassanids have all retreated inside the Sahir. The Mahak sealed the damn city gates." Gerritt's eyes chased shadows around the room. "Something's coming."

Content with my blade, I sheathed Caledin Vane in her scabbard and stood up to buckle my sword belt. I was finished walking the streets of Mahakalpe like a feckless strumpet. "The Eidolon sounded mighty displeased with the Mahak and his courtiers," I said. "His Holy Majesty is probably building a barricade around himself to escape divine retribution."

"But why bar the city?"

"You're the one who's been out and about," I said. "Stumble over any hells unleashed?"

Gerritt shook his head. "Quite the opposite, actually. Mahakalpe is blessed by the G-dhead's return. Long may he reign."

I grasped the red grip of Caledin Vane. "Hopefully not too long."

The *Cikkot* had burned through the night and most of the next day.

When the flames finally ran out of fuel, only the Altar of the Demiurge remained, its flat anvil floating atop a sea of ash. Of Luka there was no sign, but his comet's face still scorched the arc of the firmament, visible even at the height of the bright Ohtahpi day. With the Jassanids gone from their stations, the pilgrims of Mahakalpe swarmed the plaza to paint their faces with the ash of their G-dhead's rebirth. By the time they got their fill, there wouldn't be a single mote left for the urban magistrates to sweep.

Gerritt was pacing again. "Sylphid pleas; murdering Inaghke; the threat of hells unleashed... How are you so calm right now?"

I tightened the straps on my leather vambraces and pulled on my gloves. It felt good to be back in my skin. "None of that concerns me."

"That gash on your cheek says otherwise." He reached out to poke me, and I caught his finger.

"Those two got in my way," I said, releasing him. "I sent you out into the streets to find Luka, not to obsess over locked gates and every thread of loose arcanum."

"You and the Demiurge are on a first-name basis now?"

I might have been projecting calm, but that didn't mean I was in a mood for Gerritt's cheek. "Where is he, Gerritt?"

Gerritt moaned in frustration. "I could really use a scrying right about now. Damn fine time for my thaumaturge to get himself deltafixed."

"Nobody has seen Luka since the syzygy?"

Gerritt scoffed. "*Everyone's* seen him. They're passing stories around every arak still and market strip. He's healing the sick and restoring the lame. Drawing skritglyphs on newborn wains and breaking the shackles on Middle City slaves. I swear there's a stray cat wandering the bagra with a fat rodent in its mouth, mewling that the G-dhead put it there."

"He's still in the city, then."

"For now," he said. "He isn't apt to remain much longer, though. He's got a long road ahead of him." Gerritt reached out and grabbed my hand. "Please, Rux. If you're not concerned about whatever hell is coming for Mahakalpe, then we should get out of here. Tonight. I can find us a way through the gates. Your sword will work just as well on the Shevuot. We can ambush the G-dhead's caravan on the road."

I shook him off. "I won't let him leave this city. I need to kill him now—before he does any more *good*."

Gerritt drew a deep breath, preparing to mount another protest, but he was interrupted by a knock at our moldering door. His chest deflated. "You expecting someone?"

"Not expecting but always prepared." I cracked my knuckles and unsheathed Caledin Vane.

"You think it's Jassanids?" Gerritt asked.

The knock returned, more insistent.

"That's certainly one candidate." I nodded to the door, urging him to open it.

After so long separated from my blade, I was perhaps too eager to test her edge. Gerritt pulled open the door, and I lunged. Our visitor squealed as Caledin Vane's point nicked her beneath the chin. The beauty mark upon her cheek gave me pause, otherwise I would have run her through.

Wide hazel eyes stared back at me down the length of my blade.

"Liyah?" I withdrew my swordpoint from her throat, but didn't sheathe the blade.

Trembling, my former sister-wife touched the nick on her chin and gasped at the droplets of blood reddening her fingers. I hardly recognized her. She'd traded her bridal slip for a modest shalwaz. An embroidered headwrap concealed her short, dark hair but for the barest fringe along her brow.

Gerritt poked his head around the door, glancing from Liyah to me. "Friend of yours?"

"Possibly..." I said, still grasping the hilt of Caledin Vane. "What are you doing here, Liyah?"

The girl checked her chin again, more indignant this time. The bleeding had already stopped. I barely nicked her. She took in my armored visage, and I saw a glint of fear in those vibrant eyes, but she held her ground in the entryway. I noticed that her olive cheeks were flushed, and her chest heaved with exertion. A thin patina of sweat misted her brow beneath that stifling headwrap.

"Are you going to come in?" I asked.

Her eyes jumped to my exposed blade. "Are you going to stab me?"

Sighing, I sheathed Caledin Vane and raised my empty palms. Liyah took three tentative steps into the dormer and Gerritt quickly closed the door behind her, restoring the latch.

"How did you find me?" I asked.

"I—I followed you," Liyah said. "I saw you on the rooftops last night, but I don't think you saw me. I followed you out of our bagra camp. I wanted to know where you were sleeping."

"Keeping tabs on the harpy, is it?"

Liyah averted her eyes, shamed to be confronted with the rumor she'd fueled.

"It's all right," I said. "I've been called far worse."

Gerritt interposed himself between us. "Someone want to bring me up to speed?"

"This is Liyah of the Yusakot Creche," I said, still eyeing the girl. "One of the pardoned *lehakva*."

"Ah."

"Why are you here?" I asked again. "Did you miss me that much? I didn't think you'd taken to my company."

"I didn't know where else to go," Liyah said. "My tribe is under attack."

Gerritt turned his hooded gaze my way.

"Do I look like the City Watch?" I said. "Take it up with the urban magistrates."

"What magistrates?" Liyah tugged at the wrap of her shalwaz, hazel eyes wild. "They've all retreated inside the Sahir along with the Mahak and his Jassanids. We need *you*."

My own eyes narrowed skeptically. "Why me?"

"Because you already killed two of those daemons. I watched you do it with your bare hands."

"Daemons?" Gerritt cocked one eyebrow.

"She means the Inaghke," I said. "Are you saying there's another one in Mahakalpe?"

A shiver passed over Liyah, and she managed a stuttering nod. "That *creature*... It's been stalking the western bagra since the syzygy, defiling our temples and preying on our young. Our clerics penned it inside the old kodesha with Karochan wards and trope, but they can't hold it much longer."

I should have sent her away. I had a G-dling to kill and could little afford this distraction, but Liyah's report made my jaw tighten and my sword hand twitch. This Shade had to be the same one who escaped my wrath in the Sahir, and I did not like leaving any job half-finished.

Gerritt and I shared a meaningful look before I turned back to Liyah. "Show me."

We made haste to the edge of the bloc, hurrying past the climbing piles of shemechas and through a narrow alley cloaked in shade. I sensed the disturbance long before we reached our destination. The high sun dimmed unnaturally over this small corner of Mahakalpe. As we entered the dead-end plaza, I felt the small hairs on the back of my neck prickling with static and my ears began buzzing with a low hum. We'd entered one of the oldest sections of the city. Stone buildings stood in place of mudbrick hovels, and the small temple at the plaza's head looked to have been carved at the same time as the Mysin walls. A wide dome capped the boxy kodesha, brown spires rising like polearms from its wings. Spiderlegs of black lightning crackled across its facade, and around its lone entrance, three skritglyph wards glowed with endemic light. The wards looked like they'd been traced with a finger or a stick, carved hastily into the solid dirt of the hard-pack road.

Three Karochan clerics in their dun red headwraps sat around a wooden Ark of the Tractate positioned so that its grammaton skritglyphs faced the warded kodesha.

Liyah stopped short of the holy congregation. She raised her arm, pointing at the temple facade webbed with crackling sorcery. "It's in there..." she said.

I could've gathered that.

Gerritt stepped toward the temple, fascinated by the Karochan sorcery at work. He rolled up the sleeves of his tunic revealing the merton bangles around his forearms. He tensed his fists, sending beams of light racing up and down his bangles' swooping Ibreic engravings.

I left Liyah to walk to his side. "Something else I need to worry about besides the Shade?"

Gerritt watched the sealed entrance to the kodesha without blinking. "Not really my expertise," he said. "But let's proceed with caution."

I nodded. "Come on."

The clerics sat around the ark with their legs crossed, hands propped over knees with their palms facing upward. They practiced circular breathing, lips moving with ferocious speed to maintain their muttered stream of atonal trope. Whenever one paused to refresh his lungs, the other two picked up his dropped phrase, permitting no interruption to the spell. I saw the strain of the casting painted on their weathered faces. Karochan clerics all possessed some small art, but these desert teachers lacked the puissance of trained kantors. Veins throbbed from their necks and temples. Stinging sweat poured from their brows, threatening to drown their wide-eyed focus.

I recognized the cleric I joined on the bagra rooftop to watch the *Cikkot's* immolation and knelt beside him.

"The cavalry's here, Teacher."

Only his eyes moved to me as he continued his chanting.

"It's only one of them in there?" I asked.

I took the sharp jerk of his head for confirmation.

With a groan, I stood back up. Gerritt was already approaching the temple.

The cleric suddenly dropped his chanting with a gasp, and the other two seamlessly swelled their voices to replace him. "We will need to undo the wards!" he shouted, breathless. "You won't be able to cross them."

"I'll save you the trouble," Gerritt said, still watching the temple entrance. He raised his hands overhead, fingers tied in improbable knots. When he dropped them, the claws of black lightning released their grasp on the kodesha, vanishing with a clap of thunder. Pillars of white light erupted from the skritglyph wards, banishing those arcane symbols just as surely from the face of the hardpack road.

The chanting clerics all fell back from the ark, coughing and wheezing.

I stood before the temple entrance side-by-side with Gerritt. His dispel had silenced the plaza, but the kodesha still seemed like a thing alive, throbbing with some vital infestation.

"Ladies first," he said.

We passed through a small vestibule filled with shattered urns and cracked stone pedestals. Blood spattered the walls in clawed streaks—*red* blood that did not belong to the Inaghke. Caledin Vane sang from her scabbard as I walked up the short stone cursa and into the central kodesha. The ancient temple would have been black as pitch if not for the weak light cast by four stone braziers, each one astir with purple flame.

The temple had been defiled. Wooden pews torn up from their rivets and splintered. Glass windows shattered. Stone idols pulverized to chalky dust. I saw bodies and parts of bodies mixed among the detritus, limbs and torsos still covered by scraps of shredded shalwaz robes. Red blood pooled in every divot of the uneven stone floor.

At the apex of the kodesha, a black mound quivered before the bima. I took a step toward it, raising Caledin Vane, but Gerritt caught me by the shoulder.

"Wait," he cautioned.

Sibilant laughter crept out of the mound, filling the kodesha to its domed cap.

"Shibboleth..."

The black mound expanded, a mass of tentacles rising out of its umbral heap like some birthing clutch of serpents. The Inaghke flourished its black cloak and turned its burning eyes our way. Claws fanned out at either side, dripping viscid gore.

Its round mouth shaped Mysinic speech with great effort. Every syllable came out strained, crowded by its exposed fangs. "You are the one. The one who interfered with my ssspawn."

I pushed forward with Gerritt in tight formation at my shoulder.

"Didn't take much," I taunted. "I wish I could say they fought well, but..."

The Shade's lamprey mouth quivered, producing another sibilant laugh. "I thought our effortsss foiled. If only we knew your G-d would perform our tasssk for usss. We would not have wasssted so much Inaghke blood."

"You speak nonsense," I said. Eldritch creatures all trend to madness. Long lives accrue weight over time, and minds do not bear the burden well. "You tried to slay the *lehakva*. The Eidolon spared us."

The Inaghke's tentacles writhed, and the coals of its eyes flared brighter, casting a waxen pallor over its sickly gray skin. "Two pathsss to the same nexusss."

A tremor shook the kodesha, and I stumbled. Dust and broken stone rained down from the dome. The Shade glanced up at something only it could see. "She comesss," it moaned.

I'd heard enough. I would not grant this creature the dignity of dying beneath a collapsing temple. I would rather feed it to Caledin Vane.

The creature unleashed a shrill cry and raised its claws as I charged up the broken pews, angling my sword for its heart. Black shrouds of sorcery boiled out from the bima, arcing over the Shade's pointed shoulders, cascading in helical loops to meet my charge. Gerritt appeared at my side in an instant with his bangles crossed. A white ward flashed open in front of us, catching the malicious spell and quenching it with a clap of thunder. A wave of negative pressure pulled me inward, and I went to my knees, shielding my eyes from the clash of sorceries.

I heard Gerritt's ward shatter and looked up to find the Inaghke collapsed over the bima.

"Now, Rux!" Gerritt shouted.

Another tremor rattled the kodesha, more insistent than before. The old stone walls of the temple began to bow, lines of mortar cracking.

I charged over unstable ground, through showering rock and detritus. Nebulous clouds of sorcery bubbled out of the bima once again, haloing the bent Inaghke. These shrouds coalesced into four black columns, but this time they did not come for me. They shot toward the corners of the kodesha, fueling great pillars of purple flame that erupted from the temple braziers. I heard the temple cracking as I hurdled the three-step cursa, leading with the point of Caledin Vane.

The Inaghke's red eyes boiled with religious zeal. It raised its claws, perhaps by instinct, but it was not enough to stall my momentum. I landed on top of the crumpled Shade, sheathing Caledin Vane in its chest to the hilt. I felt the creature's gnarled spine snap as my sword carved its exit wound. Its head tentacles spasmed. Silver ichor spurted from the wound.

The Shade's throat rattled with its dying breath. "Yoursss isss not the only G-d reborn in Mahakalpe," it hissed.

With a blinding flash, the light extinguished from its eyes, their burning coals reduced to smoking embers.

The Inaghke's death throes spread to the kodesha, and this time the tremor did not cease. I freed Caledin Vane from the creature's chest and used the Shade's cloak to clean its ichor from her blade.

Something caught my eye atop the bima—a shattered tablet. The charm had broken into six clean shards, severing the looping knots of the *naga'tlat*.

"Rux!" Gerrit shouted over the shaking of the temple.

Over my shoulder, I saw him darting furiously around the kodesha, drawing runes with his tangled fingers and laying white sorcerous lashings over seams forming in the temple walls. The webs of his spells held for mere seconds before exploding with blasts of broken stone.

"We have to go!" he shouted.

With one last glance and the broken tablet and the vanquished Shade, I sprinted from the collapsing temple.

CHAPTER 13
ZIGGURAT

Slaying the Shade did nothing to quench whatever foul sorcery had been unbottled within the old kodesha. The ancient dome crumbled, pierced by purple columns of coldfire lancing toward the sky. Gerritt and I sprinted clear of the collapse, chased by living shadows and an expanding cloud of dust that eventually overcame us.

Tremors rattled the bagra around us. The dust quickly settled once the last stone had fallen, but the shaking continued. Through the rarefying haze, I saw vented sorcery pooling in the skies overhead, coldfire twisting in spirals, carving a purple vortex into the firmament.

The vortex grew to occlude one half of the sun, dimming the white light over Mahakalpe to match the unnatural gloaming already shrouding the defiled plaza. Violet eddies of raw mist swirled over the surface of the celestial wound. For the briefest moment, I could have sworn I saw faces in those mists, gaping mouths and absent eyes pressing against some membranous veil.

A peel of thunder shattered my focus, and the ground pitched beneath my feet. I toppled over Gerritt and heard an ominous groan—cracks spreading along the looming aqueducts. I leapt to my feet and pulled Gerritt up behind me. He ran to grab Liyah while I gathered up the clerics penned around their heavy ark.

"We have to get away from here!" I shouted at the holy men.

The clerics' eyes darted around the crumbling plaza, faces wan with horror.

The Yusakot leader clutched the painted face of the ark like a lifeboat, though I did not think it would save him. "We cannot abandon the plates!" he said.

"Then you'll be buried with them!" I grabbed the nearest cleric by the tuft of his shalwaz and dragged him after Gerritt and Liyah.

The first breach opened in the side of the aqueduct and water began to gout from the seam. A second cleric abandoned his post and followed us into the narrow alleyway, but the leader of the Yusakot remained. I caught one final glimpse of the man still clinging to his ark as the mighty aqueduct collapsed, roaring over the plaza, burying the fool and his Tractate under feet of water and crushing stone.

The water spilling from the aqueducts chased us down the alley, accelerating as momentum and grading forced the deluge into the bottleneck. We broke through into the wider bagra streets before we were overtaken. Water gushed from the alley, robbed of its ardor by the breadth of the corridor beyond. The street still flooded to the depth of our knees, overwhelming the open-air sewers, blending filth and mud until the floodwaters turned a pungent brown. The bagramate crowded the terraced passageways and rooftops of the adjacent shemechas, awed faces turned toward the dark vortex that had opened in the sky.

Our moribund party splashed through the feculent floodwaters until we reached drier ground. As soon as we stopped, one of the clerics fell to his knees and vomited. Liyah went to his aid, holding back his shalwaz and whispering calming words as she stroked his head. Gerritt turned his eyes fixedly to the horizon, fascinated by the violet wound still churning overhead.

"This will be the death of us." The voice of the second cleric, speaking to no one, eyes glazed with a thousand-yard stare. "We've lost the Word. We can never return to our creche." From the sickly cast of the man, I thought he might be on the verge of vomiting, as well. "We are *Hesserat* now. Dimly lit." He began muttering in Karochan, *"A'shana hava-a. Kariocha ehad..."*

Funeral prayers.

With no consolations to offer, I left him to his catatonic singing and joined Gerritt, who was still watching the sky.

"I told you…" Gerritt said. "I told you we needed to get out of this city."

"And miss the fireworks?"

The scorching look he shot me suggested he did not appreciate the joke. A dust cloud rose up from the collapsed corner of the city, mushrooming toward the vortex still twisting in the sky, but the violent sorcery that birthed it had reached some kind of equilibrium; the Holy City no longer shook.

"What is it?" I asked.

"I think it's a *Darwaza*," he said.

"In Mysinic, please."

"A material pocket of the Unseen World," he translated. "They're usually sealed, but this one's been good and lanced."

Sealed. I knew Gerritt used the word colloquially, but it summoned to mind the gnostic shrines I'd visited in the eastern bagra and beneath the Mahak's Sahir. An image of the *naga'tlat* flashed through my mind, its serpent coils broken by the shattered tablet upon which it had been inscribed. The coincidences were getting harder to ignore.

I shook my head. "This still isn't our problem."

"I think we just made it our problem," Gerritt said.

I knocked my wrists together, mimicking his Ibreic bangles. "Anything you can do about it?"

Gerritt shook his head. "This is well beyond my ken."

"Then we focus on the Eidolon."

"That's who we need!"

We both turned to find Liyah hovering a few feet behind us. She'd been eavesdropping but clearly misinterpreted my intent.

"Luka will fix this," Liyah said. How naive her confidence.

"You know where to find him?" I asked.

"I think so," Liyah said. "He called upon the *lehakva* to visit the orthodox ziggurat for evening prayers."

"Guess my invitation got lost in the bagra."

Liyah tossed my quip away. "Or he thinks you can take care of yourself. I think Luka is trying to protect us. Kenver came to me after the syzygy—to deliver a warning."

"What kind of warning?"

Liyah's young face twisted into the ugliest expression I'd ever seen on the girl. "The Mahak plans to round us up. He wants to complete the sacrifice."

I glanced over at Gerritt. The sorcerer took a deep breath and shook his head in resignation.

I nodded to Liyah. "Lead the way."

Our path back through the Middle City led us past the Penitent Barbican where poor Master Glavion still hung from his deltafix, now mercifully deceased. His face was no longer recognizable, chewed over by carrion birds and showing early signs of infestation. I wondered morbidly how long they would leave him there. Unless the Mahak had need of the deltafix, they might just let the scavengers pick him clean. Bones were easier to dispose of than soft remains. Cleaner, certainly.

Gerritt eyed the desiccated thaumaturge warily as we rounded the crumbling ramparts of the old barbican, turning up the stone path to the orthodox enclave and its pinnacle ziggurat. "Damn shame," he muttered to himself. "Impossible to find a good thaumaturge in Ohtahp."

A low stone wall ringed the enclave, ungated and unguarded. Mahakalpe's orthodox community lived in small free-standing houses, larger than the shemechas and domed like the merchant villas of the Middle City. Communal longhouses anchored four clusters of these homes, spreading out from the ziggurat's angular base. The ziggurat was the tallest structure in Mahakalpe—taller even than the Sahir—though its apogee barely breached the summit of the retaining wall that raised the palace over everything else.

Four firebrick terraces described the temple walls, their red faces glazed with golden skritglyphs and bisected by narrowing ramps of stairs. Triangular openings in the facade granted entry at each level but for the lowest, which was only accessible from inside the temple's core.

We found the stone pathways of the enclave empty or nearly so. Throngs of the orthodox gathered at the base of the ziggurat and around the lip of each terrace, the faces of their wives concealed behind traditional yellow veils that hung to their breasts. Tasseled tahliz scarves draped the shoulders of the men. The only exposed heads among the congregation belonged to younglings, their dark hair shaved in the same balding tonsure, plump faces framed by hanging curls. I saw nomads, as well, among the masses. Pilgrim representatives from half-a-dozen tribes. They knelt atop patterned rugs at the base of the ziggurat, pressing their foreheads to the ground in unison as they joined their voices in dissonant prayer. Nearly every face in the enclave bore the ash of Luka's pyre.

I pulled the edge of my cloak around the hilt of Caledin Vane. I was not so familiar with the traditions of Ohtahp, and I couldn't be certain how arms carried within the ziggurat might be received by the orthodox or their clerics.

Liyah stopped at the staircase, listening to the prayers of the bent. She touched her head and her heart with three fingers. "He's here," she said. "Or at least, *they* think he's here."

"How can you be certain?" I asked.

"They sing the *Karbalah Kov*," Liyah said. "Mystic prayers. These trope are only sung in the presence of the Divine."

An excited trill momentarily banished all concern for the broken *Darwaza* in the Mahakalpan sky. Caledin Vane would soon serve its tempered purpose, and there was poetry in the act of slaying G-d inside a temple of his most devout.

Gerritt's eyes moved apprehensively up the terraced layers of the ziggurat. "Awfully crowded in there."

I caught his subtle warning but would not heed it. The butcher's bill was already overdue. Escape was a problem for after it had been paid.

We climbed the staircase and entered the core of the second terrace without argument from the orthodox. The chamber bubbled with voices, their crosstalk amplified by a low ceiling and parallel walls. A deep depression centered the square chamber, its perimeter inlaid with mudbrick stairs. Only those few orthodox who gained access to the depression seemed to be engaged in active prayer. The rest of the bodies filling the terrace milled about the chamber, arranging cliques and sharing fevered conversation. I saw as many nomads as urban orthodox, and a few faces I recognized as former *lehakva*. One of these young women greeted Liyah, exchanging quick sentiments as she carved our path through the core. The former sister-wife eyed me warily, eyes stretching wide when she recognized who I was.

"*Masra elohaim!*" A portly man with chest hair squirming out from the neck of his cotton tunic elbowed his way through the crowd to reach us. He grasped Liyah's hands as soon as he could reach them. "You made it! That's ten of you. Fewer than we hoped, but each life saved is a blessing."

"Eleven, actually," Liyah said, shifting her body to reveal me.

"Ruxindra!" the man exclaimed, rushing toward me. "*Masra elohaim!*"

"Shirit?" I almost didn't believe my lying eyes. The penitent brand that once scarred his cheek had vanished, restoring luster to his supple olive skin. He looked a decade younger than I remembered, but it was certainly him.

He flashed a broad, toothy grin, no longer tugged off-kilter by the scar tissue that once deadened his right cheek. "More handsome than you remember, eh?"

"Oh, I don't know," I said, returning a tight-lipped smile. "I tend to like my men with a little wear and tear." I felt a kindling of warmth for the Uruzot disciple. As I've mentioned, my war was with his G-d, but not with him.

"I don't mean to sour this reunion," Gerritt interjected. "But our present concern is a bit time-sensitive in nature."

He was right. "We're looking for Luka," I said. "Is he here?"

"He's here." Shirit glanced down into the depression filled with adulators at prayer. "He's locked himself in the kodesha at the ziggurat's base. Gulam won't let anyone in—not even the orthodox clerics."

I noticed a handsome man standing apart from the praying adulators at the foot of the depression. He surveyed the crowd with his arms folded across his chest.

"That's Gulam?" I said, not even attempting to conceal my shock.

Shirit nodded. "I'm not the only tarnished gem newly polished by the hand of G-d, eh?"

Again, I had a difficult time believing what my eyes were showing me. Luka had cleansed the lapsed cleric of his every lesion and shaved away his leprous scales. G-d's touch restored a thick coif of light brown hair, once lost to the scars that had colonized his scalp.

Shaking off the uncanny visage, I returned to Shirit. "He'll have to make an exception. Something foul is stirring in the bagra."

Shirit's broad grin deflated. "I think he's aware. He's working on a countermeasure, but his first priority is ensuring the safety of his *lehakva*. Many of your sisters remain unaccounted for."

"I have information that might be helpful to him," I said. "I don't think we can wait."

"G-d requires your counsel, does he?"

"Have you seen the violet rent in the sky?" Gerritt asked. "I think it might behoove us to cover our bases."

Shirit's eyebrows bent inward. "Who is this?" he asked.

Liyah saved me from providing an answer. "We'd be wise to listen to Ruxindra," she insisted, grasping Shirit by the sleeve of his tunic. "She slew the creatures who brought this curse upon us."

Shirit eyed me up and down, marking my leather vambraces and greaves—perhaps even noticing the blunt point impressed by Caledin Vane's jeweled pommel inside my cloak. He tapped one finger over his lips and glanced back down at Gulam. "I'll talk to him, but I don't expect he'll change his mind."

Shirit descended the steps into the depression, and Liyah left us to find the other *lehakva* strewn about the ziggurat. I tapped my foot impatiently, awaiting Gulam's verdict.

"Is there another way inside the kodesha?" I asked.

Gerritt circled once and shook his head. "I'm not seeing *any* way inside the kodesha."

"There must be an interior passage from the core. What else is Gulam guarding?"

Over Gerritt's shoulder, a square kufi bobbed into view then dropped out of sight. The foreign headpiece grabbed my attention—as did the silver academic pin clipped to its side.

"Wait here for Shirit," I said.

"Where are you going?" Gerritt called after me.

Ignoring him, I tracked the kufi to a dark-skinned man in a purple toga bent over a mudbrick bench furiously writing in a leather-bound journal.

"Senex," I said.

Amari Desta raised a finger but not his head. He continued writing with such speed I thought his pen might burn through the parchment. He finally drew a line of punctuation at the edge of the page and looked up, blue eyes not quite tracking, mind clearly elsewhere.

"Ruxindra," I said. "We met around that gnostic shrine in the bagra. You called it a seal."

"Yes, yes... Of course..." A moment's inspiration struck him rigid, and he returned to his furious scribbling.

"What are you writing?"

"Hmm?" He didn't look up.

Frustration mounting, I reached down and ripped the journal out from under him. That got his attention. His head jerked up, eyes bright with outrage.

"I asked you a question."

"Give that back!" he shouted, grasping after the journal.

I pinned him back with a stiff arm and held its pages out of reach. "I'm trying to have a conversation with you."

"There isn't any time!" He tore off his kufi and wrung it between his hands, squirming in anguish. "I need to put this all to page—so we have some *record*. Records are the only thing that might survive!"

"Survive *what*?" I demanded.

"Are you blind, woman! Have you not seen the rent in the sky?"

"Sure, I've seen it," I said calmly. "Bit of an eyesore."

Amari Desta's eyes bugged from his skull. "The seals of Mahakalpe are *crumbling*. I stood before the bagra seal as the syzygy aligned. Cracks along its ebony face... Stones older than Mysin made brittle—falling to dust! I came to the ziggurat to check its twin, but that damned Uruzot won't grant me access to the kodesha where it's kept."

"Why would the seals be crumbling now? Why after all this time?"

Amari Desta's pink lips trembled. He squeezed his kufi, shaking his head. "All we have are—are—"

"Theories," I supplied. "Tell me yours."

The Senex inhaled a stuttering breath. "The Demiurge is a spirit of the Unseen World—an Aeon. His animus can only be dispersed, never truly destroyed. Gnostic sorcery feeds on this power, but with the Demiurge reconstituted inside a material shell, that source is no longer available. There are other ways to strengthen a bloodbind, but steps must be taken in advance of the investment... rituals observed."

"Like a virgin sacrifice by fire?" I asked.

His graven look was confirmation enough. "It's too late—now that the seals have been compromised. Disorder reigns, and time does not run back."

I nodded along. As theories went, Amari Desta's seemed like a fine one. "What was this gnostic bloodbind holding?"

The Senex's voice became very low. "I think we're all about to learn the answer to that question with empirical confidence." He extended one hand. "My folio—*please*."

I placed the journal in his hand but did not relinquish it. Our eyes joined as he tugged against my implacable grip. "I think you already know what's coming for Mahakalpe," I said.

The Senex looked pained. "*Urkaku-Azag*." The Ibreic syllables crackled in his tense throat. "I know not which one—those records are lost. Not since man's infancy has Hebdomar known the wrath of such an eldritch horror."

I released the journal, but Amari Desta did not immediately return to his writings. "We're all going to die in this city," he said. "I only hope my account will survive. Future generations need not be as blind as we are."

I left the Senex to his noble scribbling, hoping Shirit had made some headway with Gulam. If Amari Desta was right, then so was Gerritt; we needed to leave this city as soon as possible.

Urkaku-Azag...

The Azag cursed the face of Hebdomar before the Age of Men. Before cities and kingdoms coalesced. Before Mysin raised his Empire of G-d. I wasn't certain even Caledin Vane would be a match for such a creature, nor was I eager to test it.

I stepped down into the depression at the center of the ziggurat where Gerritt was watching Shirit make his fruitless case to stubborn Gulam. The former leper listened placidly, shaking his handsome head.

Sighing, Shirit turned back to me, hands raised apologetically. "I'm sorry, Ruxindra. The stubborn ox won't budge. He says Luka commanded it."

"G-d will present himself to the *lehakva* at the time of his choosing," Gulam said.

"That's a shame." I took a step back, falling in line with Gerritt. "It was worth a shot asking nicely, at least."

Four marble tiles broke the mudbrick floor at Gulam's feet. Their faces shone with glowing skritglyphs reminiscent of the wards the Yusakot clerics hastily scraped into the bagra dirt outside the old kodesha. I prodded one with my toe, felt its warmth radiating through my boot.

"These what I think they are?" I asked Gerritt

"Sure looks that way," he confirmed.

I took two more steps back from the tiles and looked over at Shirit and Gulam. "You two might want to make some space."

Shirit scrambled to the edge of the staircase without question, but Gulam remained defiant.

"Suit yourself," I said.

Gerritt widened his stance and clicked his wrists together. "*Epaphitha*," he incanted and drew a sharp slash through the air with knotted fingers. A hot streak trailed his gesture, his art warping the marble tiles with sorcerous light. Gulam did back away then, tripping over his feet to escape the locus of Gerritt's spell. Many of the orthodox adjacent to us, broke from their prayers, fleeing the depression in droves. The skritglyph tiles folded like playing cards and the floor of the ziggurat split, revealing a stone staircase descending into the bottom terrace.

Keenly aware of all the ashy and ashen faces pointed in our direction, I hurried through the broken wards with Gerritt trailing behind.

"Probably better if we aren't interrupted," I said, already well into my descent.

Gerritt muttered another incantation, and I heard the sharp snap of his arcane barrier expanding across the hatch above.

His footsteps stopped halfway down the staircase.

"Don't tell me you're getting cold feet?" I asked

He winced, allayed by some unseen attack. "They're already getting antsy up there." He glanced up the staircase irritably. "I think they've got a kantor—or a particularly ardent cleric. I'll have to stay here to brace the barrier."

"Do what you must."

Gerritt had served his purpose and served it well. This next act was between G-d and my Caledin blade.

I entered the kodesha at the base of the ziggurat, staring out from the stairwell down a corridor of stone columns and wooden pews. The temple sanctum drew toward a raised dais upon which stood the bima and a carved wooden ark. Someone had left the heavy doors to the ark ajar, exposing the hanging plates of the Tractate. One of those bronze tablets lay flat upon the bima, abandoned by whomever had been studying it. No sign of Luka—or anyone else, for that matter.

To reach the bima, I had to cross a narrow debris field of black rubble. The stone wasn't a match for any other material in the ziggurat, and when I tried to inspect a sample, the black ingot crumbled in my hand like spent charcoal. Only then did I realize what it must be—or must *have been*: Mahakalpe's final seal. Not cracked as Amari Desta described but destroyed. Disintegrated right down to its guttering gnostic core.

"It's you."

I looked up from the ruined seal.

Kenver Montaigne had claimed the dais from some hidden redoubt at the back of the kodesha. He stood over the bima like a Karochan cleric crying rites to order, golden cape dangling from the corners of his hoplite cuirass.

I felt my lips twitching, reaching for a smirk. If he was here, then Luka must be close. From the moment I first set eyes on him, I suspected my path to the Eidolon ran over this man's corpse, and the second he named his blade, I felt a sick yearning to test myself against it.

"It's me," I confirmed.

"Ruxindra."

I nodded.

"Strange name for an Azyti." He unclipped his cape and let it pool at his feet.

The threat of combat changes a space. Time slows and walls collapse inward—even on an open field with no true walls to account. I saw by the set of Kenver's jaw that he sensed the shift, as well, and that we'd both slipped from the mundane plane of the kodesha—entered that liminal space, the precipice of battle. I let my cloak fall to my side, exposing the hilt of Caledin Vane as I stepped out of the gnostic rubble and entered the aisle between the pews.

"I watched you all along," Kenver said, still rigid behind the bima. "I knew you were no true *lehakva*."

"Then you've got a better nose for fornicators than every kantor in the Mahak's Sahir."

"That wasn't it." Kenver began to circle the bima, blue eyes tracking my approach. "Violent men wear their affliction like a penitent brand. It only takes another violent man to see it."

That was true enough. I'd marked Kenver the moment he walked through the gates of Mahakalpe—just as quickly as he'd marked me. I stopped halfway down the aisle and covered my sword hilt. "You should have dealt with me while I was still unarmed."

"Where's the sport in that?" Kenver crossed in front of the bima and took two steps down from the dais. "You were never any threat to Luka."

"Where is he?" I asked.

Kenver covered his heart with a gloved hand. "He is in each of us, now."

"Don't get cute."

"What does it matter?" he asked. "You'll never leave this temple."

With the pews on either side of us, the kodesha aisle became a perfect fencing pitch, a single axis of combat. Advance and retreat. Parry and attack. Pure form.

Kenver lowered his head to me out of respect, and I returned the nicety. Our kinship extended far beyond our shared craft. His blade was a sibling to my own, which I think he knew or at least suspected. I stuck my tongue between my teeth and offered final confirmation, unsheathing Caledin Vane.

Kenver's right hand moved over his own red grip. With a long steel note sweeter than any trope, he freed her brother—her near-perfect twin.

He slid his back foot into stance as he adjusted his blade, teasing a passive form. He wanted to dictate the terms and test my mettle. I let him have a taste.

I crept and then lunged, closing the distance between us in two nimble steps. He leaned into my assault, parrying my blade with the edge of his own—*snap, snap, snap*. I withdrew a half-step, and showed a second assault, but he didn't bite on the feint, advancing forward with a quick lunge at my throat. I turned his sword away, looping Caledin Vane around his blade, reaching for his glove in an attempt to disarm him, but he withdrew before I could gain enough momentum.

He *tsk tsked*. "You think me a novice."

"Prove me wrong."

I attacked again, changing my form between steps, collapsing from Charging Ram to Black Adder. This time, Kenver did not anticipate my angle, and I drove him back several steps toward the bima as our blades clashed. Eager to press my advantage, I overextended my assault. Kenver ducked under my thrust, and Caledin Vane passed harmlessly over his shoulder. He pivoted seamlessly out of his passive stance and swung his blade in a flurry of tight attacks. I folded my body to dodge the first, then retracted my blade to parry the others. The defense forced me backward several steps, yielding the precious ground I'd only just claimed.

I caught his lateral cut on the crosshilt of Caledin Vane and tangled it to stymie the assault, but Kenver twisted free with powerful wrist work. Caledin Bolg drew a shallow score across the belly of my leather cuirass. I completed my retreat, yielding the touch, and he at last withdrew.

"That's one touch to me, I think." Kenver's blue eyes gleamed with amusement.

I smiled with gritted teeth. I was the finest swordsman at the Shibboleth, and unaccustomed to facing my equals. Moreover, Kenver's style mirrored my own, as if some master had crafted his forms to repel the art of an Apostatic Priest. Unfortunately for him, I'd spent years as a peripatetic sword, and I'd picked up plenty of idiosyncratic tricks.

He stepped forward, again showing passivity, but this time I read his game. He expected me to attack, so I obliged him, but shifted my form with every step—Charging Ram, Lunging Ostrix, Baiting Gibbon. He riposted as expected, mirroring to receive my Gibbon's thrust, but I instead swept Caledin Vane in a heavy slash, shifting my weight to add momentum. His flimsy parry folded against my saber's edge, and I stepped into him, scoring two glancing blows off his cuirass before he righted himself to deflect my lunge at his throat.

I stopped my advance to crouch, angling the point of Caledin Vane for the soft seam beneath his cuirass. This time, Kenver bit down on the feint. He lowered his sword to counter, and I sprang from my crouch with an upward slash.

Wide eyes revealed his surprise. He jerked his head by pure instinct, escaping an open throat by a hair's width. The edge of Caledin Vane caught his cheek and ear, drawing first blood, and I withdrew, permitting his tactical retreat.

Blood trickled from his ear to his chin.

"I hope you've got some more tricks up your sleeve," I taunted. "That was just a courtesy nick."

In the blink of an eye, Kenver's form vanished. He sprang at me with a wild overhand cut, trusting his cuirass to deflect my counter. Caledin Vane's edge skidded off his breastplate, and I caught his blade just in time to keep it from cleaving into my skull. He retreated one step, restoring his disciplined footwork, and pivoted back to an active assault.

Our blades clashed edge against edge as we traded ground through an extended exchange. Kenver punctuated each series of formal attacks with a wild slash or thrust intended to unbalance rather than skewer me. He hardly seemed to tire throughout the exchange, and I soon realized that this was his game. If he could not best me by skill alone, he would rely upon his superior size and weight to overpower me.

A desperate tactic. I'd killed bigger men than Kenver Montaigne.

I let him gain ground with another series of attacks from his mirrored Charging Ram, waiting for his next breach of form. The moment came after he deflected a lateral cut from Caledin Vane. Abandoning his careful footwork, he hacked at my crosshilt and lurched forward with a two-handed thrust intended to disembowel me. The attack was so clumsy. I could have seen it coming a mile away. I steered his blade away from my midriff and thrust Caledin Vane deep into the meat of his shoulder.

Kenver grimaced in pain, retreating back to form, yielding every step of the pitch he had claimed with his reckless advance. I pursued with zeal, tasting victory. Caledin Vane began to blur with the speed of my assault. I pivoted between forms, slashing and thrusting. Each parry came slower than the last as I drove him nearly to the steps of the dais. With no room left for Kenver to retreat, I chambered the final thrust of Caledin Vane.

"Kenver!"

My eyes jumped to the source of the shriek.

Luka.

The Eidolon stood atop the dais, gaping down at the battle taking place between his pews. My distraction only lasted a fraction of a second, but that was enough time for Kenver to regain his footing. He anticipated my thrust and turned it aside, advancing with a series of tight cuts and thrusts, desperate to reclaim ground.

"Stop this at once!" Luka shouted.

Neither one of us listened. I swept my feet from passive to active pose and brought Caledin Vane around to renew my assault, hoping to drive Kenver back into a corner, but his onslaught did not relent. He forced me back into a defensive posture, blade skimming my shoulder as I struggled to keep up with his frenzied attacks. I scored another glancing slash along his ribs, but he pressed through the pain, bullying me back out of position.

He hesitated. I saw his own feet begin to pivot. He must have exhausted himself. With the wounds I'd already dealt him, he could not maintain this pace indefinitely. I restructured my own form to return to the attack, but Kenver's retreat proved a feint. As soon as I took my first half-step forward, Kenver's stance hardened. He crouched and lunged, extending one leg and sweeping my feet out from under me.

I hit the ground hard and tried to bounce back up, shielding my head with my leather vambrace and the blade of my sword. I expected his blade to come down, but Kenver threw his weight on top of me instead, crashing through my forearm and butting the bridge of my nose with the crown of his head. Stars exploded across my vision as I fell flat on my back. I felt Kenver's boot crunch down on my wrist, pinning my arm and Caledin Vane to the cold kodesha floor.

I looked up at the man standing over me, blurry and bloodied, as he raised Caledin Bolg, sword point angled down at my chest. He covered the pommel with his second hand.

"My regards to the Shibboleth," he said breathlessly, chest heaving with exertion.

"Kenver, no!" Luka shouted. Not a G-d's commandment, but the frightened plea of a gentle boy.

The guardian did not obey. With all his weight, he drove the point of Caledin Bolg straight down into my chest. I felt the sharp kiss of her edge and my vision collapsed, mind racing toward oblivion.

CHAPTER 14
CATACLYSM

I have taken many wounds before, from blade and claw. From weapons more exotic and crueler, wielded by creatures both fae and foul. I've been feathered with arrows and impaled by pole arms. A charging Yaga once opened my chest with its festering cleaver. I've been bludgeoned with mauls and warhammers, knocked out by a stone tossed by a fifty-foot trebuchet. No sensation compared to the killing report of Caledin Bolg, and not even the trebuchet brought such instant oblivion.

The kodesha evaporated around me, and I felt my body compressed, sucked into a narrow tunnel like water through an aqueduct. I saw nothing. Heard nothing. Felt only a cracked-glass prickling in my chest. The pain was a distant thing. I was conscious but absent from my body.

The feeling only lasted a moment—shorter than the span of a single breath—but removed from my body, that moment seemed to encompass an eternity. My vision returned with a torrent of color and shape. Vertigo overwhelmed me, as my consciousness reached the tunnel's spout and vomited back inside my body, transported to a different time and space. I crashed back to consensus reality flailing my arms and screaming, grasping the wound in my chest.

My fingers came back bloodless, but still I flailed. The panic only abated once I realized I'd landed somewhere empty and still.

My room. Our humble bagra dormer.

I lay flat on the mudbrick floor between the two sleeping pallets. My fingers returned to the score in my leather cuirass where the killing point of Caledin Bolg came down. The breastplate had been pierced, but the blade never reached my chest—I was sure of it. My body ached, but the pain was more akin to a hundred glass splinters abrading the surface of my skin.

Hands still trembling, I fumbled with the buckles on my cuirass, struggling out of the armor to inspect the naked flesh beneath. When the leather fell away, a few yellow calcite shards fell with it, tumbling to the floor with a delicate *chink chink chink.*

I gathered a halting breath as I fished for the chain inside my undershirt. The last shard of Gerritt's ensorcelled pendant still clung to its setting; the rest had shattered. I quickly brushed the remnant shards from my chest and stared, dumbfounded, at the spent talisman.

Laughter tumbled out of me. I'd forgotten that I still wore the damn trinket; a fortunate lapse, for I certainly would have abandoned it after leaving the *Cikkot.* If I'd only thought to...

The mad laughter continued as I removed the broken remains of the pendant and tossed it aside. Gerritt's charm had saved my life, however improbably.

I was never going to hear the end of this.

A distant scream jarred me from my laughing fit. The sound died away, and an uncanny quiet rolled over the bagra in its wake. I slipped back into my leather cuirass and tightened its straps. Caledin Vane had traveled with me, still clutched in the hand that had been pinned under Kenver's boot. I picked it up from the floor, but did not return it to its sheath.

I needed to get back to the Middle City and to Gerritt, but all was not well in the bagra of Mahakalpe.

A fell miasma greeted me outside the flop house, a thick gray mist that saturated the streets, reducing my range of vision and obscuring all but the street-level shemechas. The Mahakalpan slum had always been busy with the sounds of urban congestion—hand carts creaking down the hardpack street; men and women at their labors and leisure; children playing; street merchants crying their wares. All those vital sounds had been banished, but the silence was not an easy one. I would have preferred the braying Karochan trope.

The *Darwaza* hung low over the eastern bloc, casting its violet shroud across the city, cloaking the bagra in unnatural twilight. The air smelled like thunder and decay and something else—a slick animal musk like wet skin, almost...amorous. I inched my way down the empty hardpack street, mists parting around the edge of Caledin Vane. I swore I heard voices alight on those mists, toneless whispers at the very edge of audibility. I couldn't see more than five steps in front of me, didn't realize I'd reached a crossroads until it was practically upon me.

The mists hung so thick that I could not track the Middle City's retaining wall, though surely it must have been close. Relying on my blind sense of direction, I turned north at the crossroads, toward my best recollection of the switchback ascent.

I heard raised voices in the distance. Terrified yelps lost to the mists and the guttering cries of lives violently snuffed out. Shadows flashed in my peripheral vision, and I spun, chasing them with the point of Caledin Vane. Every dark shroud eluded my direct line of sight, but they continued to skitter on the cusp of perception.

Urkaku-Azag.

Of all the idolatrous entities worshipped as false G-ds, these eldritch horrors were the most deserving of the title. Creatures out of legend and fragmentary myth. If Senex Amari Desta's intuition proved out, then Ohtahp faced a challenge without precedent in the history of man. The Azag belonged to far antiquity. According to what few myths survive from that time, the Sylphids and their fae cousins raised great armies to subdue and contain them. The war decimated their populations, reducing them to the scattered enclaves that endure to this day. If not for those losses and the victory they purchased, our ancestors might never have crawled out of their caves to inherit the reins of civilization.

If this was the hell that Luka promised, then it was a far deeper pit than Mahakalpe was prepared to endure.

Another elusive shadow darted around a bend in the street. I heard more shouting from the same direction—much closer than before. I chased the desperate sounds, entering a wide bagra thoroughfare that should have been bustling with street merchants preying on hungry pilgrims. Their carts lay shattered and abandoned. Broken bricks and splinters littered the street.

I saw it then—a black beast, half serpent and half dire wolf, eight feet tall and twice as long. The cries belonged to a tall woman and two men in bagra rags screaming for salvation as they covered four small children, backed against a row of shemechas. The creature walked on four clawed legs, its oblong head smooth and fanged. A crest of living shadow undulated along its back, bristling, extending to the base of a long tail that snaked into the mists.

The adults penned the crying children behind them as the creature flexed its jaws, sweeping the air with a long, forked tongue. I saw the flash of metal. The tall woman produced a curved knife from her belt and slashed wildly, warning the creature back. She caught the lashing tongue on the edge of her knife, and the beast reared up on its hind legs, hissing like an adder, black fluids dripping from its jaws.

I ran toward them, leading with the edge of Caledin Vane, but I wasn't fast enough. The beast unhinged its jaws and ejected its tongue like a javelin. The tall woman raised her knife, deflecting its forked tip into the chest of one of the men in her cohort. The tongue shot straight through his sternum with a burst of blood and the snap of bone. The others screamed and the woman dropped her knife, petrified. The beast retracted its tongue and the poor man with it, pulling him from his feet and crushing him between its collapsing jaws. A black light throbbed to life in the creature's core as it devoured its prey.

I reached the abomination at last—swung Caledin Vane at its raking foreclaws, severing them both at the ankles. My sword passed through its substance as easily as carving through the mists themselves, and its cut meat dissolved to vapor before it even hit the ground. The beast staggered, black blood spewing from its smoking stumps. I drove it back from the Ohtahpi with three tight thrusts, aiming Caledin Vane for the eyeless brow of its oblong head.

The creature hissed, slashing the air with its forked tongue. New claws sprouted from the severed ends of its forelimbs. I pressed my advantage, carving a dark slash across its snout. It lashed out with its tongue, but I turned that away just as easily, nearly severing its forked tip.

"Run!" I shouted at the Ohtahpi. "Head for the Middle City!"

The tall woman gathered up her knife and ushered the children down the path from whence I had come.

The creature snarled indignantly, issuing black steam from its slit nostrils. It gnashed its fangs, body coiled like an adder preparing to strike, back arching like a cornered beast. Dark silhouettes flickered in the mists behind it, and I knew reinforcements were on their way.

I charged, and the creature kicked up its forelimbs, intending to crush me beneath its claws. As its legs came down, I dropped to the ground, sliding beneath the beast until I faced its throbbing core. I buried Caledin Vane in the creature's vital underbelly, twisting her blade as I drove her to the hilt. Black fluids thick as tar gouted from the wound, splashing over me to a torrent of anguished hissing. The throbbing light returned, expanding out from the wound I'd dealt it, consuming the creature whole and melting it down to a feckless cloud of vapor and slag. The creature's vanquished remnant slipped back into the mists along the path of its snaking tail.

This was not the Azag, but rather its lowest vanguard. I had dealt the foul thing a wound, but I did not think it slain. More shadows were already beginning to coalesce in the distant mists. The gibbering sounds of their birth pierced the stagnant bagra air. I may be an army unto myself, but I could not fight this battle alone.

I wiped the filth from my eyes and stood up, dashing back toward the retaining wall and the Middle City's meager redoubt. Feral sounds rose up from every obfuscated passage—ululating barks and a white wall of hissing.

My counterattack must have caught the Azag's attention. I sensed the locus of its power coalescing, closing around me and my ill-fated path. I burst past a line of shuttered shemechas and into the wide city march that drew toward the retaining wall on its northern edge. Prickling shadows nipped at my heels. I slashed blindly with Caledin Vane to repel them.

I saw the outlines of bodies moving in the mist—the Ohtahpi I'd saved, and more of their countrymen, penned in once again against the face of the retaining wall.

The *sheer* face.

A sickening pit opened in my stomach. I sawed through the huddled masses, searching the wall's expanse for the switchback staircase that should have been there. It *should have been!* My palms found nothing but the flat plane of mudbrick—not so much as a protruding stone let alone a stair to account. The hissing grew louder, exciting the mists around us. Judging by the sounds and the vaporous outlines of stirring shadows, I knew that we were encircled, helpless, pinned against the merciless wall.

"Where is that damned staircase!" I shouted.

The tall woman looked at me, still shielding her younglings, eyes heavy with resignation. "The kantors have closed the entrances. The Mahak has abandoned us."

I punched the sheer face of the retaining wall. I knew she was right, and the craven cynicism of the tactic sickened me. A mere wall would not contain the Azag and its minions for long. The Mahak sacrificed his bagramate—offered them as fodder to occupy this fell infestation and buy the upper classes time to prepare.

Something howled in the distance. The mists withdrew, inhaled by some lurking horror. The frightened Ohtahpi tightened their knot, backs pressed against the indifferent wall. Mist curled in tendrils, peeling around the sleek bodies of three more serpent-wolves. The beasts stepped into the march from the opaque mouths of side streets consumed by mist, oblong heads sweeping side-to-side, forked tongues flicking from their jaws. Fouler minions followed in their wake, balls of tentacles twelve feet tall, their slavering mouths overflowing with jagged, cracked-glass teeth. The mouths seemed to command some sort of rank among the abominations. They mustered their pack of black chimeras, whipping them to frenzy with lashing tentacles, driving them forward like a team of hunters with their dutiful hounds.

I stepped in front of the cowering Ohtahpi, holding Caledin Vane with both hands. The Apostatic Prayer jumped to my lips. "I shall abide no walking deity within the demesne of mortal men."

The serpent-wolves scraped their claws across the hardpack ground, closing. One lashed out with its tongue, and I turned it aside with Caledin Vane. The second reared on its hindlegs, while the third opened its jaws and pounced. I raised Caledin Vane to meet it, but the crack of sorcery rended the air, and the creature crashed into a plane of blue light. The beast rebounded on impact and the spell shattered, showering the chimera with blinding daggers. Black ribbons puddled at my feet, the only remains of the annihilated beast.

I pivoted just in time to catch a tongue on the edge of my blade, severing it at the root. The forked appendage squirmed on the ground before evaporating to mist. I thrust Caledin Vane toward the serpent-wolf pawing at its wounded mouth, drove it back on its hindlegs and slashed its throat.

Another flash of blue sorcery stunned the third as it lunged for my flank, drawing lines of white fire down the back of its head. Wailing, the creature swept its head in great pained arcs, while its brother collected itself to venture a second attack. I looked around for the source of the intervention but quickly became distracted by one of the tentacled mouths lumbering into the field. A claw of black appendages reached out, ready to draw me up inside that dripping maw. I snapped to form, ready to parry them, but never got the chance.

An enfilade of blue missiles poured into the bagra from above. Each sorcerous bolt exploded on impact, cratering the creatures with glowing scars. Glass teeth raked the sky, assaulting us with gibbering cries. I backed away from the engagement, while the Azag's minions buckled under the unrelenting wave of sorcery.

Spriteling streaks bombarded the street, diving in the wake of their spells to clash with the wounded creatures. Sylphid wings buzzed through the air, churning up dust and mist as they plunged their silver spears into black throbbing hearts. I counted at least a dozen of the fae warriors. They beat back the onslaught in practiced waves, thrusting and retreating, buttressed by blue walls of sorcery raised on each flier's flanks. In a matter of minutes, they'd cleared the area of its infestation, but I already saw more shadows mustering further down the march.

The Sylphid Swarm landed in a crescent around our sorry band, the corseque tips of their silver spears sullied with black gore. They formed a thin phalanx against the gathering mists, glass wings buzzing with readiness.

I shielded my head against a descending shadow as another slim body dropped from the sky to land behind the wall of spears.

"Illusitar!" I shouted.

The Slayn's three-fingered hands still throbbed with the afterglow of her casting. She bent her head to me. "And you are Ruxindra, the curious *lehakva*. Or should I call you Priestess?"

The question caught me speechless.

"Your arcanist told me everything," Illusitar said. "And I do mean *everything*."

Damn you, Gerritt. My fingers tightened around the grip of Caledin Vane.

"Calm yourself, Priestess. Your deicidal convictions are of no concern to me. We have more dire matters to attend to, and we may yet have use for your Caledin blade."

Her assurances came as a relief, but a dim one. "The Mahak has cut the bagra off from the Middle City," I said.

Illusitar nodded. "And shut the outer gates. The people of Mahakalpe are imprisoned with these horrors."

"He's a coward."

"He is that," Illusitar agreed. "I've known Sharif a long time. His soft heart is rotten with terror. History will remember him as a faithless guardian of Mahakalpe's seal, and his spirit cannot stand the injury."

"At this rate, he won't have to stand it for long. Mudbrick walls and Karochan wards won't contain this power."

The hissing and gibbering of the Azag's foot soldiers suddenly died back. Over Illusitar's shoulder, I saw their amorphous silhouettes vanishing from the bridling mists. Illusitar's pointed ears twitched. "We cannot remain," she said. "We must regroup with the Eidolon and with your arcanist in the Mahak's Sahir—"

A cursed moan erupted from the distant mists. The sound was like a thousand widows' voices raised as one, their suffering carved up and blended into a cursed symphony. The line of Sylphid infantry began to tremble in their ranks, and Illusitar turned to face their buckling backs.

"She comes..." Illusitar said, echoing the dying Inaghke, but with far less pleasure.

The wailing returned, slamming into our cohort with such force that the adjacent hovels began to crack and crumble. The Ohtahpi covered their ears, and I wished I could do the same without abandoning my sword.

Illusitar drew back, clutching the gold necklaces that layered her chest. "We have to retreat," she said, turning back to me.

I shook my head, still staring into the impenetrable mist. "You'll get no argument from me..."

The Slayn raised her crystalline voice, chirping terse instructions in Aleel. The infantry broke ranks and began to scatter around the huddled Ohtahpi.

"Sheathe your sword," Illusitar instructed.

I did as I was told. Illusitar wrapped her slim arms around me and began to beat her wings, churning up a cloud of dust. I saw the strain in her tight-lipped expression as my toes left the ground. The other Sylphids seized the stranded Ohtahpi, offering the same winged salvation. Many more would be stranded, consigned to death in their prison slum, but every life saved is a blessing.

As we soared up the flat expanse of the retaining wall, I caught a glimpse of what stirred beyond those mists—a living mass of twisted limbs and grasping mouths, an amalgamation of the distraught and the damned. The horror drew up on unseen stalks, craning its head above the mists and the highest shemechas. Its caterwaul struck again— nearly knocked us from the sky. It turned its head to the heavens, and I caught my first glimpse of its empty face, featureless but somehow feminine, a convex abyss blacker than any moonless night. It shrank back into the mists as we crested the retaining wall—left only its impression, a black silhouette imprinted on my soul.

Urkaku-Azag.

CHAPTER 15

JUDGMENT

We landed in the central plaza of the Middle City. The mists had not yet reached this section of Mahakalpe, but I already saw them rising over the forsaken bagra, swelling with the surety of the tides. They would consume the city, if only given time.

Illusitar left my side to marshal her Swarm. Ash-covered faces surrounded us, painted with scripture and terror and awe.

"Rux!" Gerritt sprinted toward me, breaking from the gathered Ohtahpi standing witness to our frenzied escape. His eyes jumped to the rent in my leather cuirass. "You're unhurt?"

"More or less," I said. "Your trinket didn't exactly deliver me to stable ground. Did you meet with any resistance escaping from the ziggurat?"

"I had the benefit of a substantial distraction," Gerritt said. "The kantors sealed off the Middle City. I—" he hesitated. "I confessed our intentions to the Slayn—to procure her assistance."

"I'm aware."

"I think she knows more about this *Darwaza* than she's letting on."

"That's for certain." I covered the hilt of my sword with a hand and glanced up at the looming Sahir. "The Mahak can't hide from this."

Geritt sighed, combing his fingers through his brown hair already scattered by the day's tumult. He nodded his head in the direction of the bagra. "What are we dealing with down there?"

"If you're willing to take the word of a Senex—it's an Azag."

Gerritt blinked, absorbing the information with a blank expression that was uncharacteristic. He usually had the ability to maintain some of his typical whimsy—even in dire straits.

"After cutting my way through the bagra, I'm inclined to believe him," I said.

His jaw drifted open, and he quickly slammed it shut. He settled on an off-hand prayer. "*Dryghten preserve us... You fought it?*"

I shook my head. "Only its lowest foot soldiers, and that was enough. We'll need the Mahak to throw every arcane resource in Mahakalpe at this problem if his city is going to survive."

"Umbrioth..." Gerritt muttered absently.

"Excuse me?"

"Servants of the Azag," he clarified. "Or perhaps *appendages* is a better word. They aren't minions in the truest sense. They possess no unique will or animus. The Azag works directly through them."

"I'm not sure if that makes it better or worse," I said.

"Far worse, I'm afraid... Its ranks will only grow as its power waxes."

"*Her* power," I corrected, though I'm not sure why it felt so urgent to make the distinction.

Gerritt's eyebrows drifted up his brow. "Her?"

"I think so," I said. "I thought this wasn't your expertise?"

He smiled sheepishly. "I'm not entirely naive."

Illusitar rejoined us, her gathered Swarm fluttering at her back. "We need to speak with Sharif," she said. "He must be pressured to confront this threat before the rest of the city is lost. With every passing minute freed from the *Darwaza*, the Azag comes into herself."

"The Mahak has locked down the Sahir," Gerritt said. "The gatehouse is barred and there's a maniple of Jassanids standing outside the curtain wall."

Illusitar turned up her small nose, pale nostrils flared. Not a single blue hair had fallen out of place, regal bun bound back inside her circlet's emerald ring. "They will not deny me," she said with the confidence of a woman unaccustomed to denial of any kind in any land.

Together, we led our battle-hardened cohort up the cobblestone streets of the Middle City, toward the locked gatehouse footing the Sahir's retaining wall. I felt the weight of the crowd behind us, flooding toward the foreyard in our wake.

We found the situation just as Gerritt described. Twenty empty-eyed Jassanids stood sentinel outside the bronze portcullis, spearheads propped against their shoulders. The Slayn approached with Gerritt and me and at her shoulders. Behind us, the Sylphid soldiers marched in ranks, trailing an anxious mob stretching back to the Middle City plaza.

"We need to speak with the Mahak," Illusitar said. "Raise the portcullis and alert the lockheed."

Two Jassanids wearing enamel pauldrons of rank shifted their helmeted heads to each other, expressions inscrutable.

"We will not be delayed," Illusitar said with a sharper edge. It wasn't a question.

A metal crank ground into motion without signal, retracting the bronze teeth of the portcullis from the hardpack ground. The Jassanid line parted to permit the passage of a red-robed kantor, his caged mask gleaming with the *Darwaza*'s violet light.

"His Holy Majesty will permit entrance to you and you alone, Highness."

Illusitar approached until her pointed nose nearly grazed the bars of the kantor's mask. "My entourage is not an open point of negotiation."

"My orders are strict, Highness..."

Illusitar's hands tensed, their outlines crackling with sorcery. I felt the hairs on the back of my neck prickling with frisson. Her voice returned, inflected with glamor. "Sharif is not in a position to reject assistance in any form. Master Gerritt is an arcanist of no low skill. Sister Ruxindra wields a Caledin blade. You will open the Sahir and facilitate our passage. Now."

Illusitar's words drove the kantor back toward the open portcullis. I heard the shuffling of spearheads from the flanking Jassanids, and my hand went to the hilt of Caledin Vane. The bare thread of civility pulled taut, and I began counting spears—judging their arrangement. Just before it snapped, the kantor signaled the Jassanids to hold.

Through the slats of his caged mask, I saw the magus' red-rimmed eyes grow wide as the gaping portcullis behind him. Illusitar's glamor swelled, and the kantor demurred, reluctantly turning to lead us through the gatehouse and into the foreyard.

The scene awaiting us inside the Sahir did nothing to set my mind at ease. Hundreds of idle Jassanids mustered within the hypolyte, their spears reduced to mere ornaments when they ought to have been deployed throughout the city, defending the Mahak's abandoned subjects. Beyond the thin moat transecting the hypolyte, the Mahakva and her son hid behind a line of masked kantors, while what few *lehakva* they had gathered cowered on the far end of the dais under tight Jassanid guard.

My former sister-wives, pardoned and now twice-condemned, all shared the same despondent look. Maddux alone stood tall among them, her tear-streaked face the only protest against this rank injustice. I marked all of them but had eyes only for the Mahak.

The regent of Mahakalpe slouched in his throne, unattended and possessed of a vacant calm, seemingly immune to the panic gripping his hypolyte. Those eyes I'd once thought kind were now glazed with numb indifference, tracking nothing—not even the Sylphid Slayn and the two outlanders petitioning his feckless court. In that moment, I knew that we had come to the wrong place.

We'd find no kindling of resistance nor well of stoic resolve—not in this hypolyte nor anywhere else in the Sahir. The Mahak's grasping plan to corral the former *lehakva* stank of desperation. He would blithely cast these women into the same charnel pit to which he'd consigned his bagramate. And to what end? A soft heart is no sin for a regent, but softness and weakness have ever been separated by the thinnest line. I have seen monarchs beset by impossible challenges—outmatched and outnumbered—facing seemingly insurmountable threats. The fires of these trials burn away every superficial raiment of rule, and the exposure so rarely flatters. Too few deserve the allegiance they demand. Too many melt when they should be tempered. The Holy City needed its

Mahak to be galvanized in this moment, but atop that throne I saw only a puddle of slag.

The Mahak had already been defeated, and his city would fall.

"Sharif!" Illusitar bellowed. The sound of her voice finally broke through his blank stare. He corrected his posture, and I thought how small he looked, almost lost in the seat of honor he clearly did not deserve. "What madness possessed you to abandon your bagra?"

The Mahak's mouth opened, but his red-robed vizier stepped to the edge of the dais to speak on his behalf. "His Holy Majesty did only what he must to protect what remains of this Holy City. We weep for every life lost to this cataclysm, but the Azag cannot be permitted to breach the Sahir."

Illusitar scoffed. "You think your mudbrick walls and petty enchantments will hold her at bay? She is *Imajoth-Almaug*. The Unmother." The Mahak winced at the cursed Ibreic, but Illusitar granted no quarter, driving each word into him like a deltafix stake. "Even the Sahir's ancient investments are but nymphling cantrips to the Azag. She will consume your city soul-by-soul. None shall be spared her wrath."

"Do not speak its name so brazenly!" the vizier scolded, rapping the bronze butt of his scepter against the marble floor. "We know what foul thing crept out of that *Darwaza*! We have a plan to rebuild the agiaries. Even as we speak, the agents of this court are collecting *lehakva* to refresh the bindings."

A collective whimper rose up from the girls under Jassanid guard. I wanted nothing more than to storm the dais and free them, but I restrained myself. It seemed unwise to interfere with Illusitar at such a sensitive moment, and so I bided my time and my outrage.

"You are a fool, Sharif." Illusitar's gaze narrowed, eyes questing beyond the magistrate to the voiceless regent he spoke for. "The seals have been *destroyed!* The agiaries reduced to salt and ash. Your kantors don't possess the art to rebuild them. Not even if you burned every virgin girl in Mahakalpe."

The vizier slammed his scepter again. "You will show respect in this court—"

"Silence!" Illusitar's skin flashed a vibrant blue. I heard her voice in three octaves, booming with resonant glamor.

The Jassanids leveled their spears at us, and I began to wish we'd brought Illusitar's soldiers to help even the odds. We were three against an army, but a Sylphid Slayn is not so easily challenged nor casually dismissed.

"I will not speak through this servant," Illusitar bellowed. "You are the inheritor of this ancient fortress, Sharif. Descendant of Deosthenes Theocratus. Has the Blood of Old Mysin truly drawn so thin? Will you not stand and speak?"

The Jassanids kept their spears trained on us, but the eyes of the court turned to the Mahak. Even the vizier looked to his regent, likely praying for a reprieve.

The Mahak's throat bobbed as he swallowed. He grasped the silver armrests of his throne, sweat dripping from his modest headwrap and beading on his brow. Though the effort seemed to pain him, slowly, he dragged himself to his feet and approached the edge of the moat.

Such a little man, compressed by the eyes of court—outmatched by Illusitar's challenge and bereft of all courage and grit. He turned up his palms—as empty as his heart. "What would you have me do, Illusitar?"

"Fight, Sharif!" Illusitar again inflected her voice with her Sylphid glamor, and the force of it almost buckled the Mahak.

He righted himself, jaw flexing in a rictus. "We are no match in the open field! We must hold the Sahir. It is poor strategy to abandon our most defensible position!"

The Slayn's ageless face did not wrinkle—*could* not wrinkle—but the twisted expression she returned was unmistakably disgust. Her voice settled back to its mundane timbre, though it remained tight with impatience. "Leave your court in hiding. I will lead the armies of Mahakalpe in the field with Master Gerritt and Sister Ruxindra, but I will require every kantor and Jassanid spear."

The Mahak seemed to notice my presence for the first time. His eyes narrowed before snapping wide with recognition. Confusion and outrage warred on his expression until he banished them both with a shake of his wrapped head. "I forbid it!" A raised voice never sounded so pathetic. "The soldiers of Mahakalpe will defend the Sahir!"

A stirring at the back of the dais. The peacock prince shoved his way through a line of kantors to claim position at his father's side. The boy's unblemished armor glittered in the bloody hue of the dying sun, Mahakalpe's Yucca Palm embossed in gold upon its plate. With his oiled beard and gilt bracelets, he looked a better fit for a Triumph parade than a field of battle. "I will lead them, father!"

The Mahak looked upon his son with open contempt. "Shut your mouth and return to your place, Gibril."

Prince Gibril did neither. "How can you hide in the Sahir while the Holy City succumbs to this infestation? I will lead the Jassanids and the kantors at Slayn Illusitar's side. I am trained for this, father!"

"*Trained?*" the Mahak inflected the word with such disgust. "You play at sticks in the foreyard with tutors sworn to flatter you. Your brittle spirit will crumple before the Azag!"

"You dishonor me in front of the court!" Gibril protested.

I shook my head watching this menial argument play out before the august assembly. Perhaps I had misjudged the coddled prince, but only half-way. Prince Gibril's sentiments, at least, were worthy. He spoke the right words, but his gaping expression belonged to the petulant child he was and not the hardened commander he pretended to be.

It was the child to which the Mahak responded, so patronizing I thought he might turn the boy over his knee and spank his rump. "Another word and I'll have you locked in the keep, watching your court-cousin whipped."

Illusitar raised her long fingers to her temples, exasperated. We were getting nowhere, and every minute lost to this argument granted the Azag more time to muster her strength.

I leaned over to Illusitar's pointed ear. "Can you compel the Jassanids?" I asked.

She shook her head. "Not in the manner you suggest. Karochan sorcery ensures their servitude. Both the kantors and the Jassanids are bound to the Mahak's will.

Disturbed voices bubbled up from the courtiers gathered across the moat. I tracked their gazes moving past us, pulled toward the marble cursa at the foot of the hypolyte.

Torches flickered in their marble sconces. The trickle of running water bled from the court's unsettled ambience as the moat became stagnant.

Luka entered, a stone cast into the surface of a sessile lake.

Kenver followed the Eidolon onto the receiving floor, his agen helm propped under one arm, black hair bound in a warrior's top knot. The Mahakalpans averted their eyes in waves, bowing their heads in deference to the G-dhead's approach.

I cleared the path alongside Illusitar and Gerritt, yielding the floor to this undersized boy and the deity that wore him. Kenver spared me a warning glance as he passed, but I offered no challenge, content to let this intervention play out.

Luka surveyed the hypolyte, taking in every expressionless Jassanid and eclectic petitioner. I tracked his bright eyes until they landed on the Mahak. I had only seen Luka so composed once before—in the moments preceding his pardon of the *lehakva* and his investment upon the Syzygy of Avum. In this moment as before, he outgrew his diminutive frame. His presence filled the space, crowding the hypolyte to its domed rotunda. Beset by that great weight, the Mahak began to sink to his knees.

He pressed his forehead to the marble floor, and his entire court followed suit. Even the Jassanids bent the knee, compelled to genuflect before an authority much higher than the regent to whom they were sworn.

"*Masra*," the Mahak prayed. He touched three fingers to his head and his heart before returning his forehead to the marble floor. "Lord, we beseech you. We are the keepers of your holiest city—your most devout. Deliver us from this curse—that we may continue serving you in this age of your incarnation."

"Serving *me*?" Luka's small voice quivered, but I sensed no nervousness or apprehension. His was the tremor of a kindling rage, and I did not think his modest frame would long contain it. The boy balled his fists and slammed shut his eyes. He bit down on his tongue and his outrage, but the G-d within him stirred.

I am no Ibreic scholar, but I know the old tongue proffers two words for rage. *Erge* captures the anger of men in all its sundry temperatures and forms. From a parent's frustration with their disobedient get to a commander's anguish seeing his armies routed. *Erge*.

Maeniz describes the anger of G-ds—that omnipotent wrath that seasons every plate of the Tractate, that timeless pledge of vengeance from which the Empire of Mysin was raised. *Meaniz* brings entire civilizations to their knees, reduces heretics by the thousands to lifeless pillars of salt. When Luka's voice returned to him, I felt the paucity of our modern tongues for failing to recognize this distinction.

Luka's body began to *emanate*, radiating a halo of purest white—so vibrant the glare forced me to join the Ohtahpi and avert my eyes. Illusitar clutched her layered necklaces with a three-fingered hand. Even Kenver backed away, caught off guard by the sudden change in the Eidolon's bearing.

Luka inhaled—seemed to grow inside his skin with every dram of breath. His voice struck the hypolyte like a beam of cleansing light.

"Do not bow to us. Your false piety offends us, and we are not so easily offended."

Out of the corner of my eye, I saw the Mahak's hands bent in claws, nails digging into the marble.

"Rise!" A wave of pressure issued forth with Luka's commandment, washing over the Mahak and his entire court, rippling the cream fabric of his shalwaz across his bent back.

The Mahak lifted his head, squinting into the G-dhead's radiance, shielding his face with one thin arm as, slowly, he rose. I could not bear to look upon Luka, and so I stared instead at the Mahak, standing but bent, his round shoulders shaking with sobs.

"Faithless," the G-dhead's voice boomed from Luka's childish lips. The Demiurge wielded his worldly vessel like a mummer's puppet, and I wondered just how much control over this adolescent body still belonged to the boy. **"For generations, your line has denied our most ardent commandment. *Let no man abide the shedding of innocent blood in ritual or in prayer, lest he be cast from our light and forever damned to the deepest Pit of Gehenna.* Once, we forgave this trespass, but we will not abide a second transgression."**

"Masra..." The Mahak's voice returned to him, less than the meanest whimper and further reduced by contrast. "I have been a faithful steward of Mahakalpe's seal... I—I did only what was asked of me! You see the destruction she has wrought. Since the time of Old Mysin, my line has stood sentinel!"

Another wave of sorcery rippled out from the Eidolon, eliciting a frightened gasp from the crowd and silencing the Mahak's empty protestations. "**Mahak Sharif iban Deosthenes. Malka alle Mahakalpe. We judge you an apostate and a fool. You will answer for the crimes of your line, but first you will see what your ignorance has wrought.**"

The very Sahir began to tremble beneath our feet. White arms reached out from Luka's halo, ensnaring the Mahak, dragging him without resistance across the moat and the marble floor of the hypolyte to kneel before his vengeful G-d. A pale fire erupted from Luka, and the Mahak's face became a screaming mask, voiceless and stretched, as divine light poured into him from this G-dling font. His body shook with conniptions, collapsing back to the ground with a gasp once the transfer was complete.

Mortal lips began to move on the face of the G-dhead. I heard him speaking in Ibreic, which I could not understand. His intent pierced my skull's thin palisade—imposed itself on my mind, clear as Mysinic vernacular.

None here is innocent. You least of all. Would that we could reach back through the ether of time and smother your forebear that our world might be spared your birth.

I reeled from the G-dhead, clapping my hands over my throbbing ears. My mind could not shake his voice, and I was but one among hundreds. Luka held us all in thrall. Through watering eyes, I saw the congregation list on their feet, enraptured by the divine presence. That voice returned, Ibreic to my covered ears but impressed upon my consciousness—a light behind my eyes, so bright I thought it might burn me blind.

You will share in our agony. You, who have provisioned our foe. Look upon your works, ye faithless, and despair as we despair from your heresy.

The light burned ever brighter, blinding in truth, dissolving the hypolyte with its scouring glare. I felt myself falling, tossed by a maelstrom of time and space.

When the world reasserted itself, I no longer stood in the Sahir, but rather on an untamed plateau overlooking a vast killing field. Corpses and the spent matériel of war littered the plain to the distant edge of a darkling sea. A ring of armored Sylphids shared the promontory with their weapons sheathed. Among them, I saw red-maned Jinai flexing claws of fire; Undine with long trunks and webbed hands; six-legged Cherufe huddled like piles of banded rock. The Sylphids joined hands with their fae cousins.

I could neither interfere nor look away. G-d's will peeled back my eyelids and held open my ears, forcing me to bear silent witness.

This strange fellowship circled three obsidian cubes—stones not of this plateau—their symmetrical faces smooth and blank as if freshly cut. Voices joined, weaving a tapestry of mellifluous Aleel, and as they sang, I saw the light bleeding out from each of them. Still, they sang. They sang through the melting of their beaks and lips. They sang even as their husks began to wither and bend. They sang until the last fae body dropped to the ground, vesting the nascent agiaries with vitality and a burgeoning flame.

The voice of G-d bellowed from the empty Ohtahpi sky, stirring up a dry wind that scattered the ash of the fallen sorcerers. ***Behold the true Knights of Faith. The fellowship gave of themselves to vest these seals, but theirs was a sacrifice of choice. Their spell might have held another thousand years if not for your foul intercession. You have tarnished their magick, perverted it with ignorance and coercion.***

We are sickened.

My vision blurred as I was once again transported, sucked out of time and dropped in a familiar chamber, a dark temple of stone and clay cloaked in a thick, unctuous scent.

The agiary at the base of the Sahir.

A tan-skinned Ohtahpi regent, his dark beard cut square, stood over the seal, its black monolith now defaced with Karochan. Two androgynous kantors attended their monarch, their waxen heads shaved but yet uncaged. The cohort faced a young woman tied to a stake at the back of the temple. Her tight bindings pulled her arms and shoulders back, presenting her bosom in all the ripeness of youth. I tried to look away as the kantors began to sing, but the Demiurge would not permit it. His will pointed my head at the tragedy playing out—peeled back my eyelids to drink its every sordid frame.

The kantors layered their trope over the agiary, and the woman began to burn.

Her screams swelled, her skin cracking then melting from the heat. The flames consumed her—ate her entire—reduced even her final bubbling gasps to so much smoke and ash. The pyrelight cast the regent's snaking headdress in a wild light, flickering over patterns of emerald and gilt. He and his kantors watched with dispassion as the agiary stone began to throb with a violet glow, and a fresh skritglyph appeared on its ebony hide.

The original sin. The first of many. One girl for every turning of the count, burned before the agiary on the Eve of Tzipurim. Dozens more to consecrate each Eidolon that came before.

The vision collapsed and reassembled: another girl and a different Mahak, but everything so much the same. I could only watch as she burned. Could only listen as her screams faded to wet gasps, less galling than the final silence. Again, the vision cycled. Over and over through countless iterations—the same crime visited upon the women and girls of every age. Across time, the procession of Mahaks shook off their raiment by glacial increments as their kantors gradually enclosed their heads in brass. The attire changed, but the ceremony was always the same. A girl burned. A life vanquished. The agiary unsettled by a violet glow.

The scene collapsed for the final time. My mind careened back into the mundane world of the Sahir—reached my body, gasping and bent. Even the stone-faced Jassanids shared in my anguish, and I knew from the tortured expressions on every face in the hypolyte that we had all borne witness to the same shameful tale.

G-d's voice returned, echoing in the hollows of my skull, translated from the guttural Ibreic spewing forth from Luka's embodied lips. *2,217 lehakva. 2,217 lives delivered to the Unmother's foul embrace. This Holy City raised in our image courts an infernal pantheon.* **Imajoth-Almaug.** *The* **Urkaku-Azag** *of the squandered. Patron angel of every life vanquished at the ripening of youth. She is the perverse avatar of the divine feminine, the anima inverted.*

Would that you served us with the zeal you've shown her. She

feasts on every sacrifice, and the bindings you lashed across your idolatrous agiaries were ever a paltry delay.

This cataclysm is but the harvest of the sins you have sown.

Luka's penumbra evaporated with a blinding flash, and the boy staggered back, braced by the quick reaction of Kenver Montaigne. I realized I'd regained control of my limbs and shot to my feet. I did not dare approach—not yet—but I guarded the hilt of Caledin Vane with a hand, ready to unsheathe her in an instant.

The Mahak unspooled from a quivering ball of shalwaz on the floor of the hypolyte. Kenver helped Luka to steady himself, but the boy waved him off as soon as he was stable. He seemed somehow reduced—a dim shadow of the eternity he'd just unveiled. Whatever divine manifestation possessed him had retreated, and the Sahir had gone entirely sane.

The Mahak attempted to gain his feet, but Luka raised a small hand to stop him. The boy stepped toward the debased regent with his arm outstretched and laid one hand upon the Mahak's head.

"Do you confess?" Luka asked in his own small voice, barely loud enough to reach my ears.

The Mahak looked every inch the sad old man he was. His lower lip began to tremble. Luka waited patiently for this broken man to gird his response. "*Masra...* These crimes are not all my own," he stuttered.

Luka nodded sadly. "And yet, you will answer for them." He closed his hand around the Mahak's headwrap and removed it from his head. Greasy ringlets salted with gray tumbled down over his face, offering some small refuge behind their black tangle.

In the *Midras* it is written that the G-dhead bears mercy in one hand and judgment in the other. I'd already seen the first from Luka, and now that I'd seen the other, I was reminded of my task and its urgency. No matter the challenges facing Mahakalpe, the Demiurge needed to be slain.

The Mahak whimpered. Tears welled in his soft brown eyes. Intelligent eyes, surely. The craven are so often bright, but rarely wise.

Luka sighed. "So ends the line of Mahakalpe."

He withdrew, still grasping the Mahak's brown wrap, and Kenver took his place.

The Mahak looked up into the guardian's sharp blue eyes—sharper even than the blade of Caledin Bolg, which he lifted now in both hands. The Mahak searched both edges for some mercy, but Luka had withdrawn that hand, and the one he extended held only its inverse twin.

Judgment came for the dynasty of Mahakalpe.

The Mahak at last found his courage—in resignation, of all things. The irony. No longer trembling, he bent his head.

Kenver lifted his crosshilt to his lips and prayed.

The blade swung down, and the court of Mahakalpe held its breath.

CHAPTER 16
MYSTIQUE

Very little surprises me anymore.

This surprised me.

The Mahak's torso slumped to the ground. His head rolled to a stop at Luka's feet, oiled hair spread like the rags of a discarded mop, shielding his lightless eyes. In the end, not a single Jassanid raised a spear in defense of the monarch they were sworn to protect. No notes of Karochan trope sprang forth from the lips of the kantors. The court of Mahakalpe stood witness to an act of divine regicide, and the only sound in the hypolyte was the Mahakva's scream.

I paid her no heed, nor her son, though perhaps I should have. Kenver had cut down their patriarch, and with him, their only tether to power. One power remained in Mahakalpe, now. I had eyes for Luka and Luka alone. The boy seemed somehow compressed, burdened by the weight of the judgment he had rendered. I searched his visage for some semblance of the divine spark he'd just revealed but found nothing so profound—not even the weakest afterglow.

Everything hinged on whatever happened next, and for all my experience in the field, I could not predict it.

Kenver cleaned his blade on the Mahak's puddled shalwaz and sheathed it before returning to Luka's side. Gerritt and I closed ranks around Illusitar, all of us watching and waiting. She alone had declared our worth, and depending on how this conflict trended, we might need her protection.

Gerritt's eyes found mine, warning me off any rash decisions.

Wait, his eyes seemed to say. *Wait and respond.*

I hated waiting.

Luka walked to the center of the receiving floor and scanned the hypolyte anew, meeting every white eye in the chamber. This time, nobody bowed, still petrified by the revelation they had witnessed.

"The Mahak is dead," Luka said. "All vows sworn to him and his line are annulled." He turned to the hoplite maniples flanking the receiving floor. "The Jassanids and every other slave of the Sahir are delivered from their condition of servitude." He pivoted to the rows of masked kantors beyond the stagnant moat. "The Karochan chains shackling the kantors have been dispelled."

I shared in the hypolyte's silence.

The first pale hand reached for the latches at the nape of his neck and began to remove his caged mask. Luka nodded, and the cage fell to the floor with the clatter of bronze. More followed until every shaved pate upon the dais glittered with torchlight.

"I will not require that you fight for Mahakalpe," Luka said. "It would be a foul trick to grant freedom and fresh indenture with the same breath. But I do *beseech* you. You may take a moment to decide."

I saw some of the Jassanids turning their helmeted heads to their comrades. Slowly, they began to break ranks and talk among themselves. The kantors had already arranged their cadre in a circle around the empty throne, and I saw Maddux gathering up the twice-imprisoned *lehakva*, no longer penned together under guard. Of Prince Gibril and his mother, there was no sign. They'd slipped away into the depths of the Sahir along with the Mahak's vizier. I took their absence to mean the prince's offer to lead the resistance had been withdrawn.

Luka left the Mahak's rudderless court to their deliberations and walked toward us. Kenver's eyes tightened when they fell on me. He flipped back his cape, warning me with the hilt of Caledin Bolg.

"*Masra.*" Illusitar tipped her head in a shallow bow, speaking for our unlikely cohort.

"Luka, if it pleases." He managed a weak smile, the G-dless expression of a mundane boy. I noticed the small muscles of his arms and legs were trembling. The power that possessed him must have taken its toll. "We will need every Sylphid spear in Mahakalpe to confront the Unmother."

"And so you will have them," Illusitar confirmed. "As well my art."

Luka nodded graciously.

"Luka," Illusitar continued. "If you can summon the power you just unveiled, surely the Unmother can be tamed once again."

Luka winced and shook his head. "I am invested but...incomplete. Until I finish my pilgrimage, I am only the Eidolon and no true G-d. The altar is the beginning, not the end. The ritual at the Syzygy of Avum only furnished me with an inkling ghost." Luka's eyes became unfocused, seemed to drift. "I...have memories. Scraps... Disordered and unfinished." He snapped back to focus. "I do not seek to tame her. She must be vanquished, her geas severed from this plane."

Gerritt whistled. "Is that all?"

"Yes." Luka did not seem bothered by my partner's sarcasm. On the contrary, the tension in his shoulders loosened, and his trembling arms began to still. Luka squinted as if struggling to mark some blurry image on the horizon. "I think...we have what we need." He glanced over at the girls in white, my former sister-wives. They all looked lost atop the dais, unwilling or unsure if they were permitted to leave.

"The Unmother fed on the sacrificed *lehakva*," Luka said. "It is their salvation that will see her starved."

Salvation. I lingered on the *lehakva* a moment too long, missed the Eidolon pivoting his attention to me.

"You were *lehakva*—whatever your true intentions. Will you fight with me, Ruxindra?"

I felt the tension rippling from Kenver in waves as Luka awaited my response. What could I tell him? My secret intentions had already been laid bare. Every person present knew why I came to Mahakalpe, and even the child I was sworn to kill was willing to look past it to see this Azag slain.

The Shibboleth's conditioning is not so easily overcome. The deepest part of me still yearned to draw Caledin Vane and deliver her deicidal report. I could almost see Luka's red heart beating in his concave chest. How easy to pierce it. Even as he petitioned for my service, I found myself counting the paces between us—so few—and judging my own speed against the skill of Kenver Montaigne.

Faced with impossible choices, the worst thing we can do is hedge. Inaction is itself a choice, and often the most craven of the lot.

I shall abide no walking deity within the demesne of mortal men.

Many pantheons exist outside the Demiurge and his pleroma of creation. Of all those gnostic families, the *Urkaku-Azag* are one of the eldest and most foul. In its dying breath, the Inaghke warned that ours was not the only G-d reborn in Mahakalpe. *Imajoth-Almaug* is not the creator, but if she drew worship, then she was undeniably divine. Here we faced her—within the demesne of mortal men.

It is a cruel fact of life that our heaviest tasks have a way of growing in their execution.

Kenver closed one gloved hand around his sword's red grip, preparing to answer my rejection with the blade of Caledin Bolg. His satisfaction would have to be deferred.

"I will stand with you," I said. "Until this threat is vanquished or subdued."

With that vow I felt a fist inside my chest relinquish its grip. I hadn't realized how tightly it had grasped me, nor could I pinpoint the moment it first found purchase, but its banishment brought relief all the same. Kenver's own fist relaxed as well, though his hand never wandered far from his sword belt.

Many priests of the Shibboleth would name me heretic for making such a vow—however measured and limited in scope. I'd wandered from my path, but I did not think it such a mad digression. I could still find my way back once the Unmother was destroyed. Not a moment sooner, however.

I have made many mistakes and committed many crimes, but I do not count oathbreaking among my varied sins.

Luka accepted my bond with a nod that felt too small for the clemency I granted him. He turned to Gerritt. "You are a healer, I am told."

"I dabble," Gerritt said.

"We will have need of your art," Luka said. "To protect the *lehakva*. Come."

Gerritt shot a glance my way, perhaps seeking permission. I would not hold him back. He followed Luka across the moat to gather his former betrothed.

Kenver remained. No matter how many deadly Jassanids and puissant kantors loitered about the hypolyte, he judged me the superior threat. Vow or no vow, I doubted the guardian would let me out of his sight.

"I need to muster the Swarm," Illusitar said, taking her leave, as well, and abandoning me with Kenver Montaigne.

I met his stern gaze, crossing my arms over the breastplate he'd pierced only hours before.

"We have unfinished business, you and I," he said.

I nodded. "Happy to pick up where we left off once we clean up this mess."

"See that you don't cheat next time," he said, and I thought I caught a sly smile twitching in the corners of his lips.

"I'm the cheat?" I scoffed, flipping back my hair with a dismissive flourish. "If not for Luka's distraction, I would have had you skewered over a pew."

"Easy to say, but harder to prove." At last, he moved his hand from his sword belt to cup his black-bearded chin. "After all you've seen, you'd still carry out your task?" He shook his head in disbelief. "Has nothing you've witnessed in this city shaken your faith?"

My hard silence was answer enough.

Kenver's nostrils flared. "The Shibboleth is just as stubborn as reputation suggests." His sigh seemed almost weary and perhaps disappointed but undoubtedly resigned. He said something then that still haunts me. "Change is the only certainty in this world, Ruxindra. The Shibboleth must learn to bend, or else it will break."

How many times would I hear this warning echoed, and in how many condescending voices? "I once told a pretty crecheling that change is a weak foundation for any faith," I said. "I might be convinced that change is a virtue, but willful ignorance is not." I lifted my chin toward the decapitated Mahak. "Just ask him."

"It's we who are ignorant, is it?"

I tapped the side of my head with a finger. "The Shibboleth remembers so that the rest of Hebdomar can forget." I patted his breastplate with my palm. "It's a gift, Kenver. Never turn your pretty nose up at a gift."

Luka and Gerritt had mustered the *lehakva* and were now leading them across the moat. I went to join them.

In the end, every Jassanid and kantor in the hypolyte joined Luka's eclectic host, and how could it have been any other way? Their G-d had beseeched them, and their king was dead.

Our holy army assembled in the receiving yard of the Sahir—maniple rows of Jassanid spears threaded with Karochan kantors. Gerritt tended the small unit of *lehakva*, their cohort radiant in white, while I claimed the van. We marched behind Luka, though I suspected it was Kenver and Illusitar who truly led. Two kantors broke ranks to turn their stone keys, revealing the Sahir's descent. We marched to battle without fanfare or banners—a ragtag militia, albeit one assembled from formidable parts.

We reached the foreyard behind the curtain wall to discover that the Azag's miasma had risen to claim the Middle City—not yet as dense as the fog that occluded my passage through the bagra but just as unsettling. Tendrils of mist licked the bronze teeth of the barbican where we regrouped with Illusitar's Swarm. The Sylphids joined me in the van, and I was grateful for each winged foot soldier and silver spear.

Doubt crept in with the distant gibbering of the Umbrioth. We were many, perhaps the greatest assembly of armsmen the streets of Mahakalpe had seen since the time of Old Mysin. Still, I did not think it would be enough.

The mists parted enticingly around our ranks as we approached the southern plaza. I saw shadows stirring on the periphery, but none gathered their substance in challenge. The Unmother mustered herself, waiting and guarding her power, drawing us deeper within her foul demesne.

Luka stopped at the mouth of the plaza and turned to us. "I must go to my *lehakva*," he said. "Here is where we'll make our stand."

Kenver scanned the plaza, empty but for the gathering mists. The

Ohtahpi adulators had all fled from the streets, barring themselves inside their domiciles to escape the waxing miasma. "I don't like it," Kenver said. "Too many entry points. We invite encirclement."

Luka nodded. "I'm counting on it. We need to draw her out. We cannot exorcize *Imajoth-Almaug* by slaying her Umbrioth."

"You're using us as bait?" I shouldn't have been surprised. G-ds are ever capricious with their Knights of Faith.

Luka's eyes drifted, glazing with distance. "Memory is fleeting... I can only grasp it by its thinnest threads..." His voice sounded so brittle, and I found myself longing for the holy timbre that had shaken the hypolyte, vanished in the moment of our most dire need. "We need the *lehakva*...to face her. The Unmother swallows them in death, but their lives she cannot abide." He returned to us, eyes marking Kenver—and me. "Your swords. They will wound her. The maniples will hold the plaza, but you must contain the Unmother until the *lehakva* can work their spell."

All the blood drained from Kenver's face. "L-Luka," he stammered.

"I know." Luka rested one small palm on the breast of his guardian's plate. "It's all right, Kenver. I understand, and I forgive you."

Illusitar looked at Kenver warily as Luka left us to join Gerritt and the girls.

I coughed into my hand to break the tension. "That seemed awkward." The guardian shook from his trance to scowl at me. I elbowed him in the ribs. "Come, brother. We have a G-d to kill."

I claimed the arc of the mosaic sun laid into the plaza's cobblestone walk, while the Jassanids clattered into maniples, forming shield walls at each entrance from the city. The Umbrioth reacted to our entry with gibbering taunts, their black faces still lurking in the deeper mists. Beyond the retaining wall, the miasma hung thick as raw cotton, obscuring even the tallest piles of shemechas. How many thousands had already been lost within that infernal fog? How few could have possibly survived? The mist billowed over the lip of the retaining wall and vented up through cracks in the stone road, bringing with it that amorous scent—a beast betrayed by its pores, ripe with carnal heat.

Cries erupted from one of the maniples guarding the streets as black arms reached from the mist, shattering their shield wall, plunging deep into their ranks. The Jassanids recovered from the surprise sortie and spearheads rained down on the Umbrioth until it withdrew, but not before crushing the life from three Jassanids. I heard the first notes of trope rising up from gray-headed kantors, hardening the other maniples against similar assaults.

The Umbrioth tested our defenses, attempting to sow fear.

The plaza erupted with the clash of sorceries. Notes of trope prickled the mists as umbral claws slashed Jassanid spears. All six lanes into the plaza swarmed with Umbrioth, but the maniples were better prepared this time. The shield walls held against the gnashing heads of serpent-wolves and the greedy arms of tentacled maws. Karochan sorcery crackled, tattooing the Umbrioth with ethereal wards—golden skritglyphs seared into their insubstantial flesh. The mists refracted each blast of trope, peppering the plaza with ephemeral blains of diffuse light. Streams of trope sawed through the clatter of arms until the Umbrioth became so leaden with skritglyphs that their bodies burst into clouds of black smoke.

Two black claws grasped the lip of the retaining wall in front of me. Then four. Then six. Umbrioth heads crested the miasma as they hoisted their bodies over the retaining wall and lumbered into the field. Caledin Vane sang from her scabbard, harmonizing with the note rung from her brother in Kenver's gloved hand. With the clatter and cries of the Jassanid engagement encircling us, we charged into battle.

The Umbrioth climbing the retaining wall walked on two reticulated legs, knuckles dragging from muscular arms like bundles of black cord. Their jaws hung from their heads in permanent gapes, wide enough to engulf a man standing and boiling over with wan, blue light. I ducked under the first heavy fist as it swung for me, lunging for the creature's groin—the only vital seam I could reach. The creature howled as I stabbed it and nearly took off my head on the backswing.

I withdrew Caledin Vane, now dripping with black gore, and slashed again, carving through one thick thigh and buckling the creature under its own obscene weight. My attack brought me face to face with those gaping jaws, gray teeth like stalactites dripping from its gums. I swung Caledin Vane around, intending to bury her in its throat, but a klaxon scream emitted by the Umbrioth struck my body at point-blank range.

The shockwave blasted me off my feet, and the back of my head cracked against the cobblestones. I saw another massive fist plummeting toward me like a falling column. I rolled to my side to avoid the brunt of its impact, and Kenver stepped into the line of attack, severing the arm with an overhand slash. Black blood streaked the plaza ground as he whipped Caledin Bolg in a crushing series of cuts, drawing deep gouges across the Umbrioth's meat and forcing the creature to retreat.

Kenver turned to drag me up from the ground. "I thought you'd learned your lesson about losing your feet in a battle?"

"The Shibboleth is stubborn," I quipped. The moment's levity proved short-lived. Over Kenver's shoulder, I saw the first maniple of Jassanids break formation as a serpent-wolf lurched through their ranks. Its javelin tongue shot from its mouth, and I hurled Kenver out of its path just in time to split its forks on the blade of Caledin Vane. Four Sylphid soldiers seized the opening as the Umbrioth sucked its wounded tongue back inside its jaws, their silver spears falling along its flanks.

"Now we're even," I said to Knever, but I didn't have the time to wait for his retort. More of the lumbering Umbrioth were dragging themselves over the retaining wall and into the plaza, moving to catch the nearest Jassanid shield walls in a pincer. Trust sprouts readily from desperation's fertile loam, and Kenver and I quickly joined our efforts, placing our backs to each other to confront the expanding field.

Illusitar's voice rose up behind us like a crossbow cranking taut. When its coil unleashed, her incantation shot through the plaza like a glass bolt, shattering on impact with the world. I heard the brief buzzing of Sylphid wings as the Slayn soared overhead, a streaking blue sprite alight with the heat of her casting. Missiles poured from her outstretched arms, striping the Umbrioth with molten gouts, feathering their broad chests and pinning their outstretched jaws. The Umbrioth staggered back under the sorcerous enfilade, black bodies bursting in brilliant agony, others toppling over the retaining wall to plummet back into the murky pit from whence they came. Her soldiers flooded the field under arcane cover, thrusting silver spears deep into the towering guts of the Umbrioth, beating their wings to drive corseque spearheads deeper, breaching the vital light throbbing at each monster's core.

Umbrioth exploded as each Sylphid spear found purchase, but the spearmen had abandoned their maniples to answer their Slayn's call, and the Jassanid lines had begun to buckle for want of their support.

Serpent-wolves burst through a decimated shield wall, bounding down the cobblestone walk, lashing tongues at the Sylphids holding our left flank. A slavering maw, half-plastered with burning Karochan wards, split the opposite shield wall in half, gathering up the chanting kantor in its tentacles and crushing her between rows of cracked-glass teeth. Kenver and I darted in opposite directions. I hurled myself at one of the serpent-wolves that had pinned a struggling Sylphid to the ground beneath its forelimbs and brought down Caledin Vane in a two-handed slash that severed its head at the neck. Black blood gouted over the Sylphid, but the fae spearman was already dead, chest cracked open, entrails raked by the Umbrioth's claws.

Illusitar wailed at the first Sylphid casualty. Her aura flared violently to match her waxing rage. Cobblestones cracked and flew as pillars of blue light erupted beneath one Umbrioth after another, scouring each beast from existence by virtue of the Slayn's cleansing arcana. Spent by the effort, Illusitar's aura began to dim. The pumping of her wings grew sluggish as she fluttered, near insensate, to the ground and then her knees.

Relieved of Illusitar's threat, the remaining Umbrioth began to muster in pockets around the plaza. I saw Kenver's sword arm extended deep inside one of the tentacled maws, and for a moment I thought him lost, but he withdrew his arm and with it, Caledin Bolg, her bright blade blackened to the hilt with Umbrioth tar. The maw tipped back and puddled with a vanquished hiss.

I went to join him and saw his sword arm dripping with blood, raked by the teeth of the maw he had slain. "We can't keep this up much longer!" I shouted over the Umbrioth's gibbering. The sound had risen to overtake the flagging clatter of Jassanid arms. "Where is Luka with the *lehakva*?"

"He won't abandon us," Kenver insisted, nearly breathless. "We need to buy him time."

I pivoted to strike a launching tongue from the air with Caledin Vane and watched the Sylphid spearmen skewer the chimera from either side, completing the kill. "We're running out of coin," I said to Kenver.

Two more of the Jassanid shield walls broke as Umbrioth maws burst into the plaza, cracking bodies between their ellipsoid jaws, tentacles raining blows the soldiers could not repel. With carnage mounting all around the plaza, the Umbrioth focused their attacks on the remnant kantors, skewering and consuming the sorcerers faster than they could complete their cants. What few Jassanids survived the shattering of their ranks, dissolved into the melee, bravely confronting the black beasts with spears and short swords that were not up to the task. Kenver and I fought back-to-back, severing limbs and tentacles, parrying claws, muscled forelimbs, and lashing tongues. Our Caledin blades served us better than the mundane arms wielded by the Jassanids. Winged Sylphids buzzed the plaza, bodies darting like missiles, carving through black Umbrioth with spearheads prone. I felt the frenzy of battle boiling my blood inside my veins, harnessing my instincts and guiding my steps through the melee. The black shreds of flayed Umbrioth grew thicker than the mists around the whirlwind of twin Caledin blades. Each vanquished beast lit the battlefield with a brilliant flash.

I broke formation to cleave the head of a tentacled maw. Its body peeled apart from the savage wound I dealt it, and as it puddled to the ground, I peered through its vanishing substance to see the other half of the battle developing toward the plaza's head.

Umbrioth bodies blackened the battlefield as the last of the Jassanids and kantors succumbed to the onslaught. Illusitar rallied her Sylphids in counterattack, but they too were overwhelmed by the sheer vastness of the Umbrioth horde.

It was all coming undone.

Our host had fought perfectly—raised every violent asset inside the walls of Mahakalpe. Still, we had lost.

A black fist shot out from one of the lumbering Umbrioth, catching Kenver in the side of the head as he vanquished one of the serpent-wolves broken loose from the greater engagement. He fell to the ground, and I sprinted across the plaza just in time to cut the creature's second arm as it arrived to deliver the killing blow. Kenver struggled to push himself to his feet, but his arms buckled, and he fell back to the ground. I covered him with Caledin Vane, buying precious seconds while he shook off his daze.

Six Umbrioth heads closed around us, and this time we had no Sylphid sorcery to save the day. The creatures approached with caution, gnashing jaws and fangs in threat as I pivoted from one to the next, brandishing Caledin Vane—daring the Umbrioth to test her.

I could not fight them all.

The sound of refreshed trope rose up from the distant reaches of the plaza. Karochan verses swelled as new voices joined, adding their weight in layers. Not the sound of the kantors' sorcery, but more akin to a kodesha congregation at prayer.

The Umbrioth recoiled from the sound. Their black skin rippled and rarefied—shadows disturbed by a burgeoning light. Serpent-wolves coiled defensively, while tentacled maws curled up in fetal balls. Lumbering giants shook, wrapping umbral fists around their gaping heads.

I dared each of them with the edge of Caledin Vane, but the Umbrioth retracted—whipped to heel by the flexing Karochan chant.

Kenver finally regained his feet. He maintained his grip on Caledin Bolg, but I could see that he was unbalanced. The Umbrioth had drawn a deep gouge along the side of his scalp. One eye was swollen shut and blood sheeted half his face.

I lent him my arm to steady himself as all around us, the Umbrioth *withdrew*. The mists evacuated the plaza on the heels of the Azag's foul denizens. Granted fresh quarter, I scanned the carnage, searching for the source of the singing.

What remained of the Sylphid swarm landed in a protective ring around Illusitar. Less than one full maniple of Jassanids still stood, and I saw even fewer kantors among their ranks. Every karochan sorcerer in the plaza stood tight-jawed and dazed, unable to produce so much as a note of trope let alone the puissant chorus that now filled the stagnant air.

"The *lehakva*," Kenver stammered, his voice thickened by his swollen face. "They're *praying*."

Only then did I recognize the song. I'd heard it only once before—on the lips of the orthodox prostrating themselves before Mahakalpe's ziggurat. *Karbalah Kov*—a prayer reserved for the divine presence.

Distance reduced the Umbrioth's feral war cries to the mad gibbering of wounded beasts. Beyond the lip of the retaining wall, a black tide gathered on the surface of the mists. The shroud eddied and swirled, a dark reflection of the violet *Darwaza* still hanging in the sky. Illusitar led her Swarm to our side, her porcelain face brittle, green eyes listless and sagging.

"She comes…" she said, staring off at the disturbance beyond the wall.

"Can you fight?" I asked Kenver.

In answer, he grasped Caledin Bolg with both hands and raised her to the wall. I matched his defiance, sliding my feet into proper stance.

The *Karbalah Kov* continued to pour into the plaza, shaped without pause by the disembodied chorus of *lehakva*. A black mass rose from the obfuscated bagra, conjured—or else *baited*—by the resonant notes of Karochan trope. The mass puckered as with gooseflesh, reaching for the plaza with sharp ejaculations. Arms and legs squirmed to life, dozens and then hundreds of parts, an amalgamation of the tortured and the damned. The thriving bundle gathered itself over the lip of the retaining wall, threaded with stumps of fractured bone, tails of waxen hair trailing from its mass in clumps. Its apex peeled open, a flower drinking the sun. From that fertile nexus, a black head began to sprout, pushed out from the guts of the creature as a mother births her young.

Imajoth-Almaug.

The Unmother turned its empty face to the Mahakalpan sky and loosed a caterwaul worthy of her name. My ears rang with the anguish of ages—of every burned girl fueling the Unmother's geas.

Illusitar raised a terse cantrip against the Azag's cry, and a blue shield expanded overhead. The Unmother shattered it with an ejaculation of limbs, blasting the Slayn back into her ranks.

I raised Caledin Vane, and the Unmother lashed out. My sword turned her blows aside more effectively than Illusitar's sorcery, but her substance did not part with the ease of her Umbrioth's. Her twisted mass rolled toward us, and it was all Kenver and I could do to parry each blow from her collection of broken limbs. We guarded the Sylphids, but could not stall the Unmother's advance, and with every blow, Kenver was starting to slow, succumbing to his enervating wounds.

Light poured into the plaza, white and cleansing. I dared the briefest glance over my shoulder to see the *lehakva* entering in chorus, their mouths wide with the making of their song. Gerritt's art encased their cohort in a translucent pearl. I caught a glimpse of him enmeshed among the young women, brown hair whipped to frenzy, merton bangles exposed on his forearms and blazing with sorcerous heat. He clashed his bangles together, and white light scythed out from the pearl, lashing the Unmother and slowing her advance. She lowered the black nob of her head, and lurched toward us, absorbing each glancing blow from Gerritt's spell with an expressionless wince.

I raised Caledin Vane, and that empty head began to shift, surfacing a woman's face. Black matter stretched, revealing the hump of her nose and the pits of her eyes—her mouth frozen agape, fossilized in the shape of her tortured end. I stumbled back from the shock of that image, and just as quickly the Unmother's face shifted again. Her head cycled through visage after visage, revealing the breadth of her collection, her impressed menagerie of souls burned in her name.

Limbs shot out from the Unmother's amalgamated body. I cast one aside with Caledin Vane, but Kenver was not fast enough. The Unmother seized him around the waist and lifted him from his feet. I hacked at her limbs—drew one deep gouge into her substance—but the Azag's speed overwhelmed my assault. A vaginal orifice opened in the Unmother's body, black petals peeling back with a blast of lusty musk.

I could only watch as the Azag *engulfed* Kenver inside of herself, Caledin blade and all.

Buttressed by the song of the *lehakva* and the light from Gerritt's casting, I charged the Unmother, slashing through limbs and shrouds, thrusting Caledin Vane deep inside her substance, questing for some vital node that might force her to expel Kenver Montaigne. Through a flurry of dexterous strikes, I shaved off arms and legs, fingers and toes. Black matter began to pile around me, but the Unmother did not flag.

At last, I gained enough leverage to sheath Caledin Vane to the hilt in what I could only hope counted as her chest. A sharp pain in my side rewarded my valor, and I looked down to see clawed fingers raking my abdomen—two black hands buried to the knuckle in my flank. A third arm hooked me around the knee, and a fourth seized me by the throat. Frozen in the Unmother's grasp, my neutralized hand tightened around the grip of Caledin Vane. The same black orifice that swallowed Kenver peeled open once again, welcoming me with amorous lips.

I heard Gerritt's voice shouting, "Rux!" but the distance separating us might as well have been a thousand leagues.

My vision blackened at the edges as I was engulfed.

The plaza vanished. I entered the Unmother like a stone dropped in a black lake, my body submerged in freezing water, pressure drumming on my temples and my throat. My lungs pled for air. My limbs fought sluggishly against the greedy current. By no effort of my own, I breached some barrier within the Azag, bursting from the surface of its ichor with a spasmodic gasp.

Once I regained my faculties, I realized I'd landed at the base of a vast chasm, its enclosure lit by some cold, endemic light extending in a cone from a pinhole source a thousand feet above my head. My vision extended several paces in every direction, up to the edge of whatever black oblivion waited beyond my cone of light.

I no longer heard the battle that was surely raging beyond the confines of the Azag. Only the *lehakva*'s prayer penetrated the Unmother's bowels. Its muffled Karochan phrases filled the Azag like a kodesha temple, and I could sense her geas unsettled by the intrusion. As long as that music continued, I knew that our battle was not lost.

"Kenver!" I shouted, cupping my hand over my mouth.

My own voice replied, an echo rebounding from the chasm of the Azag.

"Kenver!" I shouted again.

I detected motion. Something stirred within the abyss at light's edge. The stirring jumped from point to point, and I pivoted, tracking each subtle disturbance with the point of Caledin Vane—expecting Umbrioth to converge at any moment.

A small foot entered my cone of light, followed by its pair. Another pair followed—then more. Slender bodies emerged from the abyss. Not Umbrioth, but *people*—women and girls with white legs and white arms, their shambolic bodies haloed with coldfire. The spirits encircled me, staring with the empty pits of their eyes, pale lips working noiselessly.

Lehakva.

Hundreds of them stepped into the light—*thousands*—each of them wreathed in the afterglow of their sacrificial pyres. I waited for an attack that never came as the fell congregation penned me in. I expected the spirits to fall upon me at any moment—to rend me limb from limb. The front of their advance stopped within feet of me—close enough to touch. They cocked their heads, probing with those empty eyes— almost...curious.

I circled with Caledin Vane, marking each of them—so alike in their wasting and yet possessed of some remnant vitality. Black tendrils began to drop from the roof of the chasm, grasping the *lehakva* in turn, claiming them to serve their brief terms occupying the Unmother's changeable face. None fought their possession, as one after another they were ensnared, plucked like dolls from a youngling's crate.

The Prayer of Karbalah continued to churn around us, and I saw some of the ghoulish faces confused by its music—searching the abyss for its origin.

I lowered Caledin Vane and looked one of the closest spirits straight in the pits of her eyes. "Your sisters have come to free you," I said. "But they need your help."

I saw a light then—like the flickering of the weakest candle's wick— but the Unmother did not grant me time to kindle it. A fresh tendril dropped from the chasm's mouth, and this time it came for me.

The congregation of vanquished *lehakva* became a coldfire blur as my body flew through the chasm. The tendril grasping me cracked like a whip, pressing my face against the unctuous membrane of the Unmother's face. I opened my eyes, gazing through the Azag's black mask into the plaza without. I faced the living *lehakva*, still guarded by Gerritt's art and the remnant scraps of Illusitar's exhausted swarm. In that moment, I realized the depths of the Unmother's cruelty. She wanted me to *see*—to watch. To break before the carnage she wrought.

Recognition turned to horror on every face in the plaza. Gerritt's bangles flickered as he let his sorcery slip, and my former sister-wives—

terrified by my appearance on the face of their foe—began to drop their phrases, gasps interrupting and weakening their song.

Imajoth-Almaug was too cunning by half, and I knew then that I would be my army's undoing.

Luka emerged from the fist of *lehakva*. I heard his small voice steeling my sister-wives' resolve, and they returned to their singing with only some small trepidation. Witless of any threat, Luka stepped beyond the range of Gerritt's shield, brown eyes boring into me through the semipermeable membrane of the Azag.

He did not speak, but still I heard him—that G-dling voice implanted in my mind.

Lead them, he said. ***Remind them that they are our children still, and we have not forsaken them.***

The Unmother's black substance quivered around me. With obscene suction, the Azag peeled me from her visage. My vision of the plaza vanished as I felt myself ripped from her face and hurled back into the chasm below.

The *Karbalah Kov* rang clearer than it had before, its every trope resonant, building in layers, phrase over phrase like a terraced ziggurat. The music began to breach the Unmother's thrall over these generations of vanquished *lehakva*. The burning spirits looked around the chasm, emerging from their millennial trance in daze.

I looked around, counting my legions of the wasted and slain. Caledin Vane slid from her scabbard, layering her steel voice atop the living *lehakva*'s Karochan.

"Your sisters call to you!" I shouted, raising my sword high above my head. "Hear their song. Your G-d has returned to deliver you from this torment!"

A thin sound crept out from the legion of spirits. One-by-one, then two-by-two, the vanquished *lehakva* found their voices. They tested dry throats and shriveled tongues. As their voices thawed, they began to *sing*—joining their living sisters in prayer. Trope erupted from the chasm, shaped by thousands upon thousands of desiccated lips, inflected with the anguish of eons. Their singing breathed warm life into their coldfire shrouds, and the spirits began to frenzy. As one, the girls rose up and turned on the chasm that had been their prison, tearing at its substance, stripping it to ribbons.

The Unmother's caterwaul echoed from above, pathetically reduced without the weight of so many souls to bolster it. The dread beast's bone-shattering scream became the desperate wail of an inkling ghost.

Imajoth-Almaug's tendrils rained blows upon us, but they were feckless, a poor match for the unbottled rage of her constituent parts.

Amid the torrent of thrashing limbs and screaming trope, seams of light began to form around the chasm, gaps in the Azag's internal abyss that let in the voices of the living *lehakva*. I circled in awe, watching the revolt gain momentum.

Ware the vengeance of a woman cut down at the flowering of youth. No puissant spark unleashed by her sacrifice could be worth the reckoning that awaits. Would that every shaman and necromage on the face of Hebdomar could have witnessed the fury of the *lehakva*—that they might come to fear the blood they so foolishly let.

My ears popped with the pressure of imminent dissolution. Violet fire erupted to fill the chasm, scouring away the last bright pinholes of my sight.

CHAPTER 17

PASSING OF THE BLADE

I awoke from my oblivion sore but not broken, and with the sense that no short time had passed.

Rux...

...Rux.

I was lying down—somewhere softer than the aged cobblestones of the shattered Middle City plaza. A muddy silhouette resolved, hovering over me, and at first, I mistook it for Kenver. Not an altogether unpleasant way to wake up—even if he *had* come to finish the job, though I thought him more sporting than that.

Rux...

...Rux.

My vision sharpened by increments, and the voice with it.

"There's our girl."

Not Kenver, then; Gerritt, rather—his brow wet with perspiration, narrow jawline painted with the warm light emanating from his gifted hands. The glow of his casting melted back into the merton bangles clasping his forearms.

Reading my disappointment, he folded his arms across his chest and frowned. "Nice to see you, too."

I realized my armor and underclothes had been removed and tugged

170

the ends of a cotton robe to better conceal my nudity. I'd awakened in a small marble chamber described by four fluted columns at its corners and a peaked ceiling dressed with gold leaf. A tray of soiled surgical instruments loomed unsettlingly close to my bed.

I tried to sit up, but a sharp pain in my sides collaborated with Gerritt's stern hands to push me back into my bed's plush embrace. "Easy now," he said. "You're going to pull your sutures."

Only then did I notice the thick roll of bandages wrapped around my midriff—as well two brown stains in either flank where my wounds had seeped. I sighed, guiding Gerritt's hands from my shoulders, and ventured a second, more delicate attempt to sit up.

Gerritt relented, clucking his tongue in reprimand. I had always been a terrible patient.

"Where are we?" I asked.

"We're in the Sahir," Gerritt said. "After the *lehakva* vanquished the Azag, you were—" He scratched his head. "I guess *regurgitated* is the best word for it."

Memories returned with the fractured continuity of a distant dream. Thousands of spirits forged in fire, stirred to rend their prison thread by thread, pouring their fury and their outrage into puissant song. I could have sworn I still heard the notes of Karbalah's Prayer, an echo rebounding across the cavern of my soul.

I sat up straighter, grasping my abdomen with a wince. "It's done, then?"

Gerritt nodded. "Sure seems that way. Luka said the Azag has been exorcised, and the *Darwaza* has closed. The sky looks just as dry and empty as it did before—except for that comet, of course."

One job finished, then. Onto the next.

"How long have I been out?" I asked.

"Three days," he said.

Shibboleth's mercy.

"Been a whole lot of cleanup in the bagra," Gerritt continued. "Thousands dead or missing, but thousands more survived. The Ohtahpi have their work cut out for them, but Mahakalpe will rise from this tragedy."

I found I didn't really care one way or the other what happened to

Mahakalpe. The Arrekot cleric had warned that the Holy City would outlive its usefulness, and so it would. The same could not be said for its ruling dynasty. Whatever new order rose from the ashes of Luka's judgment faced a heavy task.

Someone else's problem. I had my own to manage.

I swung my legs around gingerly and reached for the floor with bare feet.

Gerritt moved to block me. "Where do you think you're going?"

"The Azag is vanquished," I said. "The truce is over."

Gerritt shook his head and crossed his arms. "You're in no condition."

"Can't you just...?" I knocked my wrists together.

He gaped at me. "Took every ounce of my arcana just to bring you back from the brink of the abyss." He prodded my bandages painfully with a finger. "Those aren't the only wounds you sustained. That was no vitality spring you stepped into. If you had been stuck any longer..." he shook his head again instead of finishing the thought. "Luka saved you," he said instead.

"My sister-wives saved me," I corrected. "The living and the dead." I extended one hand, and Gerritt stared into my outstretched palm defiantly. "Are you going to help me up or what?"

Reluctantly, he hoisted me to my feet.

"Where is he?" I asked.

Instead of answering, Gerritt stepped aside, revealing a second feather bed across the way. Another body lay atop it, still as a corpse, guarded by my quarry.

Luka.

The Demiurge reborn.

The boy's shaved head hung low, his shoulders slumped. He stared listlessly at Kenver Montaigne—unaware of or unconcerned by the Apostatic Priestess stirring at his back. Caledin Vane leaned against the wall in her scabbard, but I did not move to claim her. I have a flexible relationship with most standards of propriety, but I would not profane this place of healing with a drawn blade.

I reached for the well of resolve I hoped to harness and found it unnervingly dry.

"Will he recover?" I asked Gerritt.

The healer compressed his lips into a thin white line. "I closed all his superficial wounds after I finished tending to you, but the Azag's poison left a deeper stain on his spirit. He's beyond my art."

I nodded.

I should have been relieved. With Kenver out of the way, my path to Luka had been cleared, but try as I might, I squeezed no satisfaction from the image of a warrior lying prostrate on his sickbed. Battle forges hard bonds, and blood let in common cause only tempers their steel. These bindings hold faster than any royal impressment or sorcerous thrall. Kenver and I had faced the Umbrioth back-to-back with sibling swords drawn. I would mourn him—even if I still intended to dress his burial in the blood of his charge.

If...

I drifted toward Kenver's sickbed, and Gerritt caught me by the arm. "Nothing rash, Rux."

I stared at his hand on my arm until he released me. It seemed the bonds of battle had hung new tethers on us all.

He raised his hands in submission. "They saved lives in this city— yours and mine among them. They deserve some respect."

"You think so little of me?" I asked.

He raised one eyebrow but left the question to dangle unanswered.

Luka hardly moved when I joined him at Kenver's bedside. His eyes were downturned, small hands clasped before his body in silent prayer.

To whom do G-ds pray? I wondered.

I watched the shallow rise and fall of Kenver's muscular chest. Bandages covered his arms from shoulders to wrists, but I did not think these were the wounds that plagued him. The warrior's eyelids fluttered, flashing glimpses of the blue light within.

Luka's head jerked up at the motion. He grasped Kenver's hand, but the guardian only moaned and settled back into unconsciousness.

"There's nothing you can do?" I asked.

Luka shook his head, tightening his grip on Kenver. "I—I made you mortal, and—and—" Sobs overwhelmed his voice. Precious breaths passed before he could finish the thought. "Time," he said, still fixated on Kenver. "Time only runs down."

How little of the G-dling spirit I sensed in him, then.

Childhood is a fortress. We raise curtain walls around our younglings, fortifications built from lies and dedication—their stones mortared with unconditional love. Time indeed runs down, and so too these juvenile walls—inevitably undermined by life and loss. Time exposes us all to the elements, and those winds are ever cold, no matter the season of their arrival. The Karochan sages claim that Luka was born of the desert, but it was not the desert that mortared his walls. For all his legions of adulators and pilgrims, they loved only the G-dling spirit that possessed him and not the child he was.

Kenver spread Luka's mortar. He alone loved Luka the way all children need to be loved. His loss would be a mighty breach.

Kenver's body tensed as another moan escaped his lips. His eyelids fluttered, and this time they remained open.

"Kenver!" Luka's face lit up like a brazier.

The warrior managed a weak smile, squeezing Luka's hand with what little strength was left to him. His throat strained as he struggled to speak. "That was... That was a *proper* battle." He drew a deep breath, winded by the effort.

"It was," Luka nearly choked on his words. "You saved the city."

"*You* saved them," Kenver corrected. "I wanted to let the *lehakva* burn, remember?"

Luka sniffed. "But you trusted my judgment in the end."

Kenver's eyes closed for a long moment, and Luka's lower lip began to tremble. "I—I can't do this without you. The path is too long, and the road too lonely."

Kenver's eyes shot back open. "Nonsense. The path before you may be long, but you will never be alone." With great effort, Kenver raised one arm and pressed his hand to Luka's chest. "You are the Demiurge— that from which all life emanates, and to which all life eventually returns. I can never leave you—not even in death."

Luka sniffed again, and I saw tears rolling down his apple cheeks.

If only we could all live lives to make G-d weep.

I suddenly regretted invading this fleeting moment between them. I felt like a voyeur, and so I started to back away. Kenver caught me with his eyes. "Wait," he said, more sharply than I thought him capable. "We need to speak." I froze as he returned his focus to Luka. "Go, now, athling. See to your flock. You will know when I return to you. You needn't witness the end with your mortal eyes."

"I want to be with you," Luka whined, the tears now falling freely.

"Others need you more," Kenver said. His intake of breath whistled in his throat. "Strong at the finish."

Luka sniffed again and wiped the tears from his cheeks.

"Say it with me," Kenver prompted. "One more time."

The words squeezed from Luka with strain, "*Strong at the finish.*"

"Good." Kenver groaned, straightening his head on the pillow. "Off with you, now."

Luka released Kenver's hand and backed away. He looked up at me warily, before speeding from the sick room.

Silence ensued once the boy's footfalls retreated down the hall.

"I think I'll see if our little G-dling needs a hand," Gerritt said, already moving for the exit.

"Keep him close," I said, still watching Kenver.

"Aye," Gerritt agreed, though I heard his resentment loud and clear.

The wounds in my side protested against my standing, but I had work yet to accomplish on this day. Kenver closed his eyes again once we were alone, gathering what scraps of strength remained to him, but already I heard the nightjar rattling in his chest. It wouldn't be long now.

His eyes fluttered open once again. "Your path is unencumbered, Priestess."

"Yes," I said.

"You remain dedicated... even after—" His face pinched with a flash of pain that stole his voice.

"I have a duty," I said, the closest thing to an honest answer I could give. I was not ready to admit that my resolve had indeed been shaken, and I could no longer say what would happen after I exited this room.

Kenver groaned as he regained control of himself. "So stubborn... He's a good boy."

Such a quaint and powerful way to describe a revenant G-d. My eyes moved to Caledin Bolg, propped in its scabbard against the wall, a perfect reflection of my own Caledin Vane. "Tell me..." I said, still eyeing the sword. "What's the Eidolon's guardian doing with a G-dkilling blade?"

Kenver's eyes rolled to the gold-leaf ceiling. "Finally, she asks..."

"Just waiting for the right opportunity."

The choking sound might have been a laugh. His voice returned to him with more clarity and strength—the last flash of a warrior's dying light. "Your Shibboleth has the right of it, but only halfway. Our world cannot endure another Mysin."

"Then why lead the boy to Mahakalpe? The risk—"

Kenver raised one trembling hand to cut me off. "Your priesthood misunderstands the threat. The living incarnation of the Demiurge is not some daemonic possession. The Holy Spirit *joins* with its host, and its disposition is colored by the soul with which it is enmeshed.

"Mysin was a warlord even before his investment. A tyrant. But Luka is not the G-d our ancestors vanquished. His pilgrimage will take him across the face of Hebdomar. He will come to know his creation as we are, and he will become the G-d we make of him. The G-d we deserve."

The G-d we deserve...

A man's dying words are not lightly given nor carelessly received. Kenver spent his to deliver this message—to me. If my resolve had been shaken by Luka's actions in Mahakalpe, then Kenver's words reduced its foundation to chalk and ash. The Shibboleth—my vow—the very cornerstone of my priesthood; it stood only as a bulwark against the resurrection of a vengeful G-d. If it could be any other way...

"You think Luka could be...different?"

"I know he will be different," Kenver said. "I pray he will be *more*."

I nodded along—despite myself and my conditioning. Change is the only eternity, and it had come to my heart as surely as the Karioch waves that ate the cliffs of Ohtahp. "You were charged to guide him to this destiny?" I asked.

"The Shibboleth is not the only priesthood that remembers." Kenver raised his hand to his mouth and coughed. When he drew away, I saw blood and bile spattering his palm. "Luka was right about one thing. He cannot hope to complete his pilgrimage alone. He needs a guardian to shepherd him through the world."

"You can't mean me."

"It must be you," he said. "Of all the priests in your Shibboleth, you alone have seen his promise and his worth. Ruxindra." He swallowed back another wracking cough. "We live in a fallen world. Who better to deliver us than the G-d who made it so?"

"The G-d we make of him..." I parroted.

Kenver's blue eyes hardened, the last light burning inside his waxen mask. "And if we turn him sour... You have your sword."

Finally, I saw this dying warrior's intentions plain. Kenver might have been a shepherd, but a shepherd with a culling blade.

Kenver's eyes shut again, and his fingers unfurled like a blooming flower. "My sword," he said.

I reached for Caledin Bolg and held it across my hands in its scabbard. Such a priceless treasure. I knew I should commandeer it—seize it on behalf of the Shibboleth and turn its power toward my priesthood's ends. I ran one finger along its jeweled pommel and placed it against Kenver's chest, gently closing his fingers around its red grip.

His chest stilled beneath the familiar weight of his sword as the final scraps of breath fled from his lips. He closed his eyes for the final time.

A true warrior only finds peace in death, and so it was for Kenver Montaigne.

CHAPTER 18
THE ZEAL OF A CONVERT

I left that chamber with no great certainty about what I would do. The Shibboleth's conditioning was not easily overcome—my vow not lightly abandoned—but a man's dying charge was neither easy nor light, and Kenver's had shaken me to my core.

A line of my former sister-wives awaited outside the sick room. For the second time, they'd cast off their bridal raiment, exchanging cream shalwaz and patterned tahliz for those narrow gowns of virginal white. They each stood a head taller than I remembered them, swollen with valor, as well they should be. Eyes in every shade of hazel, green, and brown flashed up at me as I passed. To a girl, they seemed desperate to speak to me, but the glazed look on my face held their sorties at bay.

Eventually, two of their cohort stepped into my path—Liyah and Maddux, as unlikely a pair as one could hope to wring from the harem. Liyah looked perfectly at ease in the garb of her native creche, but I thought Maddux would have been more comfortable in her mint Arrami dress.

I planted my hands on my hips and looked from one girl to the next, waiting for someone to speak or else move from my path.

"I'm sorry," Liyah said.

I arched one eyebrow at her. "For what?"

"You saved me twice," Liyah said. "I should not have doubted you. I was—I was afraid."

"Save your apologies," I said. "You were wise to fear me. I was a false *lehakva,* and I am something to be feared."

Liyah's smooth brow bunched up as her eyes pinched inward. She shook her head. "I don't think that's true. G-d called us to Mahakalpe, though the Mahak's blindness twisted his intent. He called you, too, I think."

"That's truer than you know," I said.

Maddux glanced past me to the door of the sick room, now a tomb. "Is Kenver..."

I nodded tersely, and the girl hung her head in mourning.

"Luka will need another guardian," Liyah said. "To guide him on his pilgrimage."

"He has a Holy City full of adulators to choose from," I said.

Liyah offered no counter. "What's next for Ruxindra bin Vargas?" she asked.

I snorted. "Ruxindra bin Vargas died in the *Cikkot.* Ruxindra l'Maer needs to move on from this place." I looked at both girls sternly, expecting them to move out of my way, but neither budged. "Don't you all need to gather with your people?"

"My tribe's ark is lost beneath the bagra stone," Liyah said. "We cannot return to our creche without it, so the clerics have determined that we should remain. The Yusakot will join our tribe with our bagra cousins and lend our hands to help Mahakalpe rebuild."

Change. It comes for us all.

"I wish you well in the task before you." I extended my hand to Liyah, hoping to guide this interaction to its natural close, but the girl brushed past my arm and wrapped herself around me. My hands reluctantly found their way to her back, and I brushed the braids of her shalwaz, returning the embrace, surprised by the burgeoning tenderness I felt toward the girl.

"We will pray for you as we pray for him," Liyah whispered. "Keep him safe."

Presumptuous sentiments, but Liyah was an old soul and wise well beyond her callow years. I finally escaped once she relinquished her grasp on me, but Maddux pursued me down the hall.

"Wait, Rux—"

"Mads..." I groaned. "I don't have time for this."

"I want you to take me with you!" the girl blurted out.

From one fresh hell to the next. I stared at her, deadpan.

"My mother will be furious if I return to Oksa," she insisted. "She'll pawn me off on the first slobbering Tajjar who wheels in a dowry chest, and I haven't the disposition to remain in Mahakalpe." That last part, at least, sounded true enough.

"You haven't the disposition for my path, either," I said.

Maddux puffed out her skinny chest. "*I* faced down one of the *Urkaku-Azag* and lived to tell the tale. Surely that counts for something."

"It will be a fine story to tell the children you whelp for that slobbering Tajjar."

Maddux's nostrils flared. "I can be useful to you. I am an expert haggler, and I know how to handle a longbow. I used to compete in the archery lists at Fort Okanto."

"I don't take strays," I said, and I left her to track another stray.

"I'm a merchant's daughter," Maddux shouted after me. "I don't take no for an answer!"

Shaking my head, I turned down an adjacent hall of the Sahir. I did not think I'd heard the last of Maddux DiLenus.

My footfalls echoed down the marble halls, empty but for the crash of falling water still curtaining the Sahir's clandestine nooks. I no longer sensed the kantors and Jassanids who once lurked inside these secret redoubts. So few had survived the Unmother's assault.

As the Shevuot all drew toward Mahakalpe's Mysin gates, the sweeping hallways of the Sahir all drew toward the hypolyte. I eventually reached a gallery set with diamond tiles of black and gold, and found Gerritt perched between two fluted columns, blocking a short riser to the hypolyte floor. He straightened his posture at my approach.

"He's in there?" I asked, nodding to the vast receiving floor beyond the riser.

Gerritt exhaled, eyes painting the hilt of Caledin Vane back at home on my hip. "The kid's taking Kenver pretty hard," he said.

"The *kid?*"

Gerritt sighed, tousling the brown locks of hair at the back of his head. "He is that, isn't he? No matter what else resides within him."

"I made a vow, Gerritt." Even to my own ears, the protestation sounded hollow.

"Words are smoke," Gerritt said. "It's the intention that burns."

Intention. The Shibboleth rose from the ashes of Old Mysin, our lone hedge against the pain and torment the living G-dhead had wrought upon his world. Slaying Eidolons had always seemed the surest path to salvation, but perhaps I'd stumbled upon a road less traveled—one my priesthood might even abide.

I glowered up at my mercurial partner. "Don't play at wisdom with me, mage. I know you too well."

I guided him to the side with one hand, and he let me pass into the hypolyte. In the end, the decision was mine alone, and Gerritt knew it.

Luka stood with his back to the receiving floor, staring down into the empty pit of the Mahak's former throne. After all these tempestuous days in Mahakalpe, I finally had him alone.

My boots dragged through running water as I crossed the hidden stone bridge within the moat.

"That's a nice chair," I said.

Luka glanced at me with round, wet eyes before returning to the throne.

"Thinking about sitting in it?" I asked.

"Not much sitting in my future, I don't think."

"If not you, then someone else is sure to test their claim." I sidled up next to him to gaze at the high seat. "Thrones have a way of filling themselves."

"Not this one," Luka said. "The Mahak Dynasty has ended, and it will not be replaced."

That seemed awfully wishful, even taken as a pronouncement from G-d. "Any sign of Prince Gibril or his cantankerous mother?"

Luka shook his head, big ears working like oars. "They fled the Sahir and the city—abandoned their duty in truth after abandoning it in spirit so long ago."

"Sounds like anarchy to me. How's that worked out for the other cities of Ohtahp?"

"Not anarchy," Luka said. "I trust the people of Mahakalpe with their own governance. My disciples will remain at the Sahir to help them navigate this forest."

His disciples? I tried to imagine Shirit, Hava, and Gulam meting justice and nattering over duties and tithes. Not a pretty picture, but governance so rarely is. I didn't see it then, but there was wisdom in Luka's vision for Mahakalpe, for who better to wield the plenary power of the throne than a man who has lost his freedom to that same authority? Who better understands the vital role of community than one who has been denied its sustenance by disfigurement and disease? Who better accounts the intrinsic worth of a person than a woman who has sold herself as a whore? This ruling council of the pardoned and the meek might just serve Mahakalpe at this delicate moment and serve it well.

"He's really gone," Luka said after another long pause.

"Yes."

He breathed out and turned his head to the painted rotunda arcing high above the hypolyte. I sensed him reaching, yearning to tap whatever remnant of Kenver might still persist. A small smile crept across his boyish face—the saddest expression I've seen before or since.

"I don't understand," he finally said.

I sensed the tide of conversation shifting and so waded back in with caution. "If there's a mystery beyond your ken, then I doubt I have its solution," I said.

"You are the mystery," Luka said. "I don't understand it. Why would you want to kill someone you hadn't even met?"

There it was. Confronted with my dilemma by a naked G-d. "I made a vow," I said. And with those wide, brown eyes upon me, I abrogated it. "But even vows are subject to change."

Luka knew what I was, and though he might be wise, he was not prescient. Until that moment, I don't think he knew whether I'd let him leave Mahakalpe alive. I thought my words might bring him more comfort, but with my forbearance confirmed, the rest of his path unfurled before him, and he saw that it was no placid Shevat. "I don't know how to do this without him," he said.

Kenver again.

"He told me you were on a pilgrimage."

Luka nodded. "The *Tachne* say I must climb the Twelve Branches of the Tree of Sephirot. Mahakalpe's altar is but the lowest and the first."

"Where are the rest?" I asked.

Luka reached inside his toga and unfolded a creased slip of parchment. He handed it to me as casually as an errand boy might pass a list of tasks. My eyes moved over two columns of blackstem skritglyphs that I could not read. I handed the vellum back to Luka, shaking my head, and he scanned them himself.

"Lines copied from each Ark of the Tractate," he said. "This is the reason the nomads brought them forth."

"What do they say?"

"I don't know," Luka said, and he folded the vellum, frustratedly tucking it back inside his toga. "For a former merchant, Shirit's a decrepit hand with quill and ink."

A decrepit hand?

Luka looked up at my crinkled expression and flashed a wry grin. "A joke, Ruxindra."

"Ha."

He shook his head. "And I thought Kenver too grim. I believe they are antique coordinates—impressed at the time of the Arks' construction—but I will need a cartographer of some talent to plot them, and one familiar with Mysin navigation at that."

Such a mundane request. A puzzle to be sure, but one with a worldly solution. I cupped my chin, tapping one finger against my cheek. "I think I might have an inkling where to look."

"You...?" Luka opened his mouth and just as quickly shut it.

I nodded to him. "Me."

"Why?"

"A woman's only as good as her word. I told you—I made a vow. My oath may have changed, but I will not see it broken."

I'm not sure Luka entirely understood, and how strange it seemed to befuddle an almighty G-d.

"Take the rest of the day to get your affairs in order," I told him. "We leave Mahakalpe at first light."

As I crossed the hypolyte's thin moat for what would be the final time, I marked Gerritt standing off on the receiving floor, occupying the same position he'd claimed when he first arrived to deliver me to the Mahak.

Gerritt tracked me with a curious look as I passed him. "My eyes must be playing tricks." He jogged to catch up. "That must be it. The years have finally claimed my sanity. Surely—*surely*—Ruxindra l'Maer did not just leave the Eidolon with his head whole and intact."

"Change of plans," I said.

He halted in his tracks, then jogged again to reach my side. "Back to Nurindra to plead his case?"

I shook my head. "Nurindra's the last place we'll want to be once word gets out."

"Word of the G-dhead's return?"

We swept down the marble cursa and into the receiving yard, walking a straight line for the retaining wall and the open staircase embedded within. "Word that the Eidolon left Mahakalpe after receiving his investment—with an Apostatic Priestess as his guardian."

Gerritt froze at the top of the retaining wall, and I left him there to contemplate my change of heart. Better he had some time to digest this development on his own.

He'd come around.

I did.

EPILOGUE

e left Mahakalpe a ruin, but a ruin strewn with hope. I had no doubt the Ohtahpi would resurrect their Holy City. It was not so hard to press new hovels from rubble, and soon enough life would return to some semblance of normalcy, albeit without the ruling Mahak. Mahakalpe would survive—the final front in the urban Ohtahpi's hopeless war against diaspora.

I'd had my fill of the dusty Shevuot, and I would not dare the mountain passes abutting Nurindra for fear of provoking my priesthood's wrath. I hoped to bring my sisters of the Shibboleth around to my unorthodox way of thinking, but ours was a stubborn stone, and change, however dauntless, would need time to wear its hard facade.

With Luka's recalcitrant participation, we waved his divinity like a scepter at the Mahakalpan port of Kiyat Mar and claimed a ship to convey us over the dead waters of the Karioch Sea. Our vessel was a tired craft, narrow and leaky, possessed of one mast and a single square sail checkered with patches, but its salt-encrusted hull proved sturdy enough to meet our needs.

Luka stood silently at the prow of the ship, watching the cliffs of his homeland glide by. The boy had been quiet since leaving Mahakalpe, and more than once I heard him weeping softly in the night. I kept waiting for the Demiurge to seize control of him like he did in the Sahir, but whatever G-dling fragment had invested itself upon the Syzygy of Avum kept its face buried deep. Most of the time, Luka seemed like nothing more than the adolescent boy he was—contemplative and soulful, but also excitable and naive. In quiet moments, he'd retreat inside himself for a time, only to surface clutching ancient wisdom between his teeth like a diving Kappa with a wriggling fish. The duality unsettled me, but hardly on a scale with the rapture I'd experienced in Mahakalpe.

Gerritt leaned over the starboard taffrail, scanning the horizon through a cracked spyglass he'd conned off a seaman at Kiyat Mar. Maddux whined incessantly in his ear, pleading for a turn with the device. In the end, I hadn't the heart or the energy to turn the girl away. True to her word, she'd proven herself a dogged haggler, and eventually I acquiesced—if only to claim some peace from her harassment.

I'll take you as far as Eryzitar, I told her. *After that, you're on your own.*

She smiled smugly as she accepted my terms with a spit-covered palm. I was not such a fool to believe she had any intention of keeping them.

I nudged the rudder, adjusting our eastward course, aiming to keep our little sailboat from drifting out of sight of the shore. A stone column lost its grip on the cliffside with a crumble and crash, and soon after our craft rocked on its dying wake.

I tied the rudder and crossed the deck just as Gerritt relented and passed the spyglass to Maddux. Even without the device's aid, I saw what they were ogling. A trimarine of Celukid corsairs crested the horizon's curvature—two striker pinnaces and a hulking galleon with wide, black sails.

"That ship's enormous!" Maddux squealed.

Gerritt visored his hand, still squinting at the distant ships with his naked eye. He wondered aloud, "What are they doing this far west?"

Nothing good.

Maddux lowered the spyglass and looked from Gerritt to me. "Something I should be worried about?"

"Plenty," I said. "But this ain't one of 'em."

Gerritt looked like he wanted to object but thought better of it and returned to watching the trimarine as its ships inched closer with every bob of surf.

"They won't test the waters this close to shore," I said. "We're tracking the coast all the way to Drakashan'ab. We're not worth the trouble."

Gerritt's eyes drifted to Luka, still mounted at the prow—the one thing we carried that might indeed be worth the trouble.

He might have had a point, but the unvoiced concern quickly became moot. The Celukid galleon pitched suddenly to its portside, and its escort pinnaces careened from its hull. I pressed myself between Gerritt and Maddux, curling my fingers over the taffrail to watch as a wedge-shaped head wider than either pinnace broke the surface with a turbulent splash. The head shot from the water, trailing a long, serpentine body that arced through the sky, crashing amidships on the galleon and cracking its topdeck in twain.

"*Masra aruir!*" Maddux cursed.

I snatched the spyglass from her hands and pressed it to my eye just in time to watch a line of purple dorsal fins saw through the galleon's hold. The piercing tip of a spiny, red tail flashed in my lens as the creature slipped through the breach it had created and vanished back into the sea.

The galleon's foremast canted, its broad sails deflating. We all watched the dying ship raise its bowsprit to the heavens in defiance as the sea swallowed it whole.

The creature circled, saw-tooth fins cutting the surface. Before long, both pinnaces shared their flagship's fate. The waters stilled, the trimarine reduced to a blanket of limp sails and broken jetsam bobbing lazily with the chop.

"*Dryghten's fury...*" Gerritt muttered.

"See?" I lowered the spyglass from my face and pressed it against Gerritt's chest. "Nothing to worry about."

Luka stepped down from the prow, now gazing anxiously out to sea. "I..." He clamped his lips shut before he could finish his thought.

We all stared at him.

"Something you want to tell us?" Gerritt prompted.

Luka pointed his toes together, fidgeting with his hands.

"Out with it," I said.

Luka's thin lips turned down. "I...do not think *Imajoth-Almaug* was the only eldritch horror released by my investment."

"What?" Maddux chirped. Her eyes jumped from Luka to me. "What does that mean? Surely not another Azag!"

I heard Gerritt's lips flapping as he exhaled.

Luka turned his palms up, wet eyes almost apologetic.

"This is good," I said to a pincer of gasps from Maddux and Gerritt. I doubled down, ignoring them both. "This serves us. Anything that keeps my sisters preoccupied and off our backs is a boon."

Luka's eyes narrowed. "I would not see people suffer on my account."

I nodded. "Glad to hear it."

I said it glibly but meant it in truth. Kenver had been right about his charge. Luka was not Mysin, and whatever gentle piece of him had entwined itself with the G-dling presence required nurture and careful stewardship. I only hoped it would stay that way once he'd seen more of our world and what its people had to offer.

And if it didn't?

I still had my sword.

Acknowledgments

Welcome to Hebdomar, Dear Reader. You've just completed your first journey through this fallen world, and I hope you'll come back for many more. The publishing industry will tell you that sword and sorcery is a dead genre, but much like G-ds, fiction genres are ever restless, even in death. The fact that you've reached this page means the resurrection ritual is complete.

Many thanks are due. As always, first and foremost to my loving and supportive partner, Liz, and my children, Judd and Aliyah, without whom none of this would be possible. To my first reader, story consultant, and oldest friend, Jon Koster, the first person to tell me that this book was "ready to go." To my parents as well as my brothers, Harry, Sam, and Jake.

I also need to thank David Anthony Durham, whose encouragement came at a crucial time in the ideation of this series. I've learned so many lessons from David's work and his historical rigor. No one writes better Iron Age action than DAD. Without *Acacia* and *Pride of Carthage*, there would be no Divine Heretic series. If you haven't read David's work, you really need to rectify that.

Lastly, I need to thank you, Dear Reader. You're inundated with reading options, and you took a chance on a new series from a new author. I know your reading time is a gift, and I intend to handle it with care.

Much more to come.

ABOUT THE AUTHOR

Z. Bennett Lorimer is the author of several SFF novels and short stories, including the Tales of Ciel and The Divine Heretic. A graduate of the 2014 Clarion Science Fiction and Fantasy Writers Workshop at UC-San Diego, he also holds an MFA in creative writing from Iowa State University and is the former managing editor of the international literary journal *Flyway: Journal of Writing and Environment*. A Long Island native, he currently lives in Ames, Iowa, with his partner and children.

ALSO BY Z. BENNETT LORIMER

TALES OF CIEL

Ardent Wings on Jealous Skies

Ophiuchus Flinched (Coming February 2026)

The Mark of Cain (Coming April 2026)

THE COMPACT CYCLE

The Politics of Fear (Coming June 2026)

THE DIVINE HERETIC

What Lies Between (Coming August 2026)

WANT TO SEE WHAT HAPPENS NEXT?

Scan the QR code to download your free preview of Book 2: *What Lies Between.*

And don't forget to sign up for the High Trestle Press newsletter by visiting www.hightrestlepress.com for weekly updates about upcoming books from Z. Bennett Lorimer.

www.ingramcontent.com/pod-product-compliance
Lightning Source LLC
Chambersburg PA
CBHW072129300726
48975CB00003B/991